Good Night, Sleep Tight, Sweet Dreams

Bedtime Stories and More

Michael Kugel

Artwork by Jeff Perdziak

BookLocker

Saint Petersburg, Florida

Published by BookLocker.com, Inc., St. Petersburg, Florida.

Printed on acid-free paper.

BookLocker.com, Inc.
2020

First Edition

PREFACE

(Please read before proceeding)

Active Ingredients and Use: A little bit of humor, a dash of sadness, some creativity, and just a trace of originality and values. While these paragraphs, and the messages contained within them will not relieve any pain or lower a fever, they very well might make you feel better nonetheless, and may even alter your view of the world -- then again, they may not.

Book Facts and Purpose: Despite the lack of any obvious talent, this book was created out of the dark corners of my mind in an effort to bring a few amusing and, hopefully, thought-provoking stories to light. However, they should not be viewed as illegitimate children of a literature unworthy mind since there is an abundance of widely spread literary publications that have proved to be inferior in quality, and which possessed a significantly lower dose of entertainment value when compared to the texts contained within these pages. Hence, the manufacturer and publisher of these fine stories strongly recommends that each one should be read in a quiet setting with adequate lighting, and if at all possible, with classical music (or any other that you may prefer or have within reasonable reach) playing in the background. Of course, no music at all is perfectly acceptable as well. Be sure to stock up on snacks and beverages before administration, if so preferred.

Recommended Daily Dose: Read one story per day, preferably at bedtime. However, studies have shown that it is safe to read these passages at just about any other time of the day. However, do not read more than the whole book in a twenty-four-hour period (unless you really, really, really want to).

Warning: Do not attempt to read while driving a vehicle or operating heavy machinery, as it may catch your interest and make it difficult to pay attention to any other tasks.

Keep Out of Reach of Friends: Just tell them how good it is and let them buy their own copy of this book. I need the money.

Caution: Read only when in a good mood. Absorbing this material in a foul or less than a delightful state of mind will decrease the amount of entertainment value that will be absorbed during administration. Also, any humor that you might find within these pages is intended for amusement only and should not be used in mixed company during serious conversations, especially when attempting to impress a member of the opposite sex. However, referencing back to the various concepts contained within this book may prove to be a prudent notion, and is in fact, strongly encouraged.

Follow Up: Do not call me in the morning (you can call your doctor if you want). Upon completion of each story that you enjoy, contact everybody in your area code, and anyone else you feel like calling, visiting, e-mailing, tweeting, snapchatting, instagramming, long distance mind to mind fusing, or through any other widely acceptable (or not) form of communiqué that may have come about between the time you started (or restarted) and finished the book, and tell them to invest in a copy of this fine piece of literature. If you did not like it, do nothing, since nobody likes people that spread false rumors.

GOOD NIGHT
BEDTIME STORIES

"**W**ell, Sonny, sit back, relax, and listen to the story that I'm going to tell you. It is about choices, celebration of life, and one widely enjoyed activity that some love very much. Mostly though, this story is about making sound, well-thought-out decisions that, in the short and sometimes even the long run, could affect our lives and often those around us. First though, I must say that events such as the ones that I am about to enlighten you with have been happening for hundreds of years; however, this particular story took place only a few months ago.

"It was early autumn, and millions of leaves on thousands of trees in the forest had just started to turn the various shades of red, orange, and yellow which distinguishes that time of the year as the most colorful of all. The night air turns a little cooler and a bit crisper, as the moon descends from the sky earlier and earlier. In the mornings, the fog lazily drifts through the underbrush of the forest, and engulfs open fields and knolls, while various species of birds merrily chirp away, as some of them get ready for their annual journey south for the winter, providing a melody of sorts for all other creatures to wake up and start their day.

"In what was considered to be one of the nicer neighborhoods of the forest lived a family of deer. It was a typical nuclear family that is so common (although slowly becoming rather uncommon) in today's modern world, made up of a buck – the head of the household, a doe – his wife, and their two and a half fawns – the half being the one she was expecting in another three months or so.

"While they were not the richest family in the forest (that title belonging to the bald eagle, whose royalties from the depiction of his image added up into the millions), they certainly lived comfortably and, on occasion, even helped those who were less fortunate.

"Quite often, or just occasionally – depending on which of the two parental units of the family one was inclined to believe – they engaged in various family activities such as picking berries, relaxing by large oak trees, frolicking around grassy knolls, and, sometimes, dodging cars (especially on dark curvy roads in the middle of the night). They also enjoyed shopping, movies, and ice cream socials.

"However, there was one activity that Arnold, the buck, enjoyed more than anything else in the world. The opportunity for it came only once a year and he always looked forward to it. His good friend Geary, a buck that resided in the same neighborhood with his own family, always joined him, and, more often than not, they managed to have a great time, even if the main objective of the activity was not accomplished. That's right, Sonny, it was almost open season, and both Arnold and Geary were avid hunters.

"They completed the hunters' safety class just as soon as they were old enough to do so, and were always the first in line to renew their hunter's licenses. For these two bucks, this was truly an exciting time of the year, and both felt that it was nice to get away from the laid back, relaxing, and non-chaotic environment of the forest. It was also nice to spend some time with a good friend, rub the antlers together, and get some male bonding time under their belts. Even preparing for these expeditions was a fun way to spend the time.

"During the summer, a couple of months prior to the hunting season, Arnold bought a new shotgun. It was a Remington 1100 semi-automatic with a hair trigger and a loophole scope with a laser sight mounted on top. Arnold practically drooled every time he opened the gun case and adored his newest toy. He might have been a grown deer, but he still loved toys. They were just a little more expensive than the ones he had in fawnhood. Hunting season could not come fast enough for Arnold.

"Geary, trying not to be outdone by his friend, purchased a new weapon as well. He bought a slightly used rifle that he upgraded himself, and wound up with a Savage 270 Winchester Magnum with a bipod and a 7x32 bullet drop compensating scope. He loved his new toy almost as much as he loved his adoring wife.

"A week before hunting season started, they went to the local store for supplies. The Great City Hunter catered to all kinds of outdoor enthusiasts. One could find items such as tents, hunting clothes to stay warm during the chilly temperatures and for camouflage; kayaks, canoes and oars, fishing poles and lines, bait, all kinds of guns, ammunition and weapon cleaning supplies; knives, wood, bear traps, wolf repellents, salt lick fish, and various other lures, and a whole lot of other supplies that one might require on an adventurous (or not so stimulating) trip. Arnold and Geary purchased all of their necessary supplies at a great price.

"To make the store even more appealing to customers, the management constructed a simulated city block and major roadway right in the middle of the store. The simulation depicted a typical city street complete with discarded wastes on the sidewalk, polluted air, bumper to bumper traffic, and angry pedestrians pushing their way through the crowd. Speakers, hidden within the realistically painted Styrofoam cars and cardboard buildings, broadcasted typical sounds of a morning commute – blaring horns, screeching tires, and ear-piercing shouts containing descriptive verbs, adverbs, adjectives, and occasional nouns. It was a playground for adults, and Arnold and Geary resembled two fawns in a candy store!

"The first day of open season had finally arrived. Arnold and his friend met at the edge of the forest that evening. 'I thought this day would never come!' They both wore backpacks containing all of their supplies and had their weapons slung over their shoulder. They were already wearing the camouflage clothes they purchased – jeans, T-shirts, sneakers, and baseball caps. They even bathed twice a day, every day, for the last week, and shaved to make their faces blend in a little better. Arnold had a fashionable goatee on his face, while Geary sported a closely cropped beard.

"Geary adjusted his backpack and rifle. 'You can say that again! I can't wait to test out my new toy.' They bumped antlers and without any further delays headed for the big city. According to the rumor mill, there was a lot of great game to be hunted there and they could hardly wait to see it for themselves.

"Geary spoke up again as they were making their way to their destination at an excited pace. 'Hey Arnie think you'll finally get that elusive one this year? You've been trying to get one of those big ones to put on your wall for like ... what ... almost ten years now?' Arnold just shook his head in frustration.

"Sonny, more than anything in this world, Arnold wanted to mount the head of one of his kills – a head that he could be proud of and make all his hunter friends jealous. He even had a taxidermist on speed dial and a place above his fireplace picked out. Amazingly enough, he managed to convince his wife that it was a good idea. It took him a long time to have her agree that it would add a certain amount of charm and prestige to the ambiance of the room. Every year he looked forward to hunting season and the possibility of finally getting The One. However, year after year, none of his kills were worthy to be placed above the prestigious mantle, and he was becoming increasingly frustrated and disappointed. Arnold felt even more pressure to get one on that particular night because due to family constraints, he was not going to be able to make another trip into the city this year.

"It wasn't until after the sun had set that they reached their destination. The hunter's stand was located on the roof of a two-story building overlooking the back alley in the middle of one of the city's seediest neighborhoods. The back door of a bar called The Drunken Buffoon opened into the alley and was the primary source of game for these two friends.

"Before climbing onto the roof, they quickly unpacked some of their supplies and set up the first lure: – a voluptuous mannequin cut-out of a beautiful, buxom, big-breasted blond, and they leaned her against the wall opposite their rooftop stand. Next, they walked halfway down the alley and hung pizza slices, several chicken wings, and a slice of salt lick fish. 'Nothing goes so well with beer as something salty,' Geary said with a grin on his face. Arnold could not agree more. 'Although, when the humans get drunk as much as the ones in this bar do, pizza and wings are just as good – if not better.' Geary could not argue with that valid point. Arnold then pulled out a brand-new spray bottle. 'It's vanilla - one of the most attractive scents to men. It's a natural aphrodisiac, libido enhancer, and stress reducer. Gets them really riled up, and works like a charm every time.' He quickly sprayed the perfume oil throughout the alley.

"They both looked closely at the picture of the young lady. After a few moments, they shrug their shoulders and shook their heads. 'I just don't get it. What's the big attraction that all these males have for someone who looks like this? Oh well, as long as it works. Good for us, bad for them!' With that said Arnold slapped his friend on the shoulder and they both had a good laugh. Then they climbed up to the roof, unpacked the rest of their gear, and settled into the stand. Now, all they had to do was wait.

"It was just after midnight when the first male walked out of the back door of the bar. He sauntered up to the wall opposite the door, and unzipped his pants to relieve himself.

"'Like clockwork. Never fails,' Arnold whispered to his friend as he looked over the prey through his scope. 'This one has relatively small ears though.'

"'It's alright,' Geary whispered back, 'we can still put his other parts to good use.' They watched him finish, and start to go back inside. Suddenly he turned and lifted up his head, as if trying to get a scent of something mesmerizing. The two friends could clearly see him take a few deep breaths – he was definitely being drawn to the smell. After following it for a few feet, he saw her – a beautiful woman scandalously dressed and giving a flirtatious look. He almost floated to her with a big grin stretching across his face. Her intoxicating perfume waffled across the alley and he knew exactly what he wanted. With mounting excitement, he stopped just a few feet in front of her and pursed his lips to whistle his appreciation of her looks when everything suddenly went black.

"'Nice shot,' Arnold exclaimed as Geary lowered his gun. His first kill of the season was pretty easy indeed. This male specimen, that they quickly bagged and tagged, was too intoxicated to see the difference between a real person and a lure, made the wrong decision to come and harass some unsuspecting female in a back alley, and put himself in their kill zone. 'Well,' Geary answered, 'if they're drunk enough to fall for that trap, then why make it any harder on us? I can sit here all night and pick off their dumb...' Geary quickly stopped expressing his opinions of the intoxicated humans as another male emerged into the alley and proceeded to the same spot as the previous one. Neither one of the deer wanted to make too much noise and possibly scare off their next prey.

"After finishing his business, quite sloppily too, the human began to return to the bar when all of a sudden he saw it. His salivary glands went wild and his stomach rumbled again as his eyes went wide with the amazement at his luck. Starving for the last several hours because he spent all of his money on beer, the last of which was still awaiting his return inside the bar, he drooled at the food just dangling there by the door. He wasn't sure which one to bite into first. The fish looked quite inviting and he took a lick of that. The pizza smelled really good and he took a ravenous bite, and then another. It was absolutely delicious.

"While it was going to be a slightly more difficult shot for the two hunters, he was still well within their kill zone. 'Hold on,' Geary whispered to Arnold as the trigger on his rifle was about to be pulled. 'He has a really small face. Have to let this one go – he's too young. I bet he's drinking in there with a fake ID.'

"'Yeah, you're right,' Arnold acknowledged. He slowly set his rifle back down and watched as the famished kid finished the slice of pizza, two chicken wings, and licked the fish for another five minutes. Then he looked around as if something spooked him, and quickly went back inside.

"For the next hour Arnold and Geary sat in their stand, sipping water, chewing grass sandwiches, making small talk, and joking around to pass the time. It was a great night to be in the city, and they were both enjoying themselves very much.

"It didn't take too long for another male to come out. He stretched for a bit as if he just woke up, shook himself as if a chill ran down his back, and then proceeded to cough so forcefully that the two deer seriously thought a lung was going to come popping out at any second. Eventually the subject of their interest managed to get that respiratory problem under control. He looked around, pulled out a lighter, and lit a cigarette that was dangling between his lips. After taking a few deep drags, he proceeded to walk over to a slightly different spot on the opposite wall. He finished his chore while still coughing from time to time and began to return to the bar as if the alley was no different on that night than any other. He was totally oblivious to the cutout, the perfume, and the food. Arnold suddenly realized that the reason this male was not going to fall for any of their lures was because he could not smell anything at all. He was sure that most foods probably taste very bland to him as well. It looked as if this one was going to get away as the human reached for the doorknob and began to pull open the door.

"Without wasting another second, Arnold grabbed the whistle that dangled around his neck and blew into it as hard as he could. A very soft and soothing female voice emanated from it and echoed off the walls of the alley. 'Ooooouuuuu' came the intoxicating sound, followed by a deep breath, and a light giggle that could make most any human male's heart skip a beat. The man in the alley heard those sounds and froze mid-step. He let go of the doorknob and looked down the alley to find where the engaging sounds had come from. He heard it again and squinted his eyes trying to see the source of that alluring voice. Unable to see anything yet, he turned towards the end of the alley and slowly began to walk. Before long he saw her – a big breasted woman with the sweetest voice that he had ever heard. His heart rate doubled as he came closer and closer because she was absolutely drop dead gorgeous. Of course, it took only another five seconds for him to drop dead but he was not gorgeous.

"'One for me, and now there's one for you,' Geary said as Arnold lowered his shotgun. 'He's a plump one, too.' Arnold smiled at the prospect of all the chili, jerky, steaks, and burgers he and his family will now be able to make and sell for a large profit to the bear and wolf families that live on the other side of the forest. However, the ultimate prize that he came to the city for still eluded him. "'Yeah, but his ears are just not big enough,' Arnold complained as he tagged and bagged his latest kill with the help of his friend. 'I have a funny feeling that this year I will be going home without one of those big ones yet again.' Geary tried to sympathize and reassure that the night was not yet over, but they both knew that the sun would rise in a few hours and that would mean the end of their hunting trip. The really good ones were usually spotted much earlier.

"Geary noticed that Arnold's shoulders were stooped and he was a lot less talkative as they returned to their stand. The next two hours were spent in relative quiet. There were a few more humans that made an appearance in the alley that night, but they were all either females, which held no interest for these particular hunters, or way too young, and shooting a human less than twenty-one years of age was illegal.

"As the first rays of the sun began to lift the night sky, Arnold suggested that it was time to pack up and go home. Both of them felt that there was not going to be any more game to hunt on that particular night, and besides, the bar had closed and they were getting pretty tired.

"Just as the two friends were about to start descending from their stand, a human male stumbled into the alley from the street. He swayed from side to side, and seemed very indecisive about what he wanted to do next. Finally, after tripping twice over his own feet and nearly falling, he managed to make his way halfway down the alley, lean against the wall with his forehead, and unzip his pants. Still on the roof, the two friends could hear him singing softly under his breath and from time to time yell out some slurred gibberish. After finishing up and finding the task of pulling the zipper back up too difficult, the strange male disengaged himself from the wall, took a few seconds to regain his balance, looked around sheepishly to see if anyone was watching, and began to stumble back the way he had come.

"Nonchalantly, Arnold took his shotgun and examined the prey through the scope. He saw a fully grown specimen, but decided not to bother with this one, especially since he was walking away from them. It would have been an extremely difficult shot at best. Suddenly he froze in place and squealed in delight.

"'Geary,' he whispered as fast as he could, 'check out this one. Look at his ears! They're huge! That, my friend, is an eight-pointer.' Geary picked up his scope, which he had already detached from his rifle, and examined the male in the alley. His ears, he saw, were certainly rather large, and he knew that his friend was nearly shaking with excitement. However, the guy was just a bit too far. He had to be lured to the proximal part of the alley.

"'How do we get him to notice the cutout?' Geary whispered back. 'He can't see her from there, and the other ones ate all the food. I'm pretty sure the spray has dissipated as well, and I packed the whistle at the bottom of my bag. I'll never get it out in time before he walks away.' He could see Arnold biting his lower lip. They could both see that the human had finished up what he needed to do, and after taking a few deep breaths, continued to slowly walk away in the opposite direction. Panic and frustration began to take over the two bucks, but suddenly Arnold remembered something. He quickly looked over at his friend and threw his own pack at him.

"'I totally forgot that I have one more bait. Bought it a few years ago and have never used it. Don't even know if it will work. Right in that outside pocket there. Yeah, the high heel shoes,' he said without taking his eyes off the prize and not even trying to be quiet anymore. 'Put them on quickly and walk the edge of the roof. Hurry, please!' Geary did as he was asked as fast as he could.

"Click, click, click, click. The sound reverberated through the alley. Click, click, click. Geary was swinging his hips back and forth as he walked the entire length of the edge of the roof, back and forth, doing his best to produce the sexiest clicking possible, hoping and praying that the specimen that his friend has long been searching for will hear the high heels and come back to their end of the alley. He held his breath in anticipation and saw that Arnold was doing the same thing.

"After several seconds, which seemed like much longer to the two animals, the human stopped in mid-stride and turned around. A look of curiosity was clearly etched on his face. He stood there for what seemed like forever, apparently trying to decide what he should do next.

"Click, click, click. Finally, the male took a few cautious steps toward their end of the alley, but then stopped as if he was reconsidering. Click, click, click. The sound continued to call out to him. He stood there for a while with his head bowed down low, frowning, and rocking from his toes back to his heels. Then he pulled his hands out of his pants pockets, holding a bunch of bills in one of them. He quickly counted how much money he had, and then, as a grungy grin spread across his face, began to make his way to the other end of the alley as quickly as his drunken legs would carry him. In no time at all he saw the strikingly beautiful blond, and right away knew, without a shadow of a doubt, what she was, and that he made the right decision. She was the most exotic woman he had ever seen, and exuded the promise of undulating excitement and endless fun.

"On top of the roof, Geary was frozen in one place, with one foot in front of the other, staring down at the big-eared male, too scared to make any more movements in fear of scaring off the skittish prey. Eventually, however, he did shift his eyes and glanced over at his friend. Arnold was pressing the butt of his shotgun hard into his shoulder and looking intensely through the scope with unfaltering concentration. Down in the alley, the male was quickly approaching the cutout, and making some kind of grunting noise. Geary had never experienced so much tension before a kill, and was exhaling ever so slowly when he heard his friend quietly say 'Come on. Come to papa. Yeah, that's it.' After several seconds, 'Oh, you are on my wall.'

"Sonny, I guess that what I have been trying to say is that irresponsible drinking can lead to very poor decision making – plain and simple. Often, we do or say (or both) very stupid things when inebriated, and such behavior may lead to dire consequences that, at times, may not be easily apologized for or reversed. Quite often those occurrences are simply inexcusable. Many humans have died because they, or someone else, made one of those poor decisions, and deer had nothing to do with it. So, when you are old enough, drink in moderation, and continue to make sensible choices. However, if by some chance you find yourself well beyond the point of pleasant intoxication, stay indoors until your mind returns to a normal state of sensibility, and don't forget that until that happens, make sure to use indoor plumbing. Of course, there is also an option of not drinking at all. I promise that no one will think any less of you. Who knows, you might even earn someone's admiration and respect. In other words, make a decision you can live with. Oh, and, also, don't smoke.

"Well, Sonny, that's it for this one. I hope this story gave you something to ponder. For now, get a good night's sleep. Depending on your future decisions, that may not always be possible. Oh, and remember, the restroom is at the end of the hallway on the left.

"Good night, sleep tight, and sweet dreams."

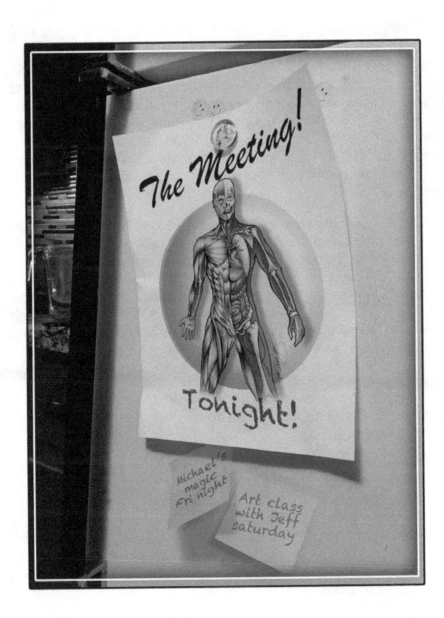

"**W**ell Sonny, sit back, relax, and listen to the story that I'm going to tell you. It's about healthy living, co-operation among team members, and mutual respect. Mostly though, it's about goals and the co-operative effort that it takes to achieve them. As you know, almost all of us have goals and dreams that we strive towards (at least we should – that's one of the things that makes us feel alive), but some do not realize all of the combined effort that it takes to get there and achieve them. Let me see if I can explain it a little better:

"It was a warm summer night and the temperature was just right for sleeping. The windows in most homes were left open as the humidity was very low and a light breeze proved to be soothing as people lay in their beds and dreamed of pleasant places and fun times. There was hardly any traffic in the streets, and even the crickets kept their noise to a minimum, seemingly aware that people were enjoying their slumber more so on that particular night than any other in recent memory.

"Everything was still as one particular man lay in bed, immersed in a deep, restful sleep. It was also a perfect night for a meeting.

"You see Sonny, all of his major organs gathered to try and settle an age-old debate and to see if they could agree on an answer once and for all. They also wanted to decide how best to proceed with a new goal. Therefore, the agenda for that night was to first, finally figure out who was the most important organ among them, and then, decide the best course of action to take in order for the man they all resided in to become physically fit.

"'I think,' the brain spoke up first as it looked down at all the other organs with an air of arrogance, 'that I am the most important organ. After all, I'm the smartest one here and make all the pivotal decisions, I control just about everything, and I'm responsible for all the higher life functions. Just look at my long beautiful neurons. Without me, all of you would become lost, and eventually none of you would be able to function properly or even exist when deprived of my leadership.'

"'You're also very humble,' the spinal cord interjected reflexively in a very sarcastic tone, and then under its breath added, 'and very bossy.' The brain chose to ignore the inferior structure that was so closely attached to it through the foramen magnum and looked to all of the other organs for affirmation. However, the others disagreed.

"'All of those are fine points brain,' the heart spoke up next, 'but I feel that it is me that should be accepted as the most important. I circulate the blood to keep all of the parts of the body happy. And let me tell you, that is a lot of hard work. Just look at how big and strong I am, especially on the left side. Sure, some of the arteries help me out with the distal circulation, but I'm still responsible for the majority of it. It is not easy to keep this steady rhythm going day in and day out. Unlike many of you, I never take breaks, and that's despite the fact that the stomach allows things through that try and interfere with my smooth functioning.' Upon completion of the heart's speech lungs took a deep breath and performed a gesture equivalent to a teenager rolling their eyes. It was pretty obvious how they felt about that proposed argument.

"'Need we bring up the fact that all of you really enjoy having oxygen around?' the lungs spoke up in unison after clearing their throat. 'Especially you brain. You absolutely despise not having enough. But what do we know? We're just dangling here in the breeze, expanding and contracting with every breath, importing all of that valuable oxygen, getting rid of just the right amount of carbon dioxide. Don't mind us constantly working on that tidal volume thing, the positive pressure balance, and the alveolar maintenance. We'll just hang here and not interfere with your vitally important debate. Where were you in the argument? Oh yes, the stomach, why do you let all those unpleasant items through?'

"All the organs stared at the lungs with blank looks on their faces. The heart just regurgitated some fluid back at the lungs and gave them a dirty look. The lungs coughed for a bit and refused to expand again. Everyone asked the heart to apologize since hypoxia quickly set in and nobody enjoyed that feeling. The heart did not want to do it at first, but eventually complied with everyone's wishes, especially since it began to feel quite dizzy within the confines of anaerobic respirations, and the lungs finally took a deep breath. As all of the organs began to enjoy the clean, fresh air once again, nobody even noticed that the lungs winked at the diaphragm in acknowledgement of its collaboration. Slowly, all of the organs turned away from the lungs and looked at the stomach.

"'Yeah stomach,' the liver eventually piped up next, 'do you have to let all those harsh things through? The majority of the stuff that the heart doesn't like, I don't like either. Couldn't you return that as garbage or something?'

"'Oh my,' the stomach replied with a nervous voice that displayed no confidence or strength. 'I've been staying up for nights worrying about that.'

"'I know,' the small intestine interrupted with a voice that clearly expressed frustration, 'my duodenum is killing me because of that. You need to relax a little more. Stop stressing yourself out so much.' Stomach bowed his cardiac sphincter in rapid succession and responded with a shaky voice.

"'Oh, I'm so sorry. Yes, I will try to be calmer, but it is so hard. I feel anxious and jittery a lot because there's so much to worry about. And, I have been known to return some of that food stuff back, especially when I'm sick, but ...' that happens very rarely. I try to do ...' Stomach's voice trailed off, and nobody was sure whether it was going to finish the sentence or not. Then, as if it had just woken up, it added, 'When I get full, I just can't tell the difference between the good stuff and the bad. I try to reduce everything to a manageable size and pass it on down as fast as I can. Even if I could tell the difference, there isn't enough time. I'm always pressured to move things along in about two hours or less. Small intestine, perhaps you could sort things out. And also, since I break down all of these huge and complex particles into manageable food and building materials that all of you rely on, and let's face it, none of you are hosting environments so harsh that it winds up eating you from within, then perhaps I am the most import ... ant ...' the stomach just trailed off once again and looked down so as to avoid visual contact with all others. Everyone waited for it to finish the sentence, but this time it made no further noise.

"'Well if that's the case,' the small intestine growled, 'then I should be the most important because none of you would have any food to eat or building blocks to build with if I didn't absorb them for you. Heart you can circulate that blood all day long, but if I don't put all those goodies in there, all of you would starve. And stomach, you don't break everything down. I have to take care of some of that stuff myself. You're too skittish to touch the fats. Don't want to get your hands greasy or something?' The stomach nervously shifted its weight, opened the pyloric sphincter but said nothing. The small intestine paused long enough to make sure that the stomach had no retort and then added, 'Yes, the liver helps me with that. Thanks for the bile, big guy. But it's not like I absorb absolutely everything. There's quite a bit that I pass on to my big brother.' At that, the large intestine moaned and then let out a long groan.

"'I feel bloated just listening to you rumble on, little brother,' the large intestine grumbled with a look of disgust on his face. 'It's actually a whole lot that you dump in me. And all that water! I have to be a good host to a majority of our guests and reabsorb all the water that you allow to escape. I don't know how important an organ the rest of you think I am, but I do know that if I ever stop working, the rest of you will find yourselves in deep … smelly trouble.' The other organs grumbled in agreement for a few seconds. The stomach took a deep breath and once again opened the sphincter, seemingly wanting to say something, but no words came forth. Then it exhaled and with a slouching posture just melted into the background.

"'Alright,' the pancreas suddenly spoke up, 'that is a very valid point you have there, large intestine. But none of you would be able to enjoy all those foods that the stomach partially breaks down, the small intestine absorbs, and the heart circulates, if it wasn't for me providing all of you with mouths so that you could eat them. Every time stomach wakes up and works, I secrete all kinds of juices as well to make small intestines' life that much easier. Let's face it, if I stop working, the rest of you would starve. And then there is the constant job of making sure that there aren't too many or too few of the sweets floating around. I think we all know how cranky the brain gets when there's just not enough sugar to his liking and how lazy some of you become when there is too much of it. Those distal nerves and the eyes do very little work when hyperglycemia hits and eventually stop working altogether. Even the kidneys shut down after a while. I think I have a very legitimate argument for the title of 'Most Important Organ.'

"'Hey man, we don't see what the problem is with hyperglycemia,' the eyes chimed in with sleepy voices. 'The work we do is not that important for survival, man. We just refocus the light and flip the image, which is pretty cool. It's not like there is a whole lot for us to do in the first place. And what is the big deal about us working properly anyway? But whatever, man. We're cool with whatever happens and whatever you give us. Like, whatever man.'

"The pancreas was about to retort vehemently, and call the eyes privileged and spoiled lazy twins who can't appreciate the importance of proper eyesight and the effort that it takes to keep them healthy, when a booming voice that seemed to have been coming from all directions at once suddenly startled all of the organs.

"'Would all of you please keep it down,' the skin spoke in a slow and measured tone. 'I'm busy thermo-regulating and all of your bickering is not helping.'

"'Sorry about that,' the liver piped up in a soft voice and looked sternly at all of the other organs. 'We didn't mean to disturb you, skin. We'll be quieter.'

"'Thank you,' the booming voice resonated throughout the body. 'By the way, none of you turn any different colors, temperatures, or textures to warn him of any problems when they arise. In no time at all I can turn cyanotic, pale, mottled, jaundiced (the liver coughed when it heard that), flushed, clammy, or diaphoretic. And if needed, I can also become warm, hot, and, sometimes, very hot. Don't make me demonstrate that last one - none of you would find that experience to be very pleasant. So, I'm pretty important as well, but I don't care about the title. Just keep it down so I can concentrate on my duties here. Thank you.'

"'I suppose an argument can be made for skin there,' the liver responded in a soft voice, having recovered from its coughing spell. 'However, I need to throw my candidacy into the ring as well. I'm pretty hard at work all day and all night, multi-tasking like no other. Let's see now, I help pancreas regulate those sweets, I, alone, remove all kinds of toxins, which is no easy task, I might add, I store a bunch of stuff that all of you might need later at a moment's notice, I manufacture some proteins and a few other useful substances, and I make sure that the clotting factors are up to code and meet the current standards. And let me tell you, my P450 cells work overtime when there is alcohol or just about any kind of medication involved. I feel like I need a vacation after those nights. But do I take a break and go on vacation? Nope, I continue working, and I work hard all the time. The rest of you would not survive for very long without me.' The small intestine kept shaking its head at everyone's arguments in obvious disagreement, but just like the stomach, offered no words of wisdom to disprove their cases for the title.

"The kidneys suddenly cleared their collective throats getting everyone to turn around and look in their general direction. With drawn out words, they presented their case.

"'Much like the liver,' they began to speak in unison, sounding like a poorly rehearsed choir speaking under water, 'we work hard day and night too. You, Heart, circulate an awful lot of blood through us and we filter all of it. We make sure there is not too much water here or too little. With the help of our headgear we regulate ...' the kidneys paused as some of the organs appeared confused about what headgear they were talking about. The kidneys inhaled deeply in frustration at the lack of familiarity with anatomy that some of the organs displayed and with a bit of anger in their voice continued, 'With the help of the adrenal glands, we regulate many electrolytes, manufacture angiotensin and corticoid steroids, and do a pretty good job of annoying the bladder. And unlike the liver that works harder only when there is alcohol or medications present, we work harder when there is alcohol, certain other types of medications, coffee, tea, sports drinks, or just a large infusion of any fluids. Boy, the bladder does not like those times at all. And let us tell all of you, it's not easy dealing with an irritated bladder. That thing is so moody. For those reasons, we feel certain that the title should belong to us. Don't let the fact that we are retro-peritoneal organs sway your decision. We deserve it just as much, and probably more, than all of you.' When the kidneys finished their speech, all the organs turned back to face each other once again, feeling that the argument the kidneys presented could not be taken seriously, and therefore, garnered no response.

"'If we stop working, you will all die.' The kidneys added in a slow and measured tone. Everyone turned back around and whole-heartedly, with overlapping voices, agreed that they are indeed vital organs and should be considered in the running for the title as well.

"Then everyone briefly looked at the spleen, but it just smiled back and clearly indicated that it had nothing to add to the debate and was, in fact, staying out of it.

"The brain was keeping back a bit, lost in thought trying to formulate his next argument when suddenly he was thrust back into the spotlight when out of nowhere the heart asked why the man doesn't exercise more and eat healthier foods. Everyone looked at the surprised organ with furrowed eyebrows.

"'Yeah, Brain,' the liver spoke again, 'a better diet would not stress me so much and give me more time to accomplish a few other useful things.'

"'I agree,' the pancreas joined in, 'I certainly would have an easier time of it as well.'

"'I'm sure all of us would appreciate that,' the large intestine spoke for all, 'and I know that most of us would be happy with at least some kind of physical activity, perhaps even a few different ones.'

"'Exercise makes me wet and sticky,' skin's voice boomed throughout the body, 'but I am all for it. That would help me stay smoother longer. I like the sound of that.'

"'I know that I would really enjoy the benefits of exercise in the long run,' heart said, 'and many of you would as well.' Some of the bones and a few of the muscles just groaned at that but said nothing; however, most of the organs agreed. The brain stood there frozen and did not speak for a few long seconds. Then he shrugged his shoulders.

"'I don't know,' he finally answered. 'I think we've been busy with so many other things, that we just didn't have enough time. However, if all of you insist on exercising, then we will start first thing in the morning.' Then after a short pause during which the brain thought extremely hard, he asked, 'Which exercises do you guys want us to do? Is working out at the gym, lifting weights, a good idea?' Once again, a good number of muscles groaned and rubbed their filaments. The brain could have sworn he heard a few of the ligaments say something unpleasant under their breath as a whole bunch of them readjusted their grips on the bones and the muscles.

"'Yeah,' the small intestine answered, 'I like the sound of that. We could also try running.'

"'Well,' suddenly they heard a voice coming from a distance as the cartilage from the left knee spoke up. 'Running is indeed a good exercise, but you know, let's not be too hasty in making that decision. We should explore all our options. Let's see, there's also speed walking, or elliptical machines at the gym, yoga, Tai Chi, or … or … cycling. That's a really good one. Oh! And how about swimming? Swimming is awesome!'

"'Oh, I like those suggestions,' the small intestine suddenly spoke up with a hint of excitement. 'Yoga sounds really nice. I mean just look at me, I'm already a contortionist.' Everyone groaned in unison at that comment.

"'Alright,' the brain answered as it gave the cartilage and the small intestine a weird look. 'Those are excellent suggestions. Any others?' Nobody said anything.

"'We will not be able to serve as a comfortable cushion to sit on for too much longer if we start all these silly exercises,' gluteus maximus muscles spoke up next in a desperate attempt to avoid hard work.

"'Now you're just being silly,' the heart responded. 'Don't be so lazy. Just think of how great you'll look once exercising gets under way.'

"'That's right,' the pancreas piped up next. 'In fact, all of you moaning and grumbling muscles will get toned at the very least, and look great.' A few of the muscles wished that they had the brain's power to think in order to come up with a better argument against exercising. After a long pause, all of them let out a collective sigh of surrender. Deep down they knew that exercising would indeed make them stronger and look better, they just didn't want to put the hard work into it.

"'Alright,' one of the gluteus maximus muscles finally spoke up again, 'but we're going to need more protein, and plenty of sleep to recover.'

"'Not a problem,' the brain said, 'I'll get a whole bunch of protein for all of you.' And then in a quieter voice added, 'and do my best to sleep more.'

"'Wait, wait, wait just a minute,' the large intestine could not get the words out fast enough. 'If you ingest too much protein at one time, my little brother dumps a lot of it on my shoulders, and there's not much I can do with it. In fact, it just goes right through me, if you know what I mean?'

"'Yeah, yeah, we know what you mean,' the liver quickly answered. 'Brain, can't you tell the small intestine to absorb more of that protein?' The brain was caught off guard at first, but was able to recover quickly.

"'Look, I just stimulate it to work. I have no control over how hard it works.' Everyone looked at the small intestine with an inquiring look. Even the stomach stuck its pyloric sphincter through the diaphragm to look at the very long organ.

"'None of you know what it's like to be me, but yet, all of you judge me. It's not so easy,' the small intestine began to explain as it assumed a defensive posture. 'When the brain signals me to work, I do. I work hard and do the best job that I can. There's just one of me you know, and I have to absorb a lot of different substances. Despite my best efforts, I can usually absorb only twenty-four to thirty grams of protein at a time. The rest moves on before I can grab it.'

"'And what about the sugars and the fats, Brain?' The kidneys suddenly spoke up again, 'we heard those should be regulated as well.' The brain frowned but did not respond. Everyone looked at each other waiting for someone to speak up with the answer. However, the only sound they heard was the turbulent blood flow through the aortic arch every time the ventricles of the heart contracted.

"'Listening to all of you argue and complain is both painful and nauseating,' a new foreboding voice startled the organs, causing everyone to gasp. The large intestine was so surprised that, inadvertently, a small air bubble traveled down the descending colon.

"The appendix was standing behind them with a look of frustration and anger clearly etched on its visage. It gave everyone a look of disapproval just like a parent would do to a child that had misbehaved. Then it just slowly shook its upper half and flared its nostrils, not that it had any nostrils, Sonny, but that was the impression that it gave to everyone else.

"'Oh my,' they all heard the stomach mumble its favorite two words from somewhere in the back, but, once again, nobody bothered to acknowledge it. The appendix carefully detached itself from the large intestine and menacingly turned towards the gathered organs.

"'All of you sound totally ridiculous arguing to see who is the most important organ.' It gave everyone another stern look and then continued on with emphasis on intonation, enunciation, and pronunciation. 'I can tell you that I am one of the smallest and least important organs in the body, but if I get really angry, the rest of you would be in mortal danger. But do I claim my case by threatening all the others? No, I do not. And do you guys and girls know why? Because nobody is more important than anyone else. All of you rely on each other for survival. It's a team effort that keeps all of us alive. Remember that concept of homeostasis? It is maintained because all of you work together as one big happy family ... well, a big family that is usually happy.

"'Each of you performs important functions that are vital to the body and the well-being of everyone else. The goal here is a healthy and functioning body. In order to achieve and maintain optimal health everyone has to work together. Almost all goals in life require efforts from multiple sources. Congruency, complimentary activities, and mutual respect are the keys in achieving almost anything from the smallest of feats to the largest achievements imaginable.' All of the organs listened intently, as understanding of the concept of teamwork began to slowly sink in. They grumbled together their agreement and looked at each other with acceptance and respect. After a short pause, appendix took a deep breath and continued.

"'Whether it is a single individual trying to reach new heights in life, a group of people trying out a new path, an organization reaching for a different direction, or a major corporation attempting to attain a new goal, it all takes teamwork. And homeostasis is no different. So therefore,' the appendix paused for dramatic effect, 'nobody is more important than anyone else.' Just as a few of the organs were about to say something more, the appendix spoke again even louder to make sure everyone heard it.

"'And when it comes to becoming more fit, anything is better than nothing. Brain, it doesn't matter which exercises we do, just as long as we do something. There are three things that go into becoming fit. And I want all of you to notice that fitness and health are goals, and therefore require a team effort as well. Number one: do something. Walk, run, cycle, swim, lift weights, play sports, martial arts, fencing, and even roller blading are just some examples of excellent forms of exercise. Find out what suits us better,' Appendix looked at Heart and then everyone else, 'and just go out there and do it. Anything is better than sitting on the couch all day. The more we do, the more of a benefit we will reap. Number two: proper nutrition. No amount of exercise that we do will benefit us in any way if we eat all kinds of junk. It is apparent that none of you are diet experts, and that's okay. All we have to do is cut down on junk food and soda. Limit the carbohydrates and fats, and increase the intake of proteins.' The appendix looked at the small intestine.

"'Yes, twenty-four to thirty grams at a time, I know. That is basically one meal that is not too large. Make it a sensible size meal, Brain, and the small intestine will be fine.' Then the appendix looked at the brain. 'Just use common sense when it comes to eating right. And if we feel we need more help or better suggestions at a later time, we could always do some research or consult a specialist.' The brain bowed his frontal cortex in agreement and understanding.

"'And that brings me to the final item.' Appendix continued. 'Number three is rest. It is very important that we get somewhere between six and eight hours of sleep every night. These muscles, though admittedly lazy, will do most of their recovery and growth during sleep. And for that matter you, Brain, will feel more energized as well, and be able to think more clearly, make better decisions, feel less stressed out,' the stomach popped its sphincter out even further when it heard those words, 'and yes, the stomach will be more confident and not worry as much.'

"'I like the sound of that,' Stomach finally piped up as the small intestine smiled and patted the stomach on the posterior side.

"All of the organs soon came to an agreement that the appendix was absolutely correct and that they're all equally important and vital to each other and the body in general. After quick apologies, they shook hands and warmly embraced.

"'Ladies and gentlemen,' the appendix spoke up again, 'I'm glad that things have settled down and you have all shown progress and maturity, and I really hate to break all of this up, but look at the time. The alarm clock is going to go off in less than two minutes, and the man will wake. So, back to your places of function and don't forget what we have learned here today.' All of the organs were surprised that it was already morning – the night sure went by fast. They all hurriedly returned to their proper places and less than two minutes later, the man woke up refreshed and energized.

"He felt better than ever before and decided to start the day off with a brisk walk to a gym. For some unexplainable reason, there was a purpose and an urge to accomplish several new goals in his life, something he did not experience yesterday. He wasn't sure what was causing him to feel like that, but he certainly liked it.

"I guess that what I have been trying to say, Sonny, is that life is one complex mechanism with many cogs, levers, and pulleys. No matter how big or small the parts are, they all serve an important function. If one of those breaks and fails, the whole thing can crumble and fall into pieces. That's why everyone needs to work together in order to sustain status quo at minimum, but hopefully with a goal towards improving. Appendix summarized that point for me fairly well. As the saying goes, no man is an island. In order to accomplish even the simplest of life's goals, a multifaceted approach is usually the answer in order to achieve satisfactory results. Optimization is almost always achieved through teamwork, and if you ever get stuck, just ask for help. Fitness is just one of those goals. Live smart in all facets of your life, and you should be able to live a healthy life for a long time.

"Well, that's all I have for you for today. I hope you enjoyed this story as much as I enjoyed telling it. Sonny, it's getting to be past both of our bedtimes. Let's try and get that six to eight hours of sleep. Perhaps we'll both be smarter and more energized in the morning.

"Good night, sleep tight, and sweet dreams."

"**W**ell Sonny, sit back, relax, and listen to the story that I'm going to tell you. It is a short story about what happened to my uncle not so long ago. It is about patience, misunderstanding, and open arms. But mostly, it is about a type of stereo that plays sweet music to a narrow mind, and unless changed, may eventually lead to chaos and anarchy. I know that it sounds pretty confusing right about now, but soon enough it will all make perfect sense. So, if you're ready, I'd like to start by reading you a letter my uncle wrote to me and let me tell you, he poured his heart and soul into this one.:

"'*Dear nephew,'*

"He never calls me by my first name, or anyone else, for that matter, but anyway, let me go on.

"'*Last week Thursday, was the most frustrating and embarrassing day of my life. I don't even know where to begin. First though, I can safely say that I am very confused and extremely upset over this whole matter. In fact, next week I am going to go see a psychologist; I sincerely hope that perhaps he can help me deal with these feelings.*

"'*I just find it so frustrating every time I think about it. We, who consider ourselves such highly educated and well-rounded individuals living in a modern, technologically advanced society, are nothing but a bunch of lowly cowards and disillusioned fanatics. I fully understand that such a bold statement should not encompass such a large population of this planet, and that there are many individuals out there who rise above such shortcomings, but by the time you finish reading my letter, you will come to realize why I feel so strongly, and perhaps even commiserate with the turmoil that is raging deep in my heart.*

"'It's just that I keep finding myself surrounded by individuals who, for some unknown reason, cannot expand their tiny minds and see things and circumstances the way they really are, and not just how they appear to be on the surface. They continue to judge a book by its cover, and I just find them to be complete and utter morons.'

"My uncle never holds back; he always expresses how he feels about everything. You see, he was born without a filter between his brain and his mouth. What makes it worse though is that he lacks tact, and I believe his chandelier does not always emit the brightest of lights – there are a few burned out bulbs up there, and nobody has replaced them. My aunt had to get out of some pretty hot situations over the years because of that, but that is a different story that I'll tell you another time."

"'It all began just like any other ordinary day in my ordinary life. I woke up bright and early, at six in the morning. After setting the coffee maker to brew, I went for a brisk jog in the park. I have always enjoyed running at an early hour because there is hardly anybody outside to get in the way, allowing me to truly enjoy the crisp, refreshing air in relative peace and quiet. The birds sing in their various choruses, the breeze feels great on my face, and the sweet smells of the neighborhood

bakery tingle my nostrils. Last Thursday was promising to be a great day.

"'By the time I returned home, the sun had firmly planted its warming rays on the city, and the clouds dispersed, revealing a light blue sky. My wife, with rollers still in her hair, was cautiously sipping the hot beverage that had finished brewing. She smiled a warm good morning in my direction. Just as always, I kissed her hello (after so many years of marriage, fewer and fewer spoken words are needed in order to communicate), and quickly began to prepare breakfast. After a great night's sleep and a good run, I felt refreshed and re-energized that morning, and looked forward to tackling the various tasks at the office and spending a nice, quiet evening with my wife. Of course, I had no idea of the events that the day had in store for me or, for that matter, the rest of the world.

"'After breakfast I showered, brushed my teeth, kissed my wife good-bye, and went to work. Pulling out of my driveway, I immediately noticed that there was something different about the street. I drove my car down the same route I always take, but somehow it felt different. It took me a few minutes, but then it finally hit me! Traffic! There was bumper-to-bumper traffic on every single street that I took – a lot more than usual. All of the main streets and side roads were heavily congested – both towards and away from downtown. I had never seen so much traffic in this city before, and I have lived here all my life. We were all crawling as if a big accident had reduced a major highway to a single lane that had to be shared *by traffic moving in opposite directions. Needless to say, I never saw the accident.*

"'I noticed something else as well. There were hundreds, maybe thousands, of people in the streets. Even the secondary streets were filled with them – probably for the first time in this city's history. I distinctly remember thinking that the number of people I saw walking and running around on the roads, sidewalks, and even lawns was far greater than the entire population of our small town. I had no idea where they all had come from, but it proved to be somewhat frustrating when quite a few of them paid no attention to cars or traffic signals when the time came to crossing the streets. It all reminded me of Times Square in New York City on New Year's Eve. By the time I reached the office, I was over two hours late, and was no longer in a good mood. I had never been that late to anything – ever. It's a good thing I'm the boss, and don't have to justify the rare occurrences of tardiness at work.

"'My secretary was already there, standing next to her desk, holding a cup of coffee, grinning sheepishly as if I was going to give her the day off. Looking at her closely, I still could not figure out why she was so happy. Last time I saw her that energized was when I gave her a raise last year. Or was it the year before?

"'I sat behind my desk and noticed that she was still staring at me. I knew that something was definitely happening, but could not, for the life of me, figure out what it was. I stared at

Michael Kugel

her for what seemed like a long time, and finally gave up.

"'What? What is it?' I said. 'Did I misfile the returns in the receipt drawer again?' She just smiled even wider and slowly shook her head.

"'You really have not heard, have you? You did not hear about it? You didn't watch the morning news on TV, listen to the radio, or read a newspaper? You really have not?' A look of disbelief covered her face, but there was no hint of surprise. I must admit that after working closely with her for the last eighteen years, she has come to know me fairly well, and on that Thursday morning I had an inexplicable feeling that she fully expected me to be unaware of the unfolding events.

"'She shook her head for a few more long moments as if savoring my ignorance and the apparent look of curiosity that must have been forming on my face and she inhaled deeply. Then she lowered her head and raised her eyebrows. Unable to explain why, it was a very intense moment for me, and I felt very inept in my apparent lack of knowledge, but I had no idea that the worst was yet to come. Very slowly and clearly, she said, 'Aliens. Aliens have come, and right to this city no less.'

"'I began to explain to her that we have had that problem in this country for many years. That our borders get crossed by those unfortunate people every day, but her raised hand quickly quieted me. She shook her head again in disbelief.

"'No, no, no,' she began. 'Every TV and radio station, every newspaper in the country is reporting that during the night there have been multiple sightings of a huge space ship in our atmosphere. It has already been confirmed by the military and civilian space agencies. We are not alone in the universe. There are a lot of speculations out there about who or what they are, and why they came here. However, the only other thing that the experts know for sure is that the current trajectory of the ship will take it directly to us – this very city. It is coming here! Isn't that exciting?'

"I sat there with my mouth wide open, hardly believing the words that my ears just heard. A state of shock enveloped me as my secretary gave me her newspaper and I read the front page. It was no hoax. Just as she had pointed out, we were about to be visited by very distant guests. I was not sure what to say, or even how to feel. Excitement, fear, happiness, and apprehension surged through me as if lightning had struck me, and all my emotions ran wild, leaving me feeling very tired and very old. I gave my secretary the day off and decided to face the rest of that monumental day with my wife.

"The drive home was slower still. It seemed that the number of cars and pedestrians had doubled, but this time, I did not care about the long ride. I tried to listen to one of the local radio stations for the latest developments, but my mind was in a trance. I was wandering off to distant planets and galaxies, wondering if the aliens would try to help us, or harm us, or perhaps neither. Would they look like us, or would we find their appearance to be significantly different, perhaps even appalling? Would they have what we would consider special powers? Would this ship be a civilian or military craft? What would their opinion be of all the creatures they would find here, including humans, and the cultures and societies that we have created on this planet? And would we still be a planet of divided countries after this?

"'Even though I was well entertained by my thoughts and imagination, I was really glad to finally pull into my driveway. I don't know how long it took me to get back home, but that is when things turned even worse. My mind was still filled with various questions and concerns: How would we communicate? Would they be able to make verbal sounds that exist on at least one of the frequencies that human ears can hear, and if so, would they be able to speak at least one of Earth's many languages? Would their cultures and customs be what we consider civilized, or would we find them cruel and barbaric? I obviously had no answers to any of these questions, and suddenly wondered why it was all bothering me so much.

"'I stepped out of my car still in deep thought, and with the welcoming sight of my front door, all of the commotion and craziness of the streets seemed somehow far away and almost forgotten. I could not wait to see my wife, to share the news, opinions, the dilemmas that haunted my mind, and to find out her thoughts and feelings on this incredible event that was about to happen, so I didn't even notice as an enormous shadow crept over my neighborhood and my house, shielding us from the warming rays of the sun. I first realized that something was happening when people began running all around me, including on my lawn and driveway. Many were hollering some words in barely understandable sentences, or just plain yelling – some in sheer terror, others in extreme jubilation.

"I raised my hand and was about to protest the unceremonious trampling of my grass, when somebody ran right into me. I never did see the person, but it was likely some overgrown, hysterical teenager who was not looking where he was going. From the impact I flew through the air, severe pain shooting down my right side. I'm not sure anymore if it was even I, myself, screaming, but when I hit the ground, landing hard on my back, I no longer felt any pain. In fact, I felt quite numb all over, unable to speak, move, or even think clearly. I was completely mesmerized, as time seemed to slow down and then come to a screeching halt.

"Hovering directly above me, not much higher than the rooftops, was a genuine, as-real-as-it-gets, Unidentified Flying Object! Stretching approximately eight to nine hundred yards in diameter, suspended about one hundred feet in the air, surrounded by a swarm of military helicopters and jets, it defied the imagination and boggled the mind. I was in an absolute state of awe.

"It was not the circular shape of a flying saucer so often depicted in the infamous cinemas and literature of the science-fiction world. Nor did it display the aerodynamic design so common to all flying apparatus developed and built on Earth. Rather it was ... irregular; no better word comes to mind. It had no apparent front or back, no noticeable system of propulsion, and no discernible points of entry. It was full of grooves and ridges, and looked as if various pieces of building materials were roughly thrown together to create this machine that now floated above my city, yet apparently it was fully capable of interstellar travel. It was hard to tell the color of the spaceship as well – whether it was green or blue, but I definitely noticed a hint of red here and there. Lying on my front lawn, staring at the spectacular sight above me, the rest of the world became immaterial. I could not see or hear any propulsion system that was holding it up in the air. As if all animals, humans, and even earthly flying machines halted and just stared in awe as well, everything around me seemed to suddenly stand still and not produce any sound. I felt as if I was caught in the deafening vacuum of outer space.

"'Then, the most extraordinary event unfolded, right in front of everybody's eyes. Directly above me, on the underside of the ship, an orifice opened up, like a stoma on a leaf. I could not see anything inside, but somewhere in the back of my mind I half expected alien guards to peek through the opening at any moment. My eyes widened in further amazement, as I expected the unexpected, and neither I nor anybody else who witnessed that spectacle had to wait for very long. An instant later, a ray of unearthly origin beamed down directly upon me, *engulfing my entire body in a circle of light and I felt my body become completely weightless. Curiously enough, I was not scared or even nervous.*

"'Exhausted by what seemed like countless hours of experiencing extreme emotions: worry, excitement, happiness, adrenaline rushes, and most recently, anger, my mind decided to no longer care or attempt to solve all those unanswerable questions and dilemmas. Perhaps that is why all of a sudden, I felt very relaxed, both physically and emotionally. Time stood still, as a split second after the strange light enveloped me, I felt my body slowly lift off the ground, gently turn in midair until I was erect, and delicately set on my feet in the middle of the lawn. Now that I think about it, it was a rather comforting experience.

"'As the beam that picked me up from the ground disappeared, the most disastrous and inexplicable event of my life, as well as all of humanity, unfolded right above my head. A pilot of one of the military helicopters unleashed its machine guns and fired a missile at the strange flying saucer. Before the first explosion could even expand into a spectacular ball of fire, all of the other military aircrafts began to fire their deadly weapons at it as if it were a menace of unimaginable evil that had settled upon Earth and required immediate eradication.

"'They say that no one is perfect, that everybody makes mistakes, and that we all deserve a second chance. I wonder if these

visitors believe in the same philosophy. As if individualism and independent thought were not a human trait, and split-second decisions could not be reversed or corrected, all of the pilots displayed quite clearly, just what kind of destructive power those various birds of prey were capable of. They did not stop until there was nothing left.

"'In horror and complete disbelief, I watched as the unsuspecting and obviously undefended spaceship began to fall apart, raining debris all around me. It was a massacre of unparalleled proportions, and I could not mistake the undeniable smell of death. Running as fast as my legs could carry me and breathing heavily with every step, I searched for any cover of safety, eventually finding it on my front porch. Gasping for air, I took a closer look at the fallen fragments, and a peculiar thought occurred to me. I realized that almost all of the ship's debris was roughly the same size and shape. As I scanned the fallen objects, I realized that every fragment, every scrap of that ship that littered the ground, resembled a humanoid body, and that there was no metal or machinery to be found of any kind at all. Every piece or chip of what I had assumed to be parts of the fallen space craft were actually bodies of the alien visitors. Everywhere I looked, all I could see was their strange short bodies, from which extended muscular arms, and very thin and fragile legs. I could see their faces, opened mouths, wrinkled noses, and unblinking eyes – a countenance devoid of life.

"'It is ever so hard to describe the tormented feeling that swept over me at that moment and forced me to experience a surge of immense pain, frustration, and anger. The helplessness that overwhelmed me, and the guilt that struck hard at my consciousness, will forever chip away at my self-esteem as a righteous human being. Words are simply not enough. All of the morals and ethics that I had been led to believe in, everything that I based and have lived my life by, were being crushed right in front of my eyes. And to think that we humans consider ourselves civilized.

"'Suddenly, out of the corner of my eye I noticed something odd. Quickly spinning my head to the left, no more than ten yards away from me, I saw one of the aliens stop its free-fall about five feet above the ground, and softly land. It was hard to miss the big wound on its leg, oozing large amount of iridescent yellow fluid. Lying prone on the ground for what seemed like ages with its head turned towards me and looking right into my eyes, I could clearly see the face of the creature, displaying unmistakable signs of emotional and physical pain. I even saw tears run down its cheeks. Gathering its strength, and putting one powerful arm in front of the other, the visitor began to crawl over to the rose bush that my wife planted over eight years ago and has been lovingly nurturing ever since. Lying there motionless in the dirt, not more than two feet tall, was another alien. With gentle, trembling hands the little one was slowly scooped off the ground, and held tightly to the bosom of the wounded alien. Physically their faces all looked somewhat similar, and I could not pick out any family resemblances, or even what sex all these poor creatures were. However, there was no mistaking the love and the special bonding that exists between a parent and its child. With tears streaking down my own cheeks, I watched as that parent held the child's green body close to its own, stroking its long blue hair. Bending its head down, the parent alien kept whispering something into the child's ear, often kissing its bright red face.

"'I wanted to go and offer my help, or a soothing word, or perhaps just put my hand on its shoulder. I wanted to show this parent that I shared its' pain and suffering, to perhaps offer a word of apology, and my shoulder to cry on. I believe that there are no language barriers when it comes to love and happiness, or hate and sadness. But, what could I say? What gesture could I perform that would explain it all, and make everything better? How could I even look this being in the eye ever again? I stood there paralyzed, watching the poor creature, as helpless as ever. As if a knife was buried deep into my heart, my chest ached mercilessly, and my knees eventually began to tremble until I collapsed onto the ground. At that moment, more than anything in the world, I wanted to be someplace else – in a different town, another country, most decidedly on a different planet.

"'I hope you understand my frustration and anger, nephew. These past few days have been quite trying, and the nightmares are not going away. They say that time heals all wounds, but ever since The Incident, every day feels like an eternity.

"*Write back soon. I want to know how you are doing. After all, it has been so long.*

"*Well, good-bye for now.*

Your Uncle.'"

"How about that crazy story, Sonny? Kind of makes you think, doesn't it? Things like that could definitely ruin a perfectly good day. I wonder how it all ended. You were probably wondering why you've never heard of such an extraordinary event? Well, Sonny, you probably have, but just don't realize it. Unfortunately, there are still quite a few narrow minds out there, and they continue listening to that type of stereo, and therefore, similar incidents like this one keep happening all around us, every day of every week. We humans, so technologically advanced, socially organized, and intellectually enlightened sometimes can't get out of our own way, and often become our own worst enemy. I guess people are people, and I wonder if they will ever learn not to be so judgmental of others.

"Sonny, it's late, and well past your bedtime. I am going to go now, and perhaps tomorrow night I will tell you another story. In the meantime, remember that when you are with others – share and don't dare, play fair, don't be a bully, and always stand up for what is right.

"Good night, sleep tight, and sweet dreams."

FRIENDSHIP

"**W**ell Sonny, sit back, relax, and listen to the story that I'm going to tell you. It is about self-fulfillment, adoration, persistence, and big dreams. Mostly though, it is about a friendship that most would find quite bizarre and very endearing. It is a story that I heard not too long ago, when everything seemed dark and empty, and I felt down and lost. It brought cheer into my life and a smile to my face. If not today, then perhaps someday in the future, it can do the same for you. Anyway, enough of the reminiscing and gooey stuff. You are probably wondering what kind of friendship would be considered so unusual. Well, a friendship between an elephant and a mouse.

"You see, there was an elephant by the name of Albert and all he ever wanted was to become a world class artiste. He fantasized about entertaining the whole world – his name in large neon lights, sold-out performances, and crowds of fans screaming with delight at the very sight of him! He could even visualize some of the adoring ladies fainting at the mere kiss that he would blow their way. Albert could almost smell and taste the excitement of being on stage with everyone's eyes fixated on him, big smiles on their faces, holding their breaths in great anticipation. He practiced signing autographs by the dozens, picked out the charities to which he would donate a substantial amount of his earnings, and wrote acceptance and thank you speeches.

"There was just one little problem. Albert had no talent as an entertainer of any kind. He could not act, sing, dance, juggle, perform magic, do impersonations, or tell a joke. He, as most elephants, was not endowed with great athleticism, and did not have a fit muscular body. Albert struggled to walk the tight rope and was horrible at swallowing sharp flaming swords. He was even timid when it came to dull cold daggers. However, none of that mattered, because Albert was determined to make it big.

"One day, he decided that it was time to do something about making his dream come true. There was to be no more eating tree leaves in the mornings, no more grass picking in the afternoons, and definitely no more holding on to the tail of the elephant in front of him while some other elephant was holding his tail during those morning and evening walks.

"'I'm going to be the lead elephant in the conga line from now on,' Albert thought to himself. He felt that the beginning of the summer was a good time to move out west where all the celebrities lived, and make his name a household word. He packed his trunks, said good-bye to his family and friends, and left the small town that he grew up in. Those that knew him tried to talk the ambitious elephant out of leaving, saying that only one out of a thousand talented hopefuls become successful enough to just barely support themselves (let alone make it big), and with his talents, perhaps one out of ten million. But he would not be persuaded to stay. His friends described the starving artist scenario for the aspiring star in great detail. However, that made Albert only more determined. Eventually his family resorted to pleading, but he just kissed them on the forehead, gave them all a big warm hug, and walked out the door and the front lawn gate towards the beginning of his new life.

"Albert spent three months on the road. He hitchhiked as much as possible, but there are only so many vehicles big enough for an elephant, and even less drivers willing to pick one up. He tried hopping trains a few times, but was mostly unsuccessful due to his lack of athleticism. Plus, he decided to stop trying that after he accidently derailed one of them. For the most part, Albert walked, which suited him just fine. Thick green forests interspersed with ponds, lakes, streams, and puddles surrounding the highways that he travelled provided all the food and water that he could ever want. The summer weather was quite agreeable with the elephant's preference for a warm climate, and the frequent rains were actually a welcomed shower that Albert enjoyed a whole lot. At night, he slept at rest areas, taking up one of the parking spots designated for tractor-trailers. Sleeping outdoors did not bother Albert in the least. In fact, he actually preferred it to being in a confined space. He would gaze at the night sky and dream about being a star.

"Eventually, he reached Hollywood. The city, and most of the surrounding areas, proved to be a breathtaking spectacle, full of tall buildings, expensive houses, blinding lights, lavish limousines, tourist attractions, and of course, countless people. After walking around the city and taking in all of the beautiful sites and scenery, Albert came to the conclusion that he needed to rent an apartment. Therefore, he had to find a job to pay for it, and since free food was scarce, he needed money for that as well.

"Finding a place that he could call his humble abode was not easy. Very few places were large enough to accommodate an elephant, and even fewer landlords allowed animals on their property. The one that Albert finally did settle into was a warehouse that had been converted into a very large studio apartment. The neighborhood was a little sketchy, but the unit came fully furnished, and had clear running water and indoor plumbing – something that Albert was highly impressed with since he did not have all those luxuries back home. Although the bathtub was too small for him to climb into, he loved filling it up with water, then sucking it into his great trunk and spraying it all over his body with forceful exhalations. It created quite a mess in the bathroom, but the cleanup was pretty easy and quick for him.

"Before Albert even signed that rental lease, he managed to find a job. It was actually a lot easier than he anticipated. Quite a few people were willing to hire him – restaurant owners, nightclub managers, bartenders, private club executives, and even some guy by the name of Little Tony whom his associates referred to as The Big Cheese. All of these establishments had rules and regulations that had to be followed, and who better than an elephant to remind patrons of that when they misbehaved. There are a very limited number of beings in this world that would be willing to pick a fight with an adult elephant. Besides, Albert was willing to work for practically peanuts!

"The aspiring star decided to work at a diner that was only two blocks away from his new home. It appealed to him because in addition to being an enforcer, which paid only slightly more than a minimum wage, he could double as a waiter, and make some extra money on tips. As a bonus, because the owner was so happy to finally have a real enforcer, since the restaurant was in the roughest part of the neighborhood, he allowed Albert to eat vegetables from the stockroom for free during his lunch breaks. The elephant worked there full-time and was earning enough money to cover all of his bills and other expenses, allowing him to live well above poverty level, unlike many of his neighbors, and occasionally send some money to his parents. With hard work and dedication, he rose up the ranks in a relatively short time and became a manager.

"However, not everything was going as great as it might have appeared to the casual observer. While Albert managed to find a good apartment and a decent job, depression loomed over him, threatening to engulf his upbeat and determined character. He was becoming frustrated, disappointed, and sad because his ultimate goal of becoming a world-famous entertainer appeared further and further out of reach. After going to numerous auditions, meetings with many agents, attending countless lunches with individuals in supposedly high places, and participating in a few acting classes, he failed miserably to impress anyone looking for talented performers. On several occasions, he walked out of the auditions, embarrassed, with his head so low that his trunk dragged on the ground. Directors broke out in hysterical laughter at the sight of his portrayal of Hamlet or Oedipus. A few screamed in terror when he tried to hit the high notes during the tryouts for a theatrical production of a popular play. He was even rejected when he tried to sign up for a ten-minute spot at a local comedy club open microphone night. Albert's future in the entertainment world was not looking promising.

"One night, Albert was closing up at the diner, but his mind was not on his work. Instead, he was heavily concentrating on the lines that he was going to recite the following morning at yet another audition. He already had them memorized, and so, just under his breath, all day long, he was practicing the proper intonation and enunciation. After everyone was gone and cleanup was completed, he turned off all the lights in the diner, stepped outside, and locked the door. After taking two steps, Albert remembered that he forgot to turn off the grill in the kitchen. He quickly unlocked the door and turned on the lights. He was not prepared for what he saw next and was thoroughly shocked.

"Albert's eyes went wide and his heart skipped a beat as he held his breath for what seemed like a long time. After all the effort he put forth over the last six months to get rid of cockroaches, ants, and other vermin, there was a mouse sitting on the counter, who appeared to be just as shocked as Albert. He could not believe that there was now going to be a mice infestation as well.

"He furrowed his eyebrows as adrenaline flooded into his bloodstream, and he mentally prepared himself for what he was about to do. In two big steps he was able to close the distance to the counter. The mouse, having finally recovered from the shock of being discovered in such a vulnerable spot, began to run towards the far end of the counter – away from the charging elephant. However, a very large pot was in its way, and going around it or above it did not pan out as an option. The little rodent quickly spun around the other way, desperately searching for a safe heaven. Suddenly, the elephant's extremely large foot cut off that retreat and his trunk eliminated yet another option. The mouse found itself trapped on the countertop with no more hope of escaping. It was boxed in between a wall, a large pot, an elephant's foot and trunk.

"Instinctively, it pressed its tiny body against the wall in a useless attempt to make itself seem as small as possible, and shaking in sheer terror, awaited the final blow. The situation seemed even more hopeless as the elephant leaned closer for a better look at the little white mammal.

"'Please don't hurt me,' the mouse suddenly pleaded, surprised to hear its own voice. 'I meant no harm. I'm just really hungry and didn't think anyone would miss a few crumbs.' Albert was surprised by the plea and leaned back, relaxing his forehead. He wasn't really sure of what to do or say next and a long awkward silence ensued.

"'I'm not going to hurt you,' he finally answered as the adrenaline and excitement of the chase began to dissipate. 'But who are you and what are you doing here?' He lowered his foot and trunk seeing that the little mouse was quite scared, and further intimidation was no longer necessary. In fact, he sat down and tried to assume the most non-threatening pose and facial expression that he could muster.

"'My name is Ed,' the mouse began still unsure of what to make of the situation, 'and I've been living here in the diner for almost a month. I made a little home for myself in that corner over there.' Ed pointed to a spot under the counter near the opposite wall. Sure enough, Albert saw a hole there that he had never noticed before. 'I come out at night, when everyone is gone, to scrape up some food and water,' Ed continued. 'You do a pretty good job of cleaning up, but usually there are still enough crumbs left over for me to survive on.'

"'I see,' the elephant began to sympathize. 'So why don't you just get a job and buy your own food? You could also get your own place then. No more living in a cramped hole in the wall and being afraid to come out during the day. And how many other mice are here anyway?'

"'Well,' the mouse felt much more at ease now, sensing that there was no imminent danger anymore, 'there are no other mice here, and I have tried so hard to get a job. I filled out many applications for various positions and went to numerous auditions, but nobody wants to hire a small mouse like me. So, I have to do what I can to survive. And the cats around here are so unfriendly. Just the other day...'

"'Hold on, hold one second,' Albert interrupted. 'Did you say auditions? As in performing on stage – in front of an audience?'

"The mouse smiled a little. 'Yes. I suppose you could call me one of those starving artists. My life-long dream has been to become an entertainer, on stage or in front of a camera, I don't care. But,' he lowered his head, 'there aren't a lot of parts for mice out there.'

"Albert smiled from ear to ear. For the first time in his life, he found somebody that he could commiserate with. 'That has been a dream of mine for as long as I can remember, and so far, I have been rejected from every audition I ever went to as well. Ever since I weighed six hundred pounds, all I could think about is the world of entertainment, and me performing for large crowds either on stage or in front of a camera.'

"Ed was genuinely surprised and intrigued. Forgetting any fear that he had earlier, he became completely relaxed, and engaged in a lengthy conversation with Albert. Both shared their feelings of frustrations and disappointments. They talked about their aspirations, backgrounds, families they left behind, crazy lifestyle that this city offered, and of course, the trials and tribulations of trying to get even a small part in any play, movie, musical, show, or skit.

"As the conversation was coming to an end, Albert took a few moments to think the situation over. He liked this little guy. There was no denying that a bond had formed between the two of them.

"'Ed,' he finally said after a short period of contemplation, 'you seem pretty decent and I like you, but I simply cannot let you stay here. If the Health Department found out that we are willingly harboring a mouse, the diner would be shut down. However, I do have a solution. Why don't you crash at my place? We have a lot in common, I have a big apartment with plenty of room, and I'll bring you all the food you want. What do you think?'

"Ed blinked in disbelief at this amazing offer. However, he quickly recovered his composure and a big grin stretched across his face. It was the easiest decision he ever had to make in his entire life. And that, Sonny, is how the strange friendship began.

"The elephant and the mouse became best buddies. Ed moved into Albert's apartment that very night. The refrigerator was full of various foods, and the smaller of the two mammals ate, well, like a pig. Ed had never seen so much food before and, for the first time since arriving in this big city, was able to satisfy his hunger. He did not stop eating until he was absolutely stuffed. Then he crawled into a queen-sized bed, thanked Albert for everything, and drifted off into a deep relaxed sleep – the kind that he did not have in a long, long time.

"The next day, Albert performed horribly at his audition. Ed was dismissed from one as well since the part called for a knight to battle a dragon, and his statuesque physique simply did not resemble either one. Both were disappointed, but this time, after sharing their feelings with someone who understood, they had no problems putting it behind them and moving on – living as happily as possible and looking forward to future auditions.

"Together, Albert and Ed devised a housekeeping schedule. One of the activities that they regularly engaged in was cleaning the apartment. Keeping tidy was very important to both of them, because while one could eat like a pig, neither wanted to live like one. Every Sunday, they dusted furniture, mopped floors, vacuumed carpets, washed windows, and removed cobwebs from ceiling and walls. Well, actually the elephant did most of that work, because Ed was just too small, but he did help in whatever way he could. He sat on the vacuum as Albert would push it back and forth, leaning forward like a dog on a fresh scent, pointing out any dust or dirt particles that the big guy missed. He would also climb on top of various pieces of furniture, and look down at the room from different angles to inspect the elephant's dusting. When Albert washed the windows, Ed would climb on the outside window ledge, and let his friend know if there were any streaks or spots that needed extra scrubbing. Albert did not mind any of Ed's constructive criticism. In fact, he found it quite amusing. He thought it was rather cute how the little mouse kept his nose just above the carpet when he rode the vacuum and how he hopped between furniture pieces – always looking so serious and intent on not missing a single speck of dust or dirt.

"Sweeping and mopping, as well as web removal, were a little different. Ed was a more active participant in those areas of clean up. After obtaining a tiny broom and mop from a dollhouse, the mouse would clean in the tight corners and hard-to-reach areas. Albert was always amazed how his little friend was able to squeeze his body into the smallest of spaces. Dust and dirt had literally no place to hide when Ed was on the job. He swept and mopped under and behind the refrigerator, the tiny space between the stove and the sink, inside the kitchen and bathroom cupboards, and even under the water heater. The elephant thought it was pretty astonishing how Ed managed to fit himself between closely positioned furniture, behind mirrors and paintings on the walls, amid the DVDs on the rack, and down the kitchen sink drain to clean out the occasional hair clogs. He worked hard to make sure that all those hidden spots remained sparkling, despite the fact that nobody could ever see them.

"Now, when it came to cobwebs, the two friends had to work together as a team in order to accomplish their goal. While Albert was able to remove a lot of it on his own, he was unable to reach the ceiling to wipe all of it away. As big as he was, the ceiling was just about two inches higher than the tip of his trunk when raised all the way up. To solve that problem, Ed stood on his hind legs on the tip of his friend's trunk and used his front paws, in which he held his little broom, to wipe the cobwebs off the ceiling. Had a zoologist witnessed that spectacle, he or she would surely have been astonished by the problem-solving ability and cooperation that these two animals displayed. Albert found it very interesting how his little friend was able to balance himself on only two legs for such a long time. He tried doing that himself several times, but could not stand erect for more than a few seconds before tumbling over. Nonetheless, Ed's perfect balance fascinated him, and Albert keenly watched how the mouse achieved that pose. He studied his friend's technique as intently as Ed sought out dirt and dust.

"There were plenty of other activities that they enjoyed doing together whenever both had free time from work and auditions. Sometimes they liked to go outside the city and take walks in the country and go to farms where they picked fresh fruit from trees. Other times they preferred to take walks in the park, where they collected leaves, gathered pine cones, and watched birds. Sometimes they stayed home, just relaxing, and watching TV. Quite often they went to the movies at the local theater where they always took the last row so Albert would not obstruct anybody's view and no female – or the occasional male – would scream in sheer terror while jumping up and down at the sight of a mouse. Every now and then, they attempted to play 'Hide and seek'. However, while Albert was pretty good at most activities that they engaged in, for obvious reasons, no adult elephant in the world is good at hiding in any part of an overcrowded city.

"Interestingly enough, the game that they liked to play the most, in the park, was called 'Survival of the Quickest.' It consisted of Albert twirling a hula-hoop on his trunk, while Ed jumped through it. They found it quite comical when one of them would make a mistake and the cycle would be broken. Albert sometimes lost his concentration and the hula-hoop would fly off his trunk and into the bushes or tree, or simply hit his big head and land at his feet. Ed sometimes misjudged the speed of the hoop, would get hit by it, and be sent flying through the air, closely resembling Mighty Mouse, but without the cape. Aside from a few minor bumps and bruises, amazingly enough, neither one of them was ever seriously injured. In fact, they spent a lot of that play time rolling around on the ground in hysterical laughter.

"On occasion, they went bike riding in the city park. Well, actually Albert was the one riding the bike. Ed just sat on the handle bars and enjoyed the breeze rushing through his fur. Now, Sonny, that seems innocent enough, but have you ever seen an elephant on a bicycle? Well, neither has anyone else. It was quite an interesting spectacle, and the two friends were always stared at by all the other visitors to the park. Some pointed in amazement at the elephant pedaling a bicycle with no safety wheels on it, while others marveled at the obvious friendship that existed between the two mammals, despite the fact that in nature those two should not be getting along. Yet, there was another group of visitors to the park that gawked at the sight of the two friends in disbelief because they could not understand how the metal frame and rubber tires of the bike held up under the combined weight of a seven-ton elephant and the eight-ounce mouse. For their part, Albert and Ed just could not understand what the big deal was. After all, bears ride bikes, so why can't an elephant ride one as well? Even a few of the bats that lived up high in the trees, opened their eyes, despite the harsh rays of the sun, to gaze upon the spectacle, always wondering what their distant cousin was doing with an elephant. The two friends, however, simply rode on, enjoying the sunshine, pleasant breeze, and fresh clean air of the park.

"One day, both felt that it was time to try something new and exciting, and it proved to be a semi-amusing spectacle for those that were nowhere near the two friends. They tried to rollerblade – it was a first for the elephant. Ed managed to borrow two pairs of tiny skates from another doll, but nobody knows where Albert managed to get four skates big enough for his feet. The visitors to the park on that fine day who happened to be passing by the two friends seemed convinced that the elephant was going to take a big spill and cause serious damage to the park. Somebody called the park's department and they quickly mobilized their repair crews in anticipation of the paved trail and possibly surrounding greenery being ruined by the fall of the giant mammal. One other individual was so convinced of Albert's upcoming plunge, that he called the National Earthquake

Center and told them to expect an earthquake in the next five to seven minutes, measuring approximately 4.0-5.0 on the Richter scale.

"Having never been on skates before, Albert did not know what to expect and tried really hard not to show his friend how nervous he was. He did not cherish the thought of plummeting from his height, which was augmented even more by the tiny wheels. Mostly though, he was deathly afraid of falling on his face, which may drastically affect his ability to look handsome and quite appealing, as well as deliver his lines, for upcoming auditions. Slowly he put the skates on all four of his legs and gingerly stood up. Albert was trying really hard to figure out what he was thinking when he agreed that going skating on rollerblades was a great idea and should be a lot of fun. He shifted his eyes very carefully to see where Ed was and what he was doing. Even moving his eyes too quickly seemed like a dangerous prospect. The mouse had all of his skates on and looked as if he was born with wheels attached to his feet. With a big smile on his face, Ed was skating forwards, backwards, making pinpoint turns, and jumping over various obstacles that a park trail may present to a little mouse. Albert wanted to ask him where he learned to skate like that, but was too scared to utter a single word.

"The mouse eventually noticed that his friend was not as mobile as one would expect a skater to be and looked at his face. Albert's wide-open eyes, clenched jaw, and flared nostrils (okay, flared nostrils on the tip of his trunk, not on his face), and extremely rigid posture clearly displayed all of the fear and apprehension that he felt. While skating between and around the elephant's legs, Ed tried to convince Albert that everything will be alright, that he should bend his knees and try to move only one leg at a time, go slow at first, and not worry about falling down. All of it was, of course, to no avail. Except for his eyes, which he shifted slowly from side to side, Albert could not move a muscle. After running out of words of encouragement, Ed even offered to catch him if he fell. Upon hearing that statement, Albert almost did fall, and would indubitably, have had a good laugh were he not so scared stiff. In desperation, Ed tried to push and then pull his friend, but there was no budging the elephant.

"After about an hour, the two friends found themselves in a strange predicament. While Ed agreed a long time ago to take off his skates and go home, Albert was now too scared to even do that. Trying to get two pairs of skates out from under an elephant that will not move a muscle is a daunting task indeed. It took Ed about two more hours to exhaust all of his theories and ideas on how to do that. He had no choice left but to call the local fire department, the local zoo, a veterinarian, and the National Department of Wildlife Conservation. This was a first for all of them as well. During the next four hours, with the help of two cranes from a nearby construction area, the wheels were finally removed, and Albert's feet firmly planted on the ground. He thanked and apologized to all one hundred and forty-one workers involved in his rescue. Then Albert had to sign a legal document promising that he would never try that again.

"When the time permitted, they went to nightclubs, because Ed loved to dance. Whenever he heard the beat of a good song, he just had to throw caution to the wind, jump on the dance floor, and shake his booty. The smile on his face during those times was absolutely priceless. He loved the adrenaline rush that a good song could produce, the feel of the vibrating floor beneath his feet (all four of them), and the creative visual stimulation of the lights and lasers that most clubs offered.

"Albert, on the other hand, was a bit more rhythmically challenged and attempted to get on the dance floor only when it was slow and there was practically no one else dancing. He felt a bit embarrassed by his clumsiness at trying to keep up with a beat, and was convinced that everyone was looking at him because he was so large and inelegant. When Albert did dance, there wasn't a whole lot of room left for anybody else anyway, and when he started swinging his hips, there was real physical danger to anyone unfortunate enough to be anywhere near the dancing elephant. Albert usually preferred to just stand off to the side of the dance floor, sip his drink, and watch everyone else dance the night away. He was comfortable as a wallflower. However, on those rare occasions when the dance floor did happen to be relatively empty, Albert tried very hard to look like he belonged out there with everybody else, always watching his little friend and trying to imitate moves that would be considered advanced even for a dance choreographer. After many months and countless trips to various clubs, there was actually a marginal improvement in the elephant's ability to dance to a beat.

"During the summer months, and at times, even during the winter, Albert loved to grill. In fact, he was quite good at it and often enjoyed impressing his friend and neighbors with delicious foods that he would cook. He would put on his "Kiss the Cook" apron and a chef's hat that Ed gave him for his birthday and cook away – sometimes for hours. He hated to cook in the kitchen, but put a grill in front of him and Albert was in heaven. Always humming or whistling as he cooked, the elephant liked to sip some red wine, flip his utensils up in the air and catch them behind his back with his trunk. He would then wink at Ed, turn the food over with both arms, and sprinkler salt and pepper (or one of the many other condiments or spices that he liked to combine for a new and exciting taste) with his trunk, all while swinging his big head back and forth to the tune of the song that he was singing.

"Despite all the clowning around and a bit of pleasant intoxication, nothing was ever burned, spices and sauces were added in just the right amounts, and the food was always scrumptious. Ed told his friend more than once that he missed his true calling in life, but the elephant kept insisting that the only place he belonged was in the world of entertainment, and that there was no convincing him otherwise.

"Every now and then, especially if the weather was cooperating, the two friends wound up spending a few hours at the beach. After all, they lived right next to the largest ocean on the planet, and trudging through hot sand and securing first degree sunburn over a relatively large percentage of the body was practically a cultural ritual.

"Albert would grab a large quilt to be his beach towel and Ed a paper towel, and they would head for one of the public beaches. They were both poor swimmers, and therefore, neither one was very fond of deep waters, however, sunbathing on the beach was a perfectly acceptable, and often desirable, way to spend their time. The two friends liked to get their feet wet and splash around a bit, but never let the level of the water get much higher than their knees.

"Albert enjoyed leaving huge imprints in the wet sand for the little kids to play in later. When he snuggled down in the sand, others often asked if he would mind if they used his large body to escape the sun and set up their blankets and towels in his shade. Of course, he never refused.

"Ed loved the way the sand felt between his toes and found the waves of the ocean almost mesmerizing. He also liked to build sandcastles with the kids. While they worked hard to construct towers, walls, and a moat, the little mouse would climb inside one of the windows and work on the interior. Interior decorating was a secret passion of his. Ed always made sure that there was a throne for the imaginary king to sit on, four chairs and a table for him and his family to eat on, and beds for the whole royalty and their guests to sleep in. He also made sure there was a television, bookcase, and fully furnished kitchen with a swinging door.

"Now, I know what you are thinking, Sonny. Where did they get the time to do all these wonderful activities? Well, they didn't do them all in one day, of course. All of this took place over a long period of time – about five years (give or take a few months). Albert still continued to work at the diner full-time and pay all the bills. Ed continued his attempts to find any kind of gainful employment, but received no calls asking him for an interview.

"Both still tried for various parts at numerous auditions, but always heard the same responses, 'We were looking for somebody smaller.' Or 'We were looking for somebody bigger.' Sometimes they said that Albert's trunk was just a little too short, or that Ed's tail was just a little too long. While it was all very frustrating, the two friends found it much easier to handle rejections and other disappointments in general when there was someone there to share them with. They talked about the problems and hurdles that they frequently faced and had to overcome, the stereotypes they had to deal with, how they felt about the world, the politics within it, the economy and inflation, their families, relationships, the morals and ethics of life in general, the value of a proper diet and health, exercise, and which toilet paper was the strongest while still retaining its soft to the touch qualities.

"Albert was no longer depressed despite his unsuccessful attempts to enter the world of entertainment. Both felt lucky to have met each other and life moved on. At times, they even went out with female companions, but neither one was able to sustain any long-term relationships with any of the girls that they dated. Once they went on a double date, but both girls jumped up on a chair and screamed when they saw whom they were double dating. The two friends broke out in loud laughter for many years to come when they spoke of that night and jumped up onto chairs and impersonated their dates.

"I know, Sonny, that you are wondering why I am describing all these activities that the two friends enjoyed. What is it all leading up to? So, here is the part of my story where it all ties together and begins to make more sense.

"One day, something special happened that changed both of their lives forever. All of the planets must have been aligned in just the right planes and their moons converged to the right positions. Perhaps opportunity became lost in the big city, wound up in their neighborhood, and knocked on their door. Albert just happened to be home and answered it.

"Ed was on the couch finishing up his first reading of a new script that he had to memorize for yet another audition when Albert burst into the loft, barely able to contain himself. His eyes were wide, his breathing fast, and the look on his face was a mixture of surprise and awe. His tail was wagging back and forth as if he belonged to the K9 family. He looked at the mouse with a huge grin.

"'What is it? What happened?' Ed asked, not sure if he should smile as well and be happy, or frown and be worried. Albert had trouble finding the right words and stumbled over his own tongue in an almost drunken attempt to explain his unexpected excitement.

"'I got it!' the words finally escaped his lips. 'I got it! I got it! I got it!' he started jumping up and down. Ed was glad they were first floor residents and the building contained no basement.

"'What?' the mouse started getting excited himself, but obviously, still unsure about what. 'Let me guess. You finally got that joke I told you the other night, right?'

"'No, no, no!' Albert could no longer contain himself and began to actually dance while jumping. 'I got the job! I mean, I got the part! I am going to be a performer!'

"'That is great!' Ed was genuinely happy for his friend. 'How? When? What are you going to be doing? And stop dancing; you're ruining the furniture and the floor!' It took quite a few minutes for the elephant to settle down, enabling him to finally start speaking coherently, although he was still pretty worked up.

"'Get ready for this,' Albert said enthusiastically. 'You are looking at the latest addition to a large cast of performers at the Circus. Can you believe it? I can hardly believe it myself. They had auditions today. I was on my way back home from the diner and saw the advertisement in the front window of that coffee house across the street. They were having open auditions today for the part of an elephant. They said I was a natural.'

"'You don't say?' Ed answered. 'A natural. Who would have thought that playing an elephant was your deeply hidden talent?'

"'Well, I would have certainly not thought of that,' Albert said. 'But they said I fit that part perfectly. I wish you could have seen it. There were an alligator, puma, and giraffe trying out for that part as well, but I was just better than they were, I guess. So now, I have to report back in two weeks to begin training for my routine. In exactly three months and twenty-four days I will be performing in my very first show!'

"'Really?' the mouse was now ecstatic as well. 'Congratulations! That is truly amazing. I have never been as happy and excited for you as I am right now! I don't even know what to say. I'm actually speechless. I mean this is so wonderful. I really am speechless!'

"Albert was well paid at his new job, and he worked very hard on his routine during rehearsals. It was extremely difficult and labor-intensive work, but he persevered. Although his muscles ached mercilessly, and Albert used to come home with his whole body sore, bruised, and extremely exhausted, he was always happy. He felt very lucky to have finally received his big break, and was determined not to let it slip through his toes. Before going to bed, he would share with his friend the stories about the long hours of exercises that all the performers had to do, the various hours of stamina training they underwent, the seemingly endless and extremely tedious time spent on choreography, and, of course, the semi-decent food they ate during the short breaks.

"Each morning, Albert woke up rejuvenated, raring to go back to the fairgrounds to improve or learn new skills. In fact, he impressed the circus owners so much, that they gave him the lead part during the elephant showcase. Eventually, he began to perform tricks that amazed even the seasoned performers and other staff who thought that they had seen every circus trick and stunt in the book. One individual claimed that he had seen some elephant perform some of those tricks in the park, but extremely poorly, displaying lousy coordination, low skill level, and very little talent for such maneuvers. However, nobody took that clown seriously. Everyone was so impressed with the elephant's performance, that his picture was added to commercials, posters, and billboards advertising the circus. He was truly beginning to live out his dream.

"The night before the big debut Albert could hardly sleep a wink. He tossed and turned nearly all night, as nervous energy and abundance of excitement circulated through his body. He knew that he was ready for the limelight, felt confident in his abilities to deliver a great performance, and couldn't wait for the curtain call.

"Ed sat in the front row of the Big Tent when the lights finally dimmed and the first act was introduced. He was very happy for his big friend and could hardly wait to see all the skills displayed that were needed to perform the difficult tricks he had heard so much about. Everyone's routine was flawless, and the crowd enthusiastically cheered all of the performers.

"Albert was finally introduced. He came out with five other elephants, but after a ten-minute routine where all of them performed a few well-choreographed moves, the other ones went behind the curtain. Albert was left alone in the middle of the ring, with the spotlight brightly illuminating his big frame. The audience, sitting quietly in the dark, held their breath in anticipation. Ed was up on his hind feet when a bad feeling settled over him.

"'Oh no! Not now,' he whispered as a look of uncertainty appeared on his friend's face. An ever-increasing aura of trepidation surrounded the elephant and Ed realized that his friend was battling stage fright. As panic engulfed the mouse and he began to feel the pain of yet another failure that the two of them were doomed to experience in the world of entertainment, Ed let out a barely perceptible plea, 'C'mon buddy. You can do it!'

"Although no one heard those words, Albert, suddenly, closed his eyes and calmness settled over him. He burst out into his first Big Trick, and Ed sank back into the seat as relief washed over him, and he watched his friend perform all kinds of amazing stunts. The crowd watched in absolute awe. Everyone felt that this was the best act of the night, and would have agreed that the elephant's number alone was worth the price of admission. When Albert finished, the applause, whistles, and cheers became thunderous under the Big Tent.

"What's that Sonny? You want to know what Albert did? Well, I'll get to that real soon so have some patience, because this is almost the end. Now, as I was saying, the show was a big success. Word spread about the circus and the amazing performances of the cast.

"Critics raved in their reviews and described the wonderfully entertaining spectacle as 'a purely impressive show of strength, coordination, and balance,' 'visually stimulating excitement,' 'an on the edge of your seat thriller,' and 'an absolutely stunning performance.' The circus became, as they say, 'the talk of the town', and all of their upcoming shows were sold out. No matter what town or country they went to on their road tours, people lined up and camped out for tickets days in advance. Their anticipated arrival generated a lot of energy and excitement in the cities where the circus was expected to put on a show.

"At the center of the circus phenomenon was none other than Albert. No one could stop talking about him. Everyone found it mind boggling that not only could an elephant perform such difficult tricks so well, but make it all look so easy – at times, even performing with his eyes closed. Virtually overnight his name became a household word. The whole world knew who he was, what he looked like, and the amazing tricks that he did.

"When the circus toured overseas, Albert saw something that stole his breath away. He saw his name in neon lights, with thousands of fans screaming his name (albeit with a bit of an accent), and huge billboards where his picture was the only image displayed to advertise the upcoming shows. After fifteen weeks of touring Europe and the Orient and dozens of successful shows, Albert realized that he had finally made it. After all of the doubts, setbacks, injuries, embarrassments, and hard work, he was now one of the biggest stars in the world. He was famous and rich, but best of all, an entertainer. For the first time in his life he felt complete and satisfied as he pondered the fact that his biggest dream, that life-consuming desire he had felt ever since he was a calf, was now a reality.

"After twenty-five weeks of being on the road, Albert returned home a very happy elephant. He could hardly wait to share his experiences from overseas with his best friend. He wanted to tell him about the abundance of amusing backstage mishaps that they all had to deal with from time to time, the numerous individuals he met and had great conversations with, the varieties of cultures and customs that he encountered during his travels, and the many different styles of cooking and unusual foods that he had tasted.

"When he walked through the front door, Ed was sitting on a sill, staring out the window. He appeared to be in deep thought and did not hear his friend's arrival.

"'Hey, little buddy,' Albert said, still smiling. 'I'm back! I have so much to tell you! How are you doing? And, oh boy, do I have great news for you!' Ed spun around, surprise showing on his face which was quickly replaced by a big smile and a look of jubilation. However, there was no hiding the eyes. They were red, puffy, holding big, giant tears. When the mouse blinked, they slid down his already slippery cheeks.

"'Albert?!' Ed began to smile. 'You're back! How did the tour go? Wow, you look great. Have a seat. Tell me all about it.' Ed scampered over to the couch and settled in to hear all about his big friend's stories of circus life, faraway places, and newly found fame and fortune.

"Albert frowned and a look of concern replaced happiness and excitement. He had never seen his little friend this upset and it was somewhat shocking. For as long as he could remember Ed always had a positive attitude, an upbeat state of mind that saw the world in a beautifully bright light with an optimistic future. No matter what unfortunate events they encountered, the mouse never despaired, complained, or frowned. Ed would always smile, sometimes give a wink, and say something to the effect of 'you can't win them all,' and 'we'll get our breaks tomorrow.' However today, Albert found his friend unhappy, even depressed, and that really bothered the elephant.

"'What is it Ed?' the elephant softly asked as he sat down on the couch next to his friend. 'What happened? Are you okay? Is everything alright? And don't try to deny it. I can plainly see that you've been crying.' Very gently, he put his arm around the little mouse. Ed knew that there was no point in denying the fact that he had been upset and crying. He felt that he might as well share his feelings with his best friend.

"'Well,' he began, 'it's actually kind of embarrassing. We have been friends for a long time.' He hesitated and appeared to be searching for the right words. 'Both of us had the same dream when we met, and we both worked very hard to get it. Throughout this whole time, you have supported me immeasurably. You have provided me with a roof over my head, all the food that I could possibly eat, and great emotional support especially on those days when things were not going so great. I know, I know, I have done the same for you, but you have done so much more, and now you have finally made it. You've become the star that you have always envisioned yourself to be. Look at me though. No matter how hard I try, I cannot get a single part in any kind of a show, can't provide any food even for myself, or contribute in any other way towards this apartment or anything else we do in our lives. I feel so frustrated and helpless. I have sponged off you ever since we became friends,' his voice began to trail off. 'I just feel so useless, and like such a burden. Perhaps, I should just leave.' Albert's vision was temporarily obstructed by the formation of his own tears, and his heart skipped a beat at the mention of Ed leaving.

"'Nonsense,' the elephant answered in a very quiet voice. 'You have been a great support for me, and I would never want you to leave. We have been through thick and thin together.' His voice became louder and firmer. 'Besides, you take up hardly any space here and you eat a lot, but, nonetheless, you still eat like...well, like a mouse. And yes, I have succeeded finally, but don't you know, I could have never done it without you?' Ed looked at his friend quizzically.

"'What are you talking about?' he said. 'You worked very hard to get to where you are now. I had nothing to do with that.'

"'Ed! Buddy! Don't you realize that my whole act, just about every little thing that I do during my performance would have been impossible without you?' The mouse looked as perplexed as ever, but the elephant continued. 'I learned to get up in my hind legs by watching you when we cleaned this apartment. I always found it amazing how you jump from furniture to furniture and crawl through the smallest of spaces. That inspired me to stand on my back legs and jump through those small hoops. Remember how we used to play 'Survival of the Quickest'? No matter how fast I would twirl that hula-hoop on my trunk, as long as you concentrated, you were always quick enough to get through it without getting hit. Well, from watching you I learned how to time my jumps, and now I jump through those small hoops while they're on fire. And where do you think I learned to dance for that cute little number when they play that upbeat music and the whole audience starts clapping along? That's right. All those times we went to the night clubs. Guess what? I danced for them at my audition. I just closed my eyes and tried to mimic you as best as I could. The director and the producer at that audition said it was the worst dancing they had ever seen, but the spectacle of seeing an elephant even try to keep a rhythm was not only entertaining, but also quite unique. They said that with some hard work, fine tuning, and lots of practice, it could turn into a great part of my routine. And it has! That's the number that helped me separate myself from all the other elephants. I would have never even tried that had you not dragged me to those dance clubs so many times.

"'Remember all those times I grilled and flipped spatulas and forks? I was just having fun and showing off to you. Who knew that juggling was going to be such a big part of my number? And when I ride my bike in the second half of my act, that came from all those times when you talked me into going bike riding in the park. Because if you remember, at first, I could hardly keep my balance on those two wheels.'"

"'Yeah, I remember,' Ed answered. 'The training wheels could not support our combined weight.'

"'Exactly,' Albert smiled. 'Shortly after they hired me, I was telling some clown about our first double date that we went on. Just like we used to do, when I reached the part about my date flipping out when she saw you, I jumped up on the chair and stamped my feet, to show him how funny and totally ridiculous she looked. We both had a good laugh. One of the guys in charge just happened to see me doing that, and so it became a part of my routine as well. You know the part I'm talking about, the one where I do all those silly things – the comedy portion.' Ed nodded his head. 'In two weeks when all of the performers reconvene back from this break, they're thinking of trying me to rollerblade because another clown remembered seeing us on TV and thought how hysterical it was to watch.'

"Albert looked his friend right in the eyes. 'Ed, you are my best friend and you have influenced my whole life. Everything I do was made possible because of you. Sure, I have fine-tuned and improved many of my skills since I joined the circus, but without your contributions and support, I would have never passed that audition and would be working at the diner to this day and the world of entertainment would still be only a dream. You have cheered me up and inspired me to keep going when I was depressed and frustrated after all those rejections, ready to quit and go back home to my family where no one ever believed in me. In fact, you were the only one who believed that I could make it big. Through good times and bad, you were always my best bud. Without you, none of this success would have been possible. Ed, please don't go.'

"Albert trailed off as tears welled up in his eyes once again and a lump formed in his throat. For a few long seconds neither one of them moved nor spoke. Ed stared up at his friend with awe and admiration. His mouth was moving ever so slightly as if he was trying to say something, but no words were coming out. He too was speechless.

"Then they embraced each other and let the emotions of the moment flow over them for a while. As it turned out, no further words were necessary.

"'Hey Albert,' the mouse finally spoke after they released each other and leaned back on the couch, 'did I hear you say earlier that you have some good news for me?'

"'Oh, yeah!' Albert exclaimed as he excitedly jumped up with a big smile stretching across his face once again. 'I almost forgot. Well, those people in the circus overheard me talking about you and began asking questions. I wound up telling them about all the crazy things we do. I even told them how you inspired me to perform many of my tricks. The more I told them, the more interested they became.

Every single one of them found it difficult to believe that an elephant and a mouse get along so well. So, guess what?' Albert paused for dramatic effect (he loved dramatic effects), while Ed was nearly exploding with anticipation. He knew what his friend was going to say next, but until it actually escaped Albert's mouth, it was too hard to fathom. After what seemed like an eternity to Ed, the elephant finally spoke.

"'They want you to come with me in two weeks to see if they can put together a routine where we would perform together. They said that if we look good as a pair, they just might come up with a whole new act – just for us. I don't know what all of it will involve, but I do know that for one of the portions of it they want you to rollerblade around me while I stand on my back legs, dancing to some upbeat music, and juggling a spatula, a wooden spoon, and a short bamboo stick. They still don't trust me with a machete, hot poker, or a large fork. Who knows, maybe someday I'll be able to perform that number on rollerblades as well. Mmm…Maybe not. Anyway, we would be the main attraction starting next season. One director even said that just seeing us perform together could become a whole show itself.'

"'Oh, and they want to bring several loads of sand and have you construct several sandcastles to be displayed at the entrance to the Big Tent. Apparently, someone had downloaded a video to the internet of you at the beach building your masterpieces. Talk about a small world!'

"Ed was once again left speechless, but this time he had the biggest smile on his face that a mouse could possibly have. Then he gave his friend the hugest hug that a mouse could give. He proceeded to leap from furniture to furniture and doing back flips, with frequent yelps of jubilation escaping his lips. Interestingly enough, that became one of his many routines in the circus.

"When the time came, both trained very diligently for their acts. Together they became even more popular than Albert had been as a single performer. Audiences across the world were astounded by their brilliant performances. Unfortunately, I never did find out what the majority of their routine consisted of, but I do know what they did for the finale. It proved to be quite a spectacle to see a mouse dance on its hind legs and juggle lit matches with his front paws, while standing on the tip of the trunk of an elephant. Albert held Ed high in the air while pedaling a bicycle. Invariably the tip of his trunk would pass just under a bunch of lit hula-hoops that the mouse jumped through without ever losing a beat. Oh, and did I already mention that all of this took place on a high wire with no safety net? In no time at all, the media exhausted all adjectives of praise that could possibly be used to describe the highly entertaining duo.

"The two friends continued to perform successfully for many years to come, and even starred in a movie and stage play loosely based on their life. Over time, they accumulated great fame and fortunes; however, they never forgot their humble beginnings or where they came from. Albert and Ed supported many charities and community-based activities, and spent countless hours visiting sick and underprivileged children.

"Of course, neither one of them forgot their families either. Every month they sent money and other presents back to their loved ones. When time permitted, they brought their families out west for a fun-filled vacation. Last I heard, each lived in a mansion, right next to each other, with their own families. Albert married a young aspiring actress elephant and they had five calves. Ed married a field mouse interested in social work and at last count they had thirty-four mouse pups.

"I guess that what I have been trying to say all along is that no matter how small or insignificant we may feel sometimes, someone out there depends on us, or is inspired by our words or gestures. Even a casual encounter may have great influence in someone's life. Everyone knows that if you put your mind to it and work really hard, you can accomplish anything – especially if there is a good friend supporting and pushing you along. Remember, friends have the ability to change our life forever. Good friends change it for the better. It is hard to judge whether you're an elephant or a mouse in any relationship, but as long as any kind of relationship exists, you are a much bigger player than you, or possibly both of you, could have ever imagined.

"Well, that's it for tonight, Sonny. I know it was a slightly longer story than what you have been used to, and you must be very tired by now. I hope you enjoyed it as much as I did when I first heard it.

"Good night, sleep tight, and sweet dreams."

"**W**ell Sonny, sit back, relax, and listen to the story that I am going to tell you. It's about politics, individual efforts, bad timing, bravery, and attitude. Mostly though, I just wanted to tell you about some relatively recent world events that I found to be quite interesting, somewhat perplexing, and reasonably amazing. I hope you'll find this story thought provoking, and yet entertaining.

"My story actually begins about two hundred and fifty years ago when several extremely smart ants established a society under a new set of rules and regulations. They built a big colony under a mighty oak tree on the west side of the forest, right between two large lakes.

"These colonial ants disapproved of any official royalty ruling over them, harbored bad feelings towards any type of monarchy and, therefore, never had a queen to govern them. To oversee the nest, they visualized, carefully developed, and eventually instituted quite a radical ideal for that period of time: Instead of handing over absolute power to one individual, these geniuses came up with a multi-party system that consisted of three branches of government and a built-in system of checks and balances. Fair and just laws were established by the ants, for the ants. They established a strong belief in the resident's rights to existence, freedom, and the quest to be joyous. Even more notable, however, is that these ants based their culture on a basic concept that proved to be the foundation of their society, and the first step towards the establishment of any modern nest. That new concept was the freedom to flap their jaws as much as they pleased.

"Any ant could discuss, degrade, debate, and denounce any topic or subject that came to their tiny minds, and not be afraid of prosecution of any kind. Jaw flapping was free from regulation, alteration, or limitation. And those that were doing the flapping were free from any confinement or practice that would be viewed as life threatening.

"They also argued that the eggs that a queen normally lays can be obtained through other means, which are just as effective. It kept the eggs from being 'put into one basket', so to speak. Therefore, after some debating, it was decided and agreed upon that all of the eggs should be distributed amongst the numerous 'baskets' of the various parts of their leadership, which proved to be somewhat complex and not always as an organized process as it was originally intended, but nonetheless, still effective and even productive. Despite such careful planning, revolutionary philosophical thinking, and ways of governing, some have argued that not only have many of the leaders in recent years become more concerned with their own wealth and prosperity rather than the rearing of the young larvae and the colonies in general, but now there are way too many leaders in the government for the amount of eggs waiting to be hatched.

"Having completed such a tremendous task, all these revolutionary ants relaxed. Some went off to find sweets and maple syrup, some sat back and drank beer and wine, and some invented, discovered, or established a few minor things like electricity, the first banking system, libraries for the common crawler, the fire ants departments, community hospitals, foundation for the modern armed forces (which later became one of the best ant armies in the whole forest), and many others that numerous larvae of today take for granted.

"Various species of ants from all parts of the forest immigrated to this colony to form new and, hopefully, better lives for themselves and their families, and to provide a brighter future for many generations to come. The colony became a multi-cultural society where many languages were spoken and various religions practiced. Eventually, however, they evolved into their own culture and, like everyone in the forest, became quite unique.

"The most popular activity that many enjoyed was a game consisting of a stick and a ball. These games drew great crowds, sold sugar cubes at exorbitant prices, and, in later years, exposed the wide use of performance enhancing maple syrup and the art of truth-bending. A great majority of the ants liked to bake pies as well. The ones made with really sweet apples became their favorite.

"Such were the conditions under which this nest survived and thrived. By the time it was nearing its bicentennial anniversary (quite young by forest standards), it was extremely large, powerfully strong, abundantly populated, and economically prosperous. All these attributes caused the nest to become an influential force throughout the world of ants. Its popularity grew throughout the lands. Its wealth and extravagant lifestyle became revered, and its core beliefs were legendary. As the years passed, the colony began to exhibit a great influence over smaller and poorer colonies, and in time they began to try and persuade them to adopt their views of life and philosophies.

"In the meantime, on the east side of the forest stood a red ant colony that was basically like the west colony in certain respects, but totally different in others. This colony was built under a birch tree with a large lake to its north and an even larger lake to its east. It was very old in comparison to the other one, and the ants that lived within it existed under a totally different set of rules and regulations.

"While they had rid themselves of a monarch as well by chopping off the head of the last queen that tried to rule them, their culture permitted no pie baking (at least not the apple kind), no games with sticks (unless played on frozen water), and absolutely no jaw flapping of any kind.

Criticisms of the leadership and disagreements with the customs of the colony (oral or written) were highly frowned upon and consequences for such actions were often swift and dire. Ironically, their structure and formula for leadership was not that much different from that of the monarchy that they fought so hard to overthrow.

"The red ants that lived there were always hard workers and everything that they worked for was divided and distributed among all of the citizens of the colony. Although there were many boisterous governmental proclamations of unity and equality among all ants, distribution of labor and products was not all that united, and was certainly not equal. As a result, certain ants, especially the really bright red ones, prospered and lived much better than certain other citizens.

"Most religions and any traditions pertaining to them were denounced and suppressed, and ants of certain religious descent were discriminated against and repressed within the society in general. However, the one activity that they all did equally well and united, and in equal numbers was the consumption of wheat syrup – often by the glass full.

"Whenever any kind of special, or even non-special, occasion occurred, wheat syrup was consumed in relatively large quantities. In fact, the red ants' consumption of it became legendary throughout the forest.

"Either due to pride, paranoid suspicions of foreigners, overdeveloped ego, or a combination of those and possibly a plethora of other factors, the red ants preferred to keep to themselves. Therefore, aspects of their culture and way of life remained a mystery to the majority of the forest crawlers. This colony continued to grow in size and by the time our story took place, it became the biggest one in the whole forest – two and a half times larger than the colony in the West.

"It influenced smaller colonies and made them believe that their way of life was superior to all others and that other colonies should establish themselves in their likeness. And Sonny, interestingly enough, one of their greatest accomplishments was the creation of one of the strongest armies the forest had ever seen.

"Now, this is where it gets interesting – or complicated – depending on your point of view. But either way, pay close attention.

"In a partially secluded distant area of the forest, separated from the others by a pond, there was yet a third colony that was much smaller than the other two and seemed quite insignificant at first glance. Unfortunately, the ants that lived there were in turmoil. The leadership was becoming very unsettled and the ants were becoming increasingly more hostile towards each other. You see, the majority of the ant nests that existed in the forest had decided to eliminate their monarchs and adopt either the life and customs of the colony from the west or the red ants' set of rules and regulations from the east.

"However, the citizens of this colony could not decide which philosophies they liked better. The ones that lived on the mossy side argued quite passionately that the red colonies way of life was superior, while the ones that lived near the marshy fields felt very strongly that the west had developed and perfected a much better lifestyle. Since neither side could convince the other to change their minds, distrust and tension between the two sides continued to escalate, and the situation began to spiral out of control. Both sides were extremely ethnocentric in their respective views and proved to be very inflexible – unwilling to yield or compromise a single idea, rule, or action.

"After a while the negotiations between the two sides stalled completely and, before long, each side began to build up their own armed forces and make threats of violence against the other. Ants from various other outside colonies tried to intervene and stave off any military action, hoping to restore order and resolve this issue once and for all. They worked earnestly to re-establish peace and harmony to the region; but, unfortunately, all of their efforts had only delayed the inevitable. The stubborn ants divided their colony into two separate camps (even though they were not physically separated) called the North Nest and the South Nest, and a civil war was started shortly thereafter.

"Now Sonny, one thing to keep in mind is that there was no love lost between the big colony in the west and the even bigger red colony in the East. They never liked each other very much right from the beginning and were it not for a healthy respect for the might of each other's military strengths and capabilities, they surely would have gone to war long before our story took place. Nonetheless, they did do their best to make the other look as appalling as possible in the eyes of all the other colonies in the forest. They often embellished and sensationalized the truths about each other, exploited various mishaps to make themselves appear in a positive light, and enlightened everyone else to the short comings of the other side. Both loved to create and spread propaganda denouncing each other and invented many slogans proclaiming the superiority of their own colony. All of that led to ridiculous stereotypes and outlandish legends that, despite their absurdity and obvious silliness, many ants not only believed wholeheartedly, but spread around as truths through rumor mills and gossiping stations.

"As you might very well imagine, the biggest pleasure for them was derived when one of the other colonies in the forest would adopt their form of leadership. Not surprisingly, both of these colonies were very much interested to see what was going to happen in the colony on the far side of the forest – particularly, what the result of their civil war was going to be. To ensure that the victory would go their way, after much debate and several splitting headaches, the colony of the west and the colony of the east decided to become actively involved in the war, but they chose different methods with which to do that.

"Since the red colony had superior weapons, technology, and war doctrines than those of the north, it decided to supply the northern army with advanced armaments, teach them the latest combat techniques and insect survival skills, and send all kinds of support supplies that any modern six-legged soldier would be very happy to have in armed conflict. That small endeavor cost the red colony a lot of money, and consumed an enormous amount of resources.

"As I have already mentioned, the leadership of the colony in the west felt very strongly about the situation in that distant colony, and even though it was not pleased to hear that the disagreement had escalated to such violent proportions, it definitely did not want to lose that colony to the red ants. Feeling that something drastic must be done to ensure a victory for the south colony, many of the ruling officials spent countless days and sleepless nights arguing, promising, proving, and manipulating the various options that they were presented with. They weighed the pros and cons of all their choices and opinions, drew up military plans, and calculated the multitude of predictions and the non-measurables. They paced back and forth in deep contemplation into the late hours of the night, until all six of their legs ached mercilessly and their jaws quivered in pain from so much flapping. Despite all their efforts and proposals, when all was said and done, still nobody had any idea on how best to handle the situation. However, they eventually settled on a solution that was controversial, but not all that revolutionary in nature.

"They decided to send their army over to the far away colony to fight alongside the inferior forces of the south army in order to ensure victory over the north. A great deal of armed forces were required for such an enormous undertaking, so to make sure that they had an adequate number of soldiers, the colony in the West drafted and instituted a policy mandating that all newly hatched ants must join the military and fight on the other side of the pond at the far away colony in the distant part of the forest. Interestingly enough, although the freedom of the colony in the west was never in jeopardy due to the unfolding events in that remote colony, all of the forces were sent under the premise that 'They are fighting and dying for our freedom.'

"Thousands and thousands of ants were deployed and engaged the enemy in grueling and bloody battles. Most of them fought bravely and honorably, performing their duties to the best of their abilities, promoting their way of life to all of the impoverished and hungry local ants that they came across (a relatively large number of the indigenous population was rather poor).

"Now Sonny, keep in mind that no war is ever pretty or easy. Despite the fact that the armies from the west colony were much better equipped and trained than their opposing army from the north (even with the help of the red colony), the northerners were much more familiar with the terrain of the colony, had collaborators blended amongst the Southerners, and often fought very unconventionally to gain any advantage possible. Therefore, the victory that seemed so inevitable and close at hand, turned out to be quite elusive and much more distant than originally believed. In fact, one could say that it was just there 'on the horizon.' You know, horizon, that imaginary line that separates the sky and earth. No matter how much one gets closer to it, it keeps moving away. As it turned out, the war dragged on for nineteen very long years. No matter how close peace seemed, it just kept moving away.

"At times it was hard to spot or even identify who the enemy was. This created numerous trust issues with the locals, and, on occasion, among the soldiers themselves. Other times, it was nearly impossible to tell where the enemy was coming from, and the blurred lines of combat made it hard to tell where the front actually was. The northern army preferred to wage a guerrilla type of warfare, which the army from the west was not as well prepared to deal with as they had hoped they would be. Many saw and experienced severe suffering and personal tragedies. The army of ants from the west colony dealt with and overcame extreme weather and environmental conditions, often poor intelligence and leadership skills, and increasingly low morale. Quite a few of the wounded wound up with physical scars, and nearly everyone that fought in the war had emotional ones too. Thousands of soldiers died, and thousands more barely dodged the bullet – often quite literally. The only two positive aspects of the whole war that they all were able to embrace were the facts that the enemy did not have any major victories in battles either, and that if they survived long enough, eventually they would be going home.

"Back home, on the west side of the forest, the events unfolding in that war were becoming unpopular among the citizens of the colony. For the first time in history, images of the war were being broadcast on the light tube during the evening news, and most did not like what they saw. This war was quite savage in nature, very dirty in all aspects of the word, and simply unnecessary. In their eyes and antennas, sending their military troops to such a distant colony was a huge waste of the lives of their young ants and larvae, and the sugar resources. They did not at all approve of or like the strain that it put on the national budget, were rather disappointed by the results that their armed forces were achieving, and, for some reason, showed a strong dislike towards anyone in a military uniform.

"Unhappy about the seemingly needless death of so many ants (military and civilian alike), the civilian ants directed all of these negative feelings at the government, vocalizing and acting out their displeasures with big gatherings, loud protests, and large slogans. Some resorted to other peace promoting activities that may have seemed controversial, but nonetheless, effective for the few that preferred that lifestyle. They spent a lot of time in brightly colored vans, driving around with two fingers raised in the air, and smoked just about anything that could have been rolled up into a cigarette. It was a turbulent time to say the least.

"No decisive victories were ever obtained by either side throughout the war until the very end. The armies from the colony in the west eventually retreated unceremoniously, being forced to give up the goals that they all fought for so long, and that so many had died for. The southern part of the colony was overrun by the army of the north, an event during which many of the local ants perished, and the whole colony became united once again in the likeness of the colony of the east.

"A rather lengthy and difficult recovery process began for many of the veteran ants of the west colony. They were very happy to be back home, however, nothing came easy. Whether the change came from within themselves or the nest that they were born into had evolved into something vastly different while they were gone, or a little bit or a lot of both, their home was not the same. After fighting in a distant colony for so long, many had a very difficult time readjusting to civilian life, and to make it even more painful, they returned to find their home environment had become very hostile and unappreciative of their efforts and sacrifices.

"Often, the returning soldiers were not seen as heroes, saviors, or even as tired and emotionally spent ants, but rather as criminals, ruffians, or wild barbarians. Many of the civilians turned out to be rude, inconsiderate, and occasionally downright mean in their behavior towards the soldiers. In fact, the whole society in general, turned out to be pretty thorny towards the veterans and a great number of the returning ants found it extremely hard to settle down and become contributing members of society, or to even fit back into the now less-than-friendly communities in any capacity. Many could not find jobs, homes, or even provide enough sugar and other vital sustenance for themselves. Quite a few suffered from various physical and psychological disorders such as depression, anxiety, post-traumatic stress disorder, and post-surgical and combat scarring. The leadership and citizens of the colony offered very little help or rehabilitative services to these soldiers, leaving many of them to fend for themselves. When you think about it Sonny, it's kind of a sad story.

"I guess that what I have been trying to say all along is that if you are going to send your fathers and mothers, husbands and wives, brothers and sisters, sons and daughters, uncles and aunts, cousins, nephews and nieces, friends and even acquaintances to fight in a distant war, and they manage to come back alive, do not treat them like evil conquerors from some barbaric wastelands bent on destroying your home and way of life. Many of these veterans have most likely experienced hardships that no ant, human, or any other living soul should ever come across or even dream about during their worst nightmares. Remember that many of them are actually really nice individuals, and some are even genuine heroes. Support them while they're gone in whatever way you can, and upon their return, along with the gratitude, kindness, and respect that they all should get, most of them also deserve a warm smile, a pat on the back, wide open arms to fall into, and a round of applause from those that are not currently busy hugging and squeezing and embracing. As I have already pointed out, the transition back to civilian life can actually be quite difficult for some, and the needs of those veterans should not be ignored. If a society truly is civilized and enlightened, it would address the myriad of needs that these veterans may possess, provide the necessary services to help them deal with their issues, and ensure a smooth transition and integration of the battle-weary soldiers to positions that are an asset to the society, instead of a burden.

"Well, Sonny, that's all I have for you right now. It's not a very long story, but it is a very interesting chain of events – at least I found them to be when I first heard of all this. I hope I have given you something to really think about. Always remember to be nice to the veterans around you – they'll appreciate it more than you realize. Alright, get some sleep now so that you can function with a purpose tomorrow.

"Good night, sleep tight, and as always, sweet dreams."

THE DYING
IMMORTALS

"Well Sonny, sit back, relax, and listen to the story that I'm going to tell you. It's about ethnocentricity, character, and a brief history of our world. Most of all though, it is about survival, and a style of self-preservation that is very common to some and, at the same time, quite foreign to many others. Pay close attention now because some of this might sound familiar.

"It all began a long, long time ago – back when our sun still wore diapers, and the planet Earth, as it is called now, was flat. You see Sonny, in the heavens, a big problem came to be, and none of the gods that lived there knew how to solve it. At first, no one even noticed it, until one day when it became apparent that they had to sleep standing up.

"They tried ignoring it, hoping it would go away on its own, but that did not work. They tried blaming it on each other, but that did not bring the answer any closer either. Then finally, the gods spent many centuries in meetings, trying to find a solution, however none was forthcoming. Many considered it a hopeless situation, and they became quite frustrated and upset. Tempers were running short, probably because their feet hurt for so long, and many experienced numbness in their toes. And to their disappointment, it did not look like they would lay down or even sit down any time soon.

"Oh, the problem, Sonny? It was overcrowding.

"As big as the heavens are, there were simply too many gods for the available space. With their insurmountable egos, exotic and often expensive tastes, and an always insatiable appetite for more, they occupied every corner of the globe, sorry – I meant to say heavens – that could be found. They were everywhere – behind, below, on top of, and in front of every cloud in the sky, even occupying puffs of smoke. And the fact that they multiplied like cockroaches did not help either. Oh yes, Sonny, I'm talking about those ugly and annoying bugs that have been here forever, and will probably be here long after our planet becomes extinct. Even back then they were pests, and the gods could not find a way to get rid of them. But that is a different story that I will tell you another time.

"One day, a god by the name of Thingsure looked down at the distended veins on his ankles and feet, and something caught his eye. He blinked several times just to make sure his eyes were not deceiving him, and a big grin stretched across his face.

"There was no mistaking it. He had found the answer.

"It was right under their feet all that time, but everybody always walked around with their chins held up and noses pointed in arrogance towards a higher cloud, so nobody had ever noticed it. Thingsure gave out a loud yell of jubilation. When nobody paid him any attention because they all assumed that it was just another all too common occurrence of a god getting his toes stepped on, he let out another cry – much louder this time and with even more feeling.

"'Listen up brothers,' he shouted. 'I believe that I have found a solution to our problem!'

"Everyone within his earshot stopped talking, turned to see Thingsure, and listened carefully with inquisitive looks on their faces.

"'Brothers and sisters,' he was saying, 'please lend me your ears and hear out my words. I believe the solution is within our grasp. Everyone, look down and see the universe below us. Do you all see the abundance of planets, moons, and stars? Just look at all the constellations! There must be thousands … no, millions and millions of worlds for us to explore and live on. We could spread out throughout the entire universe, and have plenty of room for everybody. Forever!'

"All the gods were getting very excited. As his short speech progressed, a sense of elation and hope spread through the heavens, like a wildfire through a dry forest. Their spirits soared, so to speak. Some even tried to dance out of sheer happiness, but were unable to do so because of their painful feet, and besides, their knees kept bumping into thighs, and that really hurt as well.

"'It sends a shiver down my spine to think that I will be able to bend my knees,' Thingsure continued, 'that I will be able to lean forward and stretch my back. That, without any difficulty, I will finally be able to scratch my…'

"Unfortunately, Sonny, Thingsure never finished his inspirational speech. Everyone within earshot, and gods could speak pretty loudly, sprinted for the wide-open spaces of the universe, trampling poor Thingsure under their achy feet. Others caught on immediately, and a big stampede resulted. By the time the last of the gods left the heavens, stumbling over Thingsure, a millennium had passed. When he was finally able to stand up, Thingsure took a good look around and below him, swung his hand in disgust at all those other gods, and decided to stay right where he was. After all, the heavens were so roomy now.

"Like a mushroom cloud and the energy blast of a nuclear bomb, the gods exploded unto the universe, trembling from the excitement at the prospect of finally sitting down. Some even dared to ponder lying down. Overrunning, consuming, changing, and exploiting every galaxy they went to; leaving no stone or pebble unturned, they settled down on anything that came across their paths.

Not only were they able to live out their dreams, and for many the dreams were long forgotten or hopelessly given up on, but they were able to do so in complete privacy if they so desired. Planets were modified for easier, more comfortable living, stars were rearranged for a better, more pleasing view, and whole galaxies were moved for faster, more convenient travel. They lived in complete luxury, enjoying life to the fullest, believing that it would never end.

"But they were wrong.

"Without any regard for the future, they used and abused all of the natural resources that every new world had to offer. Destroying thousands, even millions of different species on various planets, sometimes in a single day, to suit their needs became a common occurrence. It was their planet after all, they reasoned, and there was nobody intelligent enough to dispute that claim.

"However, while living outside the heavens, they needed all the natural resources available – no matter how powerful the gods believed themselves to be. And while living as lavishly as they did, most of these resources were depleted faster than you can say 'fossil fuel.' Coal, oil, petroleum, and natural gas, which took millions of years to form on certain planets, were used up or destroyed within hundreds of years; and sometimes, some of the gods did it in a matter of days. So, without thinking twice, they simply moved on to the next planet, the next star, or the next galaxy, always leaving behind worlds devoid of the life that did, or might have, prospered, and landscapes full of waste. In their wake, quite frequently, there remained disorder and devastation.

"One day, a young god by the name of Khaos, noticed something odd out of the corner of his eye. One galaxy away he saw something white, smooth, and creamy. Not having settled down anywhere special yet after completely destroying the last planet he was on, he decided to investigate.

"Quickly making his way over, he realized that what he had found was milk. A whole galaxy surrounded by a beltway of milk. 2%, I believe, it was. Being very thirsty after his long journey, Khaos drank almost three quarters of it, leaving the rest untouched. However, since the delicate balance between the amount of milk available flowing at a constant rate of speed and the really cold temperature of outer space was disrupted, the remaining milk froze into a huge icicle and drifted away. In the meantime, Khaos figured that it might not be a bad idea to settle down here and was so happy to have his thirst finally quenched that he decided to name this galaxy the Milky Way.

"What caught his eye though was how pretty the galaxy looked with its nine planets rotating around a single star, seven round and two flat; although he could not make up his mind if the chunk of ice floating on the outskirts of the galaxy was even big enough to be considered a planet. More importantly though was that the view of the universe was absolutely spectacular from there. The best part for Khaos, however, was that he was finally alone. All he wanted, after all, was some peace and quiet.

"'Yes,' he thought, 'I want this to be my home, and I shall live here forever. That fourth planet from the sun will suit me just fine; nice and flat with plenty of water. I shall call it...' Here Khaos's mind stumbled for a second and he was not sure what the name of the planet should be. While coming up with the name for the galaxy was relatively easy – it just flowed through him – coming up with a name for his new home was proving to be a little more difficult. He pondered and scratched his chin for a while, feeling a bit frustrated. Eventually though, he decided to name it after his favorite candy bar that he enjoyed so much back in the heavens. He named the planet Mars, and went to live on it.

"In no time at all he built a huge castle for himself at a random spot on the planet and a beautiful summer home on an excellent beachfront property. He was able to purchase both of those pieces of land at a great bargain – free, since the only living creatures on Mars were microorganisms, and they simply did not establish a strong economic system yet, or, for that matter, place any monetary values on any property. And thus, he reveled in his new existence in complete isolation, enjoying his new home, living up his new lifestyle to the fullest, being very happy – for about two days.

"You see Sonny, since the planet was flat, every time he went to bed, no matter what time it was, the sun would always be shining its bright light right into his face. How could anyone get any sleep with that happening? Khaos was very upset and irritated by the lack of sleep. He contemplated the problem for a while, scratching his chin once again, and finally came up with a solution. No Sonny, it was not curtains. That was way too simple for a god like Khaos. Instead, he flexed his muscles, huffed and puffed for a brief second, and made Mars round. In doing so, at least half of the planet – the part facing away from the sun - was plunged into darkness at all times, and those were just perfect conditions for an excellent good night's sleep.

"However, while that problem was resolved, a new one was created. As soon as the planet became circular, all the water fell off, killing all the microorganisms. Khaos was devastated. His thirty-six-bathroom summer home that he loved so much, no longer stood on beachfront property. With all of the water now gone, it stood in the middle of a dessert, its value suddenly greatly reduced, and all the fun of swimming and splashing around was simply gone. Even his castle seemed antiquated and boring. Khaos faced a new set of problems that he was not sure how to solve. He paced back and forth for hundreds of years, looking for a moist answer, but finding only barren rock. There were very few choices left for him. After careful considerations and contemplations, and a coin toss (heads he stays, tails he does not), Khaos made the difficult decision to move. There was only one other planet with water on it – the third one from the sun, and for no particular reason at all, this one he called Earth.

"Earth was just as flat as Mars had been, but contained a lot more water. In fact, so much so, that there was no dry land, which again posed a problem for his summer home plans.

"Khaos did not want to make the same mistake twice – at least not if he could help it. Relying on his excellent education at All High Gods Schooling Establishment, he quickly calculated a few very important numbers in his head. Remembering what he learned in such classes as Survey of Calculus and the Supernatural 101 and 102, Metaphysical Magic 605, and, of course, Sociological Economics of Superior Beings 204, Khaos worked out some formulas, balanced out a few equations, and came up with a favorable answer that he was looking for. It was safe to make Earth round without losing all the water.

"'In fact,' he reasoned aloud, 'the surface of the planet should be equally divided among land and water.'

"With a simple wave of his hand, Khaos bent the edges of our world and made Earth into the round sphere that it is today. Just as he had calculated, a big mass of water fell off the planet. What he did not bother to consider is that, just like on Mars several centuries earlier, all that water immediately crystallized in the severe coldness of space, became a huge and very fast comet, and destroyed several other planets in the next galaxy, some of which most likely had sustained life. Come to think of it, the frozen milk might have been a devastating comet as well. Sonny, that is probably why we still have not made contact with alien beings - yet.

"However, back on Earth, exactly half of the surface became land, and that is what really mattered to the young god. He was very happy. Since that went so well (somewhat to his surprise), Khaos decided to do some remodeling. He solved a few simple mathematical problems, balanced one difficult equation – however, never achieving any grades higher than a C - he ignored the fact that two does not equal three, and therefore eventually throwing off his final solution by a relatively large number. Then he flexed his muscles once more, and moved all the continents, positioning them just the way he preferred them to be. In fact, the way they are today is pretty much the way he set them up all those millions of years ago. However, because his equation did not actually balance out, a few side effects have resulted which we experience even today. The tectonic plates continue to move causing pretty serious earthquakes and tidal waves. Other disasters such as volcanoes, hurricanes, and even tornadoes are all, either directly or indirectly, results of that gross miscalculation.

"Khaos then built a new castle and summerhouse, even bigger than the ones he had before. Thousands of acres of rainforest were destroyed, killing thousands of various animals and ecosystems in order to create the space and lumber that Khaos needed for his spacious habitat. I guess, Sonny, some things have not changed over the years. He splashed around in an ocean every morning, a different one each day, and washed up in one of the seas of his choosing. He ate the rich selection of fruits that the land began to offer, and danced around out of pure joy because everything was absolutely perfect. In the afternoons he enjoyed a game that closely resembled golf – on a global scale of course, and in the evenings, he liked to sit back and stare at the stars. He marveled at the wonderful constellations he had created, and soaked in the quietness and abundance of space that surrounded him. Finally, there were no other gods stepping on his toes, quite literally and figuratively, the sun did not keep him awake at bedtime, and there was more than enough water to satisfy all his desires for all kinds of water-based activities. Never denying himself any luxury, never compromising the slightest of any comforts, and always expanding his domain, Khaos lived life to the fullest once again. Never, not even for a second, did he consider the consequences of any of his actions.

"One chilly afternoon, Khaos noticed that a new kind of animal appeared on Earth. Many of their kind were rather big, very dumb (in his opinion), and very scaly (to his eyes). At first, he thought them not worthy of his attention and very valuable time. Eventually, however, he became more and more curious of their behavior and occasional sociability. So, he tried playing around with them, training them, even adopting a few as pets. However, being an impatient individual, he quickly became bored and somewhat frustrated at their unwillingness to cooperate.

"Khaos named them 'dinosaurs', after the dog he had as a little boy. That K9 wouldn't listen to anything he had to say either, and proved to be quite un-trainable under Khaos's tutelage. And in case you're wondering Sonny, the answer is yes: all dogs do go to heaven.

"On rare occasions, Khaos amused himself by teasing them in some annoying way, but generally, they were too simple a being for him to bother with. For about five million years they all lived on, each minding their own business, and thriving in their respective environments, being happy to roam the world.

"But circumstances do change, Sonny.

"One night, while lying in his bed tossing back and forth under a clear starry sky with a full moon shining brightly down onto Earth, Khaos finally figured out why he could not sleep well for the last ten thousand years. Dinosaurs!

"Yes, dinosaurs were the problem. With their unceasing desire to run, play, eat, pull, tear, and of course growl and roar, they simply made too much noise. It even reminded him of the old days in the heavens. How could anybody be expected to get a good night's sleep when all of those intolerable creatures were such unbelievable pests? It was absolutely abhorring! He flipped back his covers, went to the window, and, with a frown on his face, observed the noisy beasts. As far as the eye could see, and as far as the ear could hear, there were dinosaurs – many of them moving around and making all kinds of racket. Deep in thought, he rubbed his chin, slapped his forehead, and let out a loud burp (he had a fizzy juice earlier that night, and it made him gassy). There was only one way to solve this problem. With a wave of his right arm and a flex of his left hand, Khaos simply made all the dinosaurs vanish, and that, Sonny, is the truth behind the mystery of their disappearance so long ago.

"Calmly Khaos returned to bed, and spent the rest of the night in a deep sleep. The new day began with bright sunshine, and a refreshing dip in his favorite sea – I believe it was the Caribbean – and a delicious breakfast. It was quiet around him once again, and Khaos was so energized and cheerful that he even sang a song he once heard on a different planet. Centuries went by, but for Khaos, who was so happy, time stood still.

"One day while swimming in the Pacific Ocean, he noticed something peculiar on shore. Hurrying back to his house he grabbed the telescope and observed a new kind of life form. They walked upright on two legs, talked to each other in order to communicate, and possessed an opposable thumb. They were different, more so than any other creature Khaos had ever encountered. They were making a variety of tools, building diverse structures to serve multiple purposes, and began organizing themselves into complex societies.

"'These creatures are definitely smarter, perhaps even more advanced, than all the others,' he thought. 'Even the ones that still live in caves can make fire. I shall call them hummus … No, no … Let them be known as humans.' And thus, he sat at the window for hours at a time, spending countless years observing the humans and their incredibly swift evolution.

"It was sometime around the first snow fall, and Khaos was sitting on his deck, watching and studying the erect animals through his telescope. He found them to be very fascinating, especially because, despite their obvious intellect, they still waged war on each other and fought over seemingly irrelevant matters.

"Suddenly, Khaos felt a chill as the temperature outside plummeted and he saw through his telescope that the ice which covered a pretty significant portion of the northern hemisphere had thickened.

"'It is freezing,' he said to himself and flapped his arms for warmth. At this point, Sonny, it simply became too cold for him to enjoy his favorite activities, after all, gods wear only togas, you know.

"'There are icicles outside,' he reasoned, 'and at this rate my morning swim and bath might freeze over, and summer is just too far away.' That thought sent a shiver down his back, leaving Khaos to, again, think very hard. It upset him that things could never be easy. He was highly agitated that, unlike in the heavens, his surroundings never stayed as he would set them up but, rather, they were always evolving and changing into something new, and always presenting him with novel problems that were never easy to resolve – nothing ever was! He repeatedly had to be an innovative being in order to solve these dilemmas, and thinking that hard frequently gave him headaches. However, complaining about it did not bring a solution any closer – he remembered that lesson from the heavens. Pacing back and forth to keep him warm, Khaos searched for the answer. It came to him several eons later and it was such a brilliant solution that he jumped up in the air and clicked his heels.

"'I should have done that a long time ago,' he uttered.

"Carefully looking up into the sky, he waited until the sun was facing the other way. He then reached quickly up into space, and with a growing grin on his face, yanked the diaper off of the sun.

"An interesting chain of events soon unfolded. Being totally naked the sun became very embarrassed, began to blush, and could not bear to turn and face Earth again – even to this day. In fact, if one was so inclined as to fly to the other side of the sun, one might be able to see (if one was to wear a really good pair of sunglasses) its face and the apparent embarrassment that is still evident on it. In the interim, the sun started to glow brighter and brighter, until it hurt to look at it directly. Since it was so bright, a lot more heat was generated, the solar flares became bigger and bigger, and things really began to warm up. Khaos was overjoyed, but as always did not bother to consider the consequences. As the temperature rose, the polar caps began to melt and the ocean levels to rise, changing the surface of his planet. At first it seemed insignificant – almost unnoticeable – at least to Khaos. He did not realize there was a problem until he came back from his morning swim and found his beautiful summer home completely submerged in water, with strange fish swimming through it.

"'Well,' Khaos thought, 'that explains all those human screams reaching my ears from the direction of where the city of Atlantis is supposed to be.' In the meantime, the great city of Atlantis was submerged beneath the Atlantic Ocean, Earth became more water than land, and millions of ecosystems and species were either wiped out or greatly altered. And, of course, the latest Ice Age was finally over. A new era had begun – and although he didn't know it yet, it was a new era for Khaos as well.

"Annoyance welled up deep inside, and Khaos became extremely outraged. Every time he settled down into a seemingly harmonious existence, something would invariably disrupt the majestic serenity of his peaceful life. Somehow, in some bizarre or unconventional way, the absolutely perfect paradise that he always surrounded himself with would get ruined in an ugly way, often by the most insignificant of events or creatures. It was becoming quite preposterous. He had lost yet another summer home (the forty-fifth I believe, since leaving the heavens), and that made him quite angry. He quickly packed his bags and was looking up into the sky to see where to go next when an idea flashed through his head. He would go live among the clouds where the relaxing chirping of the birds was the only noise to hear, where flooding is never a problem, and no mortal creature would ever disrupt or corrupt his beautiful dwelling, and he would still be able to enjoy all of his favorite activities – especially swimming and human watching.

"And thus, he moved.

"He built a new home for himself high amongst the clouds – the biggest one he ever had. It was a kingdom he could truly be proud of. There were magnificent towers with tall columns and breathtaking buttresses, and lavishly decorated palaces with marble floors, mahogany walls and roofs, and all of it was adorned with the most divine crystals and gold that could be found on the planet below. It was his best work ever, and Khaos lived there for many centuries without as much as a single worry to stress his ever-relaxing mind.

"One thing, however, still fascinated him more than anything. The humans were the most complex and mind-boggling creatures he had come across on Earth. He found them to be highly unpredictable, extremely destructive, very innovative, and incredibly entertaining to watch. Staring at the numerous constellations and playing golf (even with a low handicap), no longer satisfied his desire to be amused. An insatiable yarning to contact the two-legged creatures consumed his every thought, and, at night he dreamed of nothing else but the erect animal, their social interactions and steadily increasing mental capacity. He even learned their languages.

"One day, Khaos reached a decision that he had contemplated for a long time. Sometime in the middle of the summer as the sun was just beginning to set, he gathered his thoughts and made his first return trip to Earth to contact the humans. This proved to be a very nerve-wracking experience even for a god of Khaos's caliber. Fear of rejection, embarrassment, and humiliation haunted his consciousness and his hands shook slightly. He even recalled that asking one of the young goddesses to a school dance for the first time was far less nerve wracking than this. As he approached the closest man, his knee caps trembled so hard that he almost fell over. However, it actually turned out to be a very touching, tear-jerking, experience.

"The humans welcomed Khaos with open arms, offering him plenty of food, water, and shelter. They even invited him to join them in a big celebratory feast – although he could not figure out just what they were celebrating. He felt that all of the dishes he was served were quite splendid, but his favorites were the bread with porridge, mutton, melons, dates, beef, duck mixed with goose, and especially the beer that they washed it all down with.

"There was also a lot of singing and dancing, games, costumes, and skill contests. The feast lasted for days, and Khaos, forgetting all of his apprehensions, enjoyed himself immensely – in fact, it was the best time he had ever had anywhere in all of his life. In return, he decided to offer them some undiscovered knowledge. He taught the humans some basic engineering techniques, slightly advanced math, and a few scientific formulas. They listened carefully, paying close attention to every detail, because, Sonny, back then libraries were in rather short supply and they could not look up things on the internet.

"The very next day, after Khaos left, they began to utilize their newly acquired knowledge to honor their leaders. They built many triangular-shaped structures (among other things) as the final resting place for their rulers and other closely related noble men. Khaos decided to call this thriving land Egypt, after that first girl he asked to the dance, and the people became known as Egyptians.

"Several days later he descended from the clouds again and made his second human contact on a different continent. Everything went pretty much the same. The dinner was absolutely spectacular and the dancing invigorating. The appetizers consisted of tomatoes, tamales, honey, beans, tortillas, chili peppers, avocados, chilies, octli, and various other drinks. The main meal, made with turkey, iguana, maize, squash, fish, and sweet potatoes, was absolutely delicious. Khaos loved every morsel of it.

"The festivities were capped off with a surprise – They sacrificed a man from their tribe to a god whose name Khaos had never heard before. He was pretty sure though that it was not any of his cousins. It did not really matter though; after the sacrifice, they proceeded to eat the man as a means of absorbing his spirit and strength – and a pretty tasty dish he turned out to be too, Khaos thought. The whole evening was simply, as you young people say, 'a blast'.

"He shared with them the same knowledge he shared with the Egyptians, which they gladly accepted. While trying to name these humans, he ran into a small problem. He had two names picked out, and could not decide on one. The names belonged to two of his best friends that he used to skip school and hang around with when not doing his homework. After some deliberation, he named half of them Aztec and the other half Mayans.

"And the fun was only beginning!

"The next day, he was walking around a forest when he heard loud splashing, as if a god was taking a very long and luxurious morning shower. He came forth and saw not a god, but a very beautiful and powerful waterfall in the middle of a river. There was a long, breathtaking rainbow canopy stretching across this majestic scene. Its gentle curve hugged closely the angry, yet mesmerizing, foamy white turmoil that the fall of the rushing water created. Khaos took a long, deep breath. It reminded him of a long-forgotten love. Her name was Niagara, and Khaos stared at it for days.

"As he continued to explore the region, he noticed people living there who wore large bird feathers in their hair, were excellent hunters, preferred to live in tipis, and appeared to be in tune with nature. He made contact with them immediately. It was a warm and friendly meeting as well. They shook hands like he was long lost family, patted each other on the back, and then they exchanged gifts.

"They gave him feathers and war paint for his hair and face; Khaos decided to present these wonderful people with food instead of the knowledge he shared earlier. Not knowing exactly which foods to give, he decided to rely on his experience with other humans. However, he could only remember a small portion of the wide variety of culinary items that he was served, and therefore, presented them with turkey, maize, beans, squash, bread, and his favorite, the sweet potatoes. The dinner party went on for three days, until everyone was simply exhausted. Khaos named these people after the rulers of the tribes he visited earlier. He called them Chiefs. Of course, many centuries later, an explorer made a mistake and gave them a different name, by which they are commonly referred to today.

"'These humans,' he reasoned, 'have proven to be very entertaining and time worthy creatures. Although still not as intelligent as I am, they are a lot more fun to play with than those dinosaurs.' He was glad that he did not leave the galaxy after all. Besides, there was one more game that he wanted to play – a game of imagination and wit. In fact, he became upset at himself for not thinking of it earlier. Humans presented a perfect opportunity to live out his long-forgotten fantasy. He looked down at the Earth from one of his towers, and picked out a new group of people. He really liked their architecture, philosophical way of thinking, and their taste in the latest clothing fashions. It also helped that they lived on a continent that he had never been to before. His game would not have worked with the ones he had already met. Without much ado, and barely able to contain his excitement, Khaos slowly descended to these people – clouds and all.

"It was a warm, sunny day when they first noticed him. Everybody stood in awe, their eyes and mouths wide open, intently staring and pointing at the overpowering and extremely regal sight of a seemingly superior being. The aura that Khaos created mystified all who laid their eyes on this glorified scene. One by one, they all went down on their knees, and bowed their heads to the ground. Feeling extreme jubilation, Khaos proceeded to proclaim himself god of all. For the next seven months, with only occasional breaks, he began telling them stories of gods and the heavens the likes of which have not been attained since. Once he started, like a snowball rolling downhill, and his imagination working overtime, he just kept going and going, and the stories were getting bigger and better by the minute. Unfortunately, a lot of what he said was forgotten, lost, or incorrectly recorded. However, most of the main ideas that he expressed continue to survive to this day – although somewhat skewed and simplified.

"Khaos began telling everyone about the difficult childhood he had with his three brothers, Zeus, Poseidon, and Hades. He told them how they always picked on him as a child and occasionally ridiculed him as an adult, simply because he was adopted. Then he began telling them that Earth was their common property and that all of the gods shared Mount Olympus, located in the heavens, as their common dwelling. Everyone listened intently.

"Khaos continued with great enthusiasm. He and his three brothers, and a few other gods, had apparently spent many years fighting bitter wars against the Titans for control of the world. The gods eventually prevailed, with no small part played by Khaos and his many brave acts of valor. Then they started to fight each other to see who would be the king of all gods. However, Khaos, at Zeus's request, happened to be away for several centuries on a very important god business; therefore, Khaos could not affect the outcome of that war in any way.

"Upon his return, he found Zeus seated as the king on Mount Olympus, married to Hera, a goddess that Khaos loved and was engaged to be married to before leaving on his journey. Even though she was a very annoying and jealous woman, she was still very endearing, and Khaos still loved her very much. To rub it in even more, Zeus told him in great detail of the spectacularly extravagant wedding they had, and bragged about their daughter Athena, goddess of wisdom, who was conceived and born while he was away. What made the whole thing worse was that Zeus cheated on his wife many times with Aphrodite, the goddess of love, and even several human females, one of whom became pregnant with his child.

"His brother Poseidon, he set up as the king of the sea, and Hades as the ruler of the underworld. Even Zeus's best friend, Bacchus, was made god of debauchery. Khaos discussed many gods – rulers of different elements and realms, with diverse personalities, talents, agendas, and philosophies on life and humans in general. He told them of the powers they possessed and the wars that they invariably still waged; of the love that filled some of their hearts and the jealousy that would turn their eyes green.

"'Here is the problem,' Khaos was saying to the gathered masses. 'Neither Zeus nor any of his brothers have any real interest in seeing the humans prosper and live well. Anytime there is no rain and the sun is too hot and all your crops die, or there is too much rain and your crops and homes flood, locusts attack them, or the ground becomes less fertile, all of that is Zeus's doing. In fact, once he tried to destroy all of humankind with a flood, and the extremely prosperous city of Atlantis sank during that deplorable act. Luckily, I managed to stop him before he could finish with that plan.

"'Whenever, a storm comes over the sea and your ships cannot sail and they sink, whenever tidal waves come ashore and kill so many of your loved ones, that is Poseidon's handiwork. When the ground shakes or volcanoes erupt and both of those wreak destruction and havoc on your villages, that is Hades having fun in his lair. I promise that with your support and prayers, I will overthrow Zeus, kick out Poseidon and Hades, and bring you fortunes, victory over your enemies, and make your people prominent here on Earth and Mount Olympus.'

"He continued by stressing that he is indeed the most powerful god of them all, and that it is only a matter of time before he claimed the throne and had Hera back at his side. They all listened very carefully, captivated by the drama that was unfolding in the heavens and on Earth.

"Khaos seemed to be strong of spirit, powerful in words, and capable of great magic. And besides, he promised wealth and prosperity, to drive all disease far way, and to finally balance the budget and reduce the national deficit. The people accepted him with open hearts, and spent the next several centuries praying for his good will.

"Khaos took his time naming these people. He felt they were special, and therefore, deserved a special name. He spent hours trying to think of something good, and finally named them Grakos, after his favorite sandwich in the heavens. Since the land seemed so peaceful to him, he named it Grace, but somewhere in history someone misspelled it and it has been known as Greece ever since. And the people became known as Greeks.

"He thrived in the euphoric state that evolved and surrounded his very being. With all of the attention that humans gave him through their prayers and rituals, Khaos felt very special and important. He began to see himself as a vital part of everything that existed around him, eventually believing that life on Earth, this galaxy, and even the universe could not exist without him.

"He lived in pure happiness for many years, reveling in his fantasy. However, Sonny, all good things must come to an end.

"One day he decided that it was time to come back down to Earth from his castle in the sky and make contact with yet another group of people. He felt that it was time to increase his following. For whatever reason, the group he chose this time preferred to isolate themselves from the rest of the world and that suited Khaos just fine. He came down on a magnificent cloud like before, and they were all amazed just as the other ones had been. He proceeded to tell them the same stories with a lot of effort, strong feelings, deeply caring voice, dramatic tone, and exaggerated hand gestures. He told all of the tales that he so brilliantly made up, but, upon completion, they all laughed. Everybody believed they were the most amusing adventures they had ever heard. They wanted him to tell the stories again, and when Khaos finished the second time, they laughed even harder. Khaos could not figure out what was so funny about the difficult events that he had gone through, and the perils and hardships that he still had to endure. The harder he tried to convince them of the sincerity in his plots, the harder they laughed, pointing their fingers at him while trying to catch their breath between fits of laughter, and the more of a jokester they found him to be. They even began to see him as a fool. Their reaction caught Khaos off guard and for the first time in his very long existence, he experienced shock and was at a complete loss for words. He simply didn't know what else to say or do.

"For the first time since leaving the heavens, he no longer felt like he was in control, and knew that no amount of pacing would bring about a plan of action. These people not only did not accept him as their god, they ridiculed him for trying to convince them that he was even worthy of their worship. An unfamiliar feeling engulfed his heart and mind, one that he had never experienced before. He felt humiliated, alone, and utterly hurt.

"Lowering his chin to his chest, Khaos turned around and slowly walked away, dragging the magnificent cloud behind him. He turned his head several times to gaze back at those people as if they might change their minds, but found them still pointing at him and laughing hysterically. Filled with shame and doubt, Khaos made his way home, reconsidering everything that he had done with the humans. He began to wonder if it was really worth it. All the effort and time the humans needed, all of the aggravation and frustration that they evoked, all of the love and tenderness that they demanded was simply getting to be too much. There were nights when he lost a few minutes of sleep because of them, several times his appetite decreased a little, and he had not played a good game of golf in years. It was no longer any fun, and definitely began to be aggravating. Even the Grakos were beginning to question him and, over the last several centuries, began to worship all of the other gods, especially Zeus and Jupiter, in increasingly greater numbers. Most of them couldn't even remember his name anymore.

"Khaos felt emotionally drained. The drive to flourish and incessantly frolic around came to a screeching halt. The invigorating flame that spurred him onto new, bigger, and sometimes better ideas; creative, although not always orthodox, problem solving; and often dangerously impulsive behavior was extinguished, like the Olympic torch at the end of the games. He even finally noticed that the natural supplies on Earth, that he was so dependent upon, were significantly diminished. It was just too much to handle all at the same time, and Khaos became what today is commonly referred to as clinically depressed. Too bad there was no psychiatric counseling available for higher beings at that time.

"Experiencing the cruel feelings of being ridiculed and betrayed, the harshness of loneliness, and a host of other unpleasantly extreme emotions, Khaos went back to his castle, locked the door, and climbed into his comforting bed. He did not want to see or talk to anybody. He did not want to eat, bathe, or get involved in any of the recreational activities that he used to enjoy so much. For many centuries to come, he just stayed in bed sleeping or pouting. It was really sad to have a grown god waste away like that. As I understand it, he even cried from time to time. After a while, there was hardly any emotion to be found in his eyes. They just stared blankly at the world around him. Khaos became a torpid being, believing himself to be very tired and very old.

"A long time had passed before he felt any better. He no longer spent all his time in bed, but he still refused to leave the reassuring confines of his castle. He found warmth and comfort in having the familiar walls of his home around him. Often, he enjoyed sitting at his favorite window on the north wing, staring at the delicate clouds, enjoying the fresh air, the warming rays of the sun, and the beautiful singing of the birds. He was very content with the quiet that surrounded him, and even began to show early signs of a thriving being once again in the serenity that enveloped his existence and finally brought peace to his heart. However, he wanted nothing else to do with any of Earth's creatures or landscapes. He vowed to himself to never set foot on that planet ever again, and thus many blissful centuries went by.

"One fine day, after another exhaustive morning of doing nothing and once again feeling sleepy, Khaos lied down to take yet another nap. He just started to enjoy his first dream when a distant, but annoying, buzzing reached his ears. At first, he ignored it, hoping it would go away. However, as it came closer and closer, it became louder and louder, until Khaos just had to jump out of his bed and run over to the window to see what kind of a bird would make such an ear-piercing noise. He had to brace himself as the whole castle shook – right down to its foundation. Squinting, he could not see anything, but then, out of the corner of his eye, he noticed an object slowly materializing into view. As it came closer, his eyes widened in surprise and his jaw dropped to his chest in total amazement. An aura of disbelief swept over him, and anger welled up from deep inside. For what seemed like an eternity, he froze in place as a long cold shiver ran down his back.

"Khaos saw something he never expected, or believed was even possible. Inside of a metallic cylinder with wings, propelling forward at an exceptionally high rate of speed by powerful engines, were the loathsome humans. Flying without any apparent regard for what's around them in the sky, they flew way too close for Khaos's comfort, and did not even notice him or his beautiful castle.

"'They didn't even stop to apologize!' he cried as he grabbed his hair into his fists, turning his knuckles snowy white. 'The nerve of these loathsome creatures! They will stop at nothing! Even up here I cannot get away from them! Is nothing sacred to them anymore?' In frustration, he began pacing back and forth once again.

"Before long, the flights became much more frequent, much louder, and produced much more turbulence. The exhaust was getting worse and worse as well. Khaos had to glue down all of his possessions and reinforce the walls of his castle after witnessing the collapse of the west wing. He could no longer sleep more than eight hours at a time because of the noise that these stupid machines created. Breathing by an open window had caused multiple respiratory problems because of the pollution that was generated by those loud and obnoxious monstrosities. He even developed convulsions and a twitch in his left eye.

"Khaos tried to stop the horrible flying cylinders by creating hurricanes and throwing lightning bolts, but none of that worked. For every plane that he caused to crash or simply disappear (Emilia flew by incredibly close), three or four new ones would appear – bigger, better, and faster than the ones before. The supersonic ones even ruptured his ear drums a couple of times. Like a cold in the middle of a winter, there was just no getting rid of the wretched humans.

"For the first time in his life, Khaos realized that he was outmatched with no hope of a solution. He no longer had any desire to see it through to the end. Humans had become technologically advanced very quickly, and he had nobody to blame but himself. He believed, beyond a shadow of a doubt, that by sharing the undiscovered knowledge and science secrets with them during those parties, and more specifically during those drinking binges, that he had set the wheels in motion. Khaos packed his bags, and, in disgust, left the Milky Way galaxy forever.

"To this day, nobody really knows where he went. Some say he went back to the heavens, while others believe he is in the next galaxy over. However, one very old man once told me that he heard someone say that he wanted to be 'as far away from the humans as possible.'

"I guess, Sonny, that all I have been trying to say is that every little thing we do, like the butterfly effect, counts in the long run and just may have an impact on a much bigger picture. Even with our best intentions to make this a better place, often we wind up disrupting world's harmony and its natural perfection. No matter how insignificant something appears to be, when our lives touch it, it affects many others, be they humans, animals, or gods. So, be more aware and cautious the next time you step outside – for your own, and everyone else's, sake. It is a big and wonderful planet we live on, Sonny. Instead of constantly changing it and adapting it to yourself, learn to love it the way it is. You will do a great service to the universe and every creature within it. In the end, everything we do or say, sooner or later, like a boomerang, comes back to us - just the way it happened to Khaos.

"Well, that is all for tonight. Next week I'll tell you another story. It will be very interesting, and I just know you will enjoy it.

"Good night, sleep tight, and sweet dreams."

The Morals and Ethics of Yellow

"**W**ell Sonny, sit back, relax, and listen to the story that I'm going to tell you. It is about ethically sound behavior, morally justifiable acts, heart, and shiny yellow nuggets. Mostly though, it's about a history lesson that, as it would appear, has fallen on the deaf ears of some people, preventing these poor individuals from learning or benefiting from it in any way. Maybe this little story will help to shine a light on some of the darker corners of their shallow minds and bring forth the concept of accountability and a brighter future. If all of this sounds confusing, I promise that it will make sense soon enough.

"You see, it all happened a very long time ago. Back then, animals ruled the planet and humans were few and far between. Most of the humans were too busy just trying to survive and preserve their own species, and had no time left in their schedules to dominate the planet or enforce their will on anyone or anything else. As time went on, the animals began to evolve into intelligent and culturally advanced societies. They became involved and began to create various forms of art – such as painting, architecture, sculpture, literature, theater ... and war. They also achieved new heights in engineering, construction and manufacturing. Believing themselves to be highly intelligent, well educated, and possessing an exceedingly advanced culture that was far superior to all other species, they developed diverse laws and philosophies dealing with life, the purpose of their existence, and the cosmos. Over the centuries they managed to construct a very intricate system of government, a relatively complex structure of checks and balances, and several distinct social classes.

"After many weak rulers, Lion became the king that everyone loved and respected. He was a very firm, but fair ruler, and was always willing to please most of his subjects. The animals also established a Senate, which helped to govern this huge empire. However, at the time that this story takes place, the members of this Senate separated themselves into two feuding parties that were widely divided on almost every issue – which proved, in the end, to be quite ineffective as a ruling body (but that is a different story that I'll tell you some other time).

"At the heart of this society was an event that made the king very popular among his animals and brought everyone together in a big celebration. That was the weekly gladiator battles which were held in the Capital's center. Every Sunday, from early morning until dusk, the Great Stadium was filled to capacity as the animals that came from all over the land to gawk and cheer at the great spectacle of other animals fighting humans to the death. The bloodier the battles became, the more the crowd became energized, got louder, and enjoyed themselves. The happier the crowd was, the more they were willing to pay for their entrance tickets, and the more money they spent at the various concession stands. That, in turn, made Lion very happy since all of that money went directly to the royal treasury. Each and every one of the fans could not get enough of the ferocious battles that forced these warriors to fight with all the skills that they could muster – strength, speed, flexibility, endurance, and quick wit – in order to defeat the beasts that were in the ring, ready to tear them apart. The best part, for most of the spectators, was not knowing who would die and who would live. Often, some dumb luck would either hinder the human and cost him his life or help him prevail over the animal. The more evenly matched a battle turned out to be, the more the gathering masses pumped their paws into the air and the louder they clapped, yelled, and whistled.

"Everything was going great for years, until one day a small problem reared its ugly head. You see Sonny, since humans began to be increasingly victorious over the previous months and even years, there was a shortage of animals that were qualified to fight. There were plenty of battle-worthy humans by that time, but the animals born and raised for these games were in danger of becoming extinct, and had to be placed on the endangered list.

"One day, while the royal servants were giving their king a manicure, Lion had, what he considered, a great idea. He wondered if humans fighting and killing each other would be better. He thought, 'Let them duke it out among themselves, doubling the spectators' pleasure of watching them display their wonderful skills.' He reasoned that the fights would be just as full of action and drama as the ones that had taken place over the last couple of decades when the animals were involved. While he liked the idea of sparing the lives of his remaining relatives (except for one of his cousins who tended to really annoy him from time to time), he was not sure how well the public would receive this concept. After all, if they did not like it, he may lose his popularity among the animals and respect among the humans, and neither was acceptable. His popularity and respect being the defining aspects of power, as he saw it, always came first and that meant keeping his public happy at all costs.

"He pondered this inspirational scheme for a little longer, and then, seeking a second opinion, or actually more a confirmation, of his brilliant plan, consulted his main advisor, Snake. Not wanting to wind up facing one of the gladiators himself, Snake smoothly proclaimed that it was an incredibly wonderful idea, one that could only be materialized in the mind of none other than a pure genius. It was then decided to implement this new modification of the games the very next Sunday.

"The king felt quite apprehensive about the possible negative reaction of the crowd. He tossed and turned throughout the nights, constantly disturbing the four lionesses that shared his bed. Like I said Sonny, he was very concerned about his popularity and at that time he was quite popular. On the morning of the big day, he woke up early, and went to the dining room. When the chef brought out his usual Sunday morning feast of freshly prepared rack of lamb, Lion just stared at it for a relatively long time, but then walked away without trying a single morsel. Becoming nervous that he had offended the king with his culinary skills, the chef nervously asked 'Burger, King?' However, Lion horizontally shook his head and just walked around the palace slowly and aimlessly. Everyone saw that he was in deep thought and did not want to disturb him any further for fear of arousing his anger. After strolling listlessly for a couple of hours, he went back to his private chamber and began to primp and prepare for his public appearance at the Great Stadium. By ten in the morning he was finally pleased by his appearance and ready to go. With his trusty Snake at his side, Lion proceeded to the center of the Capital.

"The stadium was filled to capacity once again. The roar of the crowd ricocheted off the walls as everyone cheered loudly when His Majesty entered the arena and stood in front of his seat in his purple and gold private box. He generously waved to the gathered masses in acknowledgement of their adoration, and then signaled for everyone to sit as he made himself comfortable in the makeshift throne. After a few lowly jester monkeys performed their short skits in an attempt to amuse and warm the crowd, it was time for the gladiators to come out and perform in the main event. Everyone hushed in puzzlement when they saw only humans in the middle of the arena and no animals. That is when Lion stood up, raised his right paw, cleared his throat, and addressed the thousands in the stands with slight trepidation in his voice:

"'My fellow animals, lend me your ears. I have decided that from this day forth, we will no longer sacrifice animals in this ring. I believe that humans fighting each other for glory and honor will be more breathtaking, provide edge of your seat drama, and elevate the thrill of the fights to a whole new level! Just imagine the abundance of skill, bravery, and bloodshed that we will witness when the gladiators square off against each other. I think we have all witnessed the increasingly greater and greater skills and agility that most of them have developed over the years.

"'My fellow citizens, close your eyes and imagine clashes the likes of which you have never witnessed, combat that the gods themselves never participated in or could even have dreamed of. Despite the uncertainty that some of you may feel towards such battles, I call unto all of you to join me in this event today and to enjoy these fights as much as, I'm sure, I will! Oh, and as before, I also promise to reduce the taxes and address the education problems.'"

"Lion held his breath awaiting the response of his animals. After a brief pause, three consecutive cheers rumbled from the stands and reverberated all the way down to the underground tunnels, chambers, and the underdeveloped subway system.

"'Hail to the King! Hail to the King! Hail to the King!' The chant was followed by a booming round of applause and cat whistles, as everyone blindly accepted the words of royalty and anticipated a spectacular display of willpower, skill, and death. The king had finally exhaled a breath of relief, feeling once again that as far as his animals were concerned, he could do no wrong. He was even mildly surprised, as was I, at the excellent quality of the speech that he had come up with.

"Sure enough, just as he had predicted, or rather had hoped, the humans put on a spectacular display for the crowd, pleasing even the most skeptic of spectators. Everyone found the brutality of human versus human quite mesmerizing and entertaining. Some were actually surprised at the cruelty that some gladiators displayed, and all were pleased with the larger than usual bloodshed and death count. They loved to see the horrible death in all its glory; clapping and cheering louder and louder as swords and other weapons pierced and sliced through the gladiators' bodies – rarely bringing a quick and painless death to any of the warriors. Thus, started the tradition of humans fighting humans. This weekly ritual went on for years, bringing the king's popularity, according the latest polls, soaring ever higher, and driving up the price of tickets for these events to a record high.

"No Sonny, this is not the end of the story, but I am almost done. As I was saying many years went by and the gladiator fights were as popular as ever. However, a disaster was looming on the horizon, and threatened to shake that society to its core.

"One evening just before sunset, the Snake speedily slithered to the royal chamber and burst through the doors in a frenzied state. Surprised by the rude interruption, Lion let out a loud growl of displeasure, and asked the two lionesses in the chambers to excuse him while he taught his advisor proper manners.

"'Oh SSSire, oh SSSire,' Snake hissed as fast as he could, seeing his master advance toward him with his claws popping out. 'The humanss SSSire, the humanss are refusssing to fight next SSSunday.' The Lion stopped dead in his tracks and sat down.

"'What do you mean they are refusing to fight? Why? Are they not happy with the newly refurbished and furnished dungeon that I have provided for them? Why do they refuse to fight?'

"'Well SSSire, I don't undersssstand everything they sssay, but it hass to do with moralss and ethicsss." Snake hissed on, 'They are ssaying ssomething to the effect that it iss morally wrong for human beingss to kill or even harm other human beingsss. SSome babble about ethical conduct worthy of intelligent creaturesss. SSSire, they are ssaying ssomething about evolution and higher intellect that I do not undersssstand, and it appearsss that they actually care about each other. Thiss iss horrible SSSire, absolutely horrible!'

"To say that Lion was shocked and at a loss for words, let alone action, would be a gross understatement. He did not move for a long time as shortness of breath indicative of a panic attack threatened to steal his confidence and self-control. Snake, afraid to say another word, just lay motionless in front of him. After a while, the king began to pace and mumble something to himself that Snake could not make out clearly, but thought it sounded a lot like certain words that he had not heard in a long time. When Lion was finally able to gather his emotions under control and could think clearly once again, he stopped pacing and turned to look at Snake with such piercing eyes that it sent a shiver down his long body.

"'You will go to the humans' he said in a slow, measured tone, 'and figure out what it will take for them to become, how should I say this...less enlightened. You will find out how I can make them care less about their morals and ethics. I want to know what I need to do to change their minds. The crowds will never approve of them fighting my relatives again – the ratings will surely drop. The battles that they have been having among themselves have just been too good. Go down, slither into some dark corner in their quarters, observe closely, learn what the answer is, and bring me back the news that I need. Hurry along, because if you do not come back with the information that I desire by Saturday night, we will all find out the precise spot of where the body on a snake ends and the head begins.'

Swallowing hard, the king's loyal advisor bowed his head and disappeared off into the darkness on his hair-raising (if he had any) mission.

"Late Saturday night, Snake suddenly appeared in front of the king, as he sat on his throne, deep in thought, worry, once again, clearly apparent on his face. With a diabolical smile that clearly displayed his fangs, Snake slithered up to the king's feet, sheepishly looked up at him, and began to hiss,

"'SSSire, I have found the ansswer to your...our dilemma.' Lion's ears perked up as he leaned forward in great anticipation. He could hardly contain himself at the prospect of solving the pesky human problem. 'They are not as deeply ethical asss they believe themselvesss to be, SSSire.' The Snake continued, 'In fact, they are quite eassily manipulated. They are willing to do just about anything for that yellow metal. All you need to do is offer those usselesss coinsss to whoever shall emerge as the winner, and they will continue to fight. They will tear each otherss throatsss out, if necesssary, for that ssilly sstuff.'

"The king was very surprised. 'Are you telling me that all I have to do is offer a bucket full of those yellow coins? Those useless coins that our basements are overstuffed with? Is it that simple? Is it really that easy to change their core beliefs? You are not mistaken?'

"'Abssolutely SSSire, there is no missstaking thisss,' the Snake hissed back. 'I lay quietly coiled up in a dark corner where they could not sssee me and ssstudied them. In a relatively short amount of time, I figured out that you do not need a whole bucket full, jussst two pieces per fight will do nicely. I apologize for taking ssso long, SSSire, but I just wanted to be completely sure. I ssstayed and watched sssome more to confirm sssuch bizarre phenomenon, and now I feel fully assured that it will certainly work.'

Michael Kugel

"As the information began to sink in, Lion broke into a quiet chuckle that became a throaty laugh as he thought more and more about the shallowness of the humans. Snake, feeling quite proud of himself, joined in with a sinister laugh of his own. Eventually their lofty laughter was heard resonating throughout the palace. The following morning was looking to be very promising, indeed.

"By the time the king arrived, the Great Stadium was once again filled to capacity. As Lion looked over the spectators, he thought that the huge crowd appeared livelier than usual. He waited for the gladiators to appear with great anticipation as he nervously shook his legs. Although doubt nagged at the back of his mind about the reliability of the information that Snake had delivered, his heart was telling him that his advisor was right and he would succeed once again.

"Finally, the gladiators came out into the middle of the arena, but carried no weapons. The King suddenly began to feel even more nervous and doubtful since it was quite obvious to everyone present that the humans had no intention of fighting. The gladiator's chosen spokesman came closer to where Lion was sitting and in a loud voice declared that from this day forth they will no longer battle and kill each other because it was too barbaric and that they were far above such atrocities and cruelties. He spoke of love and compassion towards others, and good will for all. Cheered on by all other gladiators, the human talked about honesty and fairness, freedom of choice, right versus wrong, and the need for affordable health insurance for their tired, broken, and mangled bodies.

"Deafening silence fell over the stadium as the one-time gladiator returned to stand among his companions. Holding their breaths in anticipation, the members of the crowd could not believe what they just heard. Slowly shifting their wide-open eyes from the humans to the King, they awaited his response. It was at that moment that Lion realized that the future of his political career was about to be decided in the next few minutes. Thick tension enveloped the Great Stadium. Lion knew that perhaps even his own life may be in jeopardy since the assassination of unpopular leaders had been on the rise in recent decades, and therefore, even his life may depend heavily on his next words and actions.

"He could feel his heart beating ever so hard in his chest, as sweat beaded on his forehead and slowly rolled down his cheek. Taking a deep cleansing breath, he raised himself and without taking his eyes off the humans, held up his paw. Clearly holding up a bucket full of yellow coins, he loudly announced, 'For every fight, the victor shall have two of these!' He then took out two coins and held them up in his other paw. He need not say more; as soon as the bucket was displayed in plain view and his ten words uttered, the answer as to whether Snake was right or not became quite clear. Lion had absolutely nothing to worry about. He looked over at his advisor with a big smile on his face, sat back down, and watched with satisfaction the events that unfolded before him.

"Every human that stood in that arena changed his demeanor as if possessed by an evil spirit. Their eyes glazed over with greed; menace and bad intent was suddenly spotted upon their faces, and with their bare hands they proceeded to rip each other apart. They punched and scratched, bit and kicked, and even lowered themselves to throwing sand into their opponent's eyes, and whipping rocks at each other. They were so ferocious towards each other that even the strongest, most menacing and hungry lions could not have matched the killer instinct that these humans displayed. All of the other animals could hardly believe their eyes. It was the most wonderful spectacle of backstabbing that any of them had ever seen, and the crowd absolutely loved it. Much to the king's pleasure, in one swift move, while keeping his claws crossed, the Sunday fights became even more entertaining, thus raising the price of the tickets higher still, and making him even more popular and powerful than ever before.

"What can I say Sonny? For many years to come, as long as the king was paying out the yellow coins, the humans continued to battle each other to the death – usually with weapons, but sometimes with bare hands as well if that was called for. Many of them even began to cheat in order to get an upper hand. Sometimes they would sneak poisons or drugs into their opponents' food or water so that they would feel extremely drowsy, or would inflict some kind of a serious, but non-fatal, wound before a fight in order to weaken them. It is, I mean was, a really ugly time for humans.

"Some of the humans eventually managed to form various groups that later became known as 'corporations'. These people were particularly ruthless. To earn those lousy yellow coins, they began poisoning water supplies and even air, not caring who was affected by their actions or to what capacity. As long as the coins were won in the Stadium, no act of treachery was too severe or too big. In time, even the animals became very sick, and creatures of all species began to die prematurely – especially the ones that lived near the corporations.

"There was also a much higher rate of stillbirths, congenital defects, and various other diseases that are too numerous to name – for both the animals and the humans. It became so bad, that as the years passed, the whole society began to fall apart, until there was nothing and no one left. There were no more gladiators, no more corporations, no more animals. Ironically enough, none of them, whether they were members of a corporation or not, were ever even able to enjoy those yellow coins that they worked so hard to hoard.

"The king died many years later in a secluded house somewhere in the middle of a forest. He was in complete misery because there was no society left in which to be popular and prosperous. None of the surviving animals even knew his name.

"I guess what I have been trying to say is that some of the values we carry can become dull when facing bright sparkly things. Now that we humans control the world, it is nice to see that animals are not sinking down to those levels that these humans did so many years ago. Just remember that ethics are only as good as your morals – the more committed you are to one, the higher value you'll place on the other. Sometimes the cost of power and wealth is not worth the compromise of principles and beliefs that we attempt to hold onto when getting on the first step of the ladder of success. Of course, to some the 'light' of enlightenment continues to be dim, and the corners of their minds continue to exist in relative darkness. Just keep in mind that the brightness of small yellow objects and other sparkly things is directly proportional to the amount of good health one is able to accumulate. After all, what's the point of the former if one is willing to sacrifice the latter in order to obtain it? How is that for a deep thought? See, and you thought I could only tell simple stories!

"Well, that's all I have for you today, Sonny. I hope you liked this little account of events and perhaps even learned something. I promise that tomorrow I will tell you another one if you're in the mood.

"Good night, sleep tight, and sssssweet dreamsss."

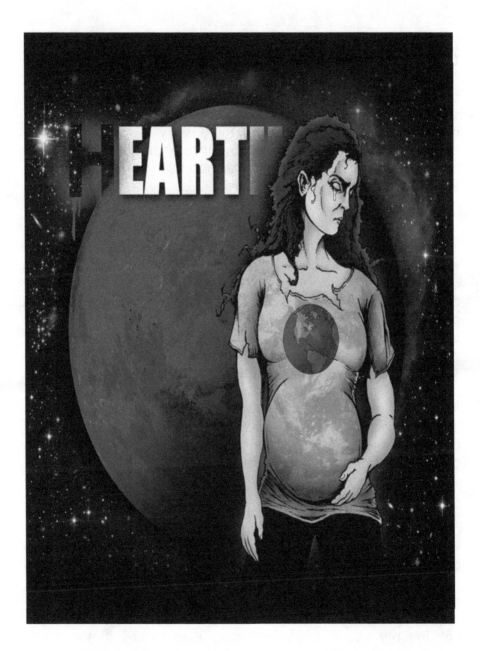

"**W**ell Sonny, sit back, relax, and listen to the story that I am going to tell you. It's about trust, mistakes, friendships, and faith in others. Mostly though, it is about decisions and the importance of making the right ones. You see, sometimes even the most insignificant of choices, if made poorly, may affect you for a very long time. Maybe even for the rest of your life. The interesting aspect to all of this is that the right decision is not that difficult to make, and therefore, the consequences can easily be avoided.

"You see, a long time ago, when everything was young and new, there existed a recently formed planet. She was only a few million years old, well, give or take a few centuries, and was mostly made up of rock and water with a pretty thick atmosphere of various gases. These gases constantly shifted, and as eons went by, they changed, and the atmosphere evolved into mostly nitrogen, oxygen, and small traces of a whole bunch of other gases. I see the smirk on your face. Yes, she was a pretty gassy planet. However, all that is not important for my story. What is important is that this planet was young, ambitious, and pretty. However, she was also immature, and on occasion proved to be somewhat temperamental, mildly impatient, and borderline rebellious. Her name was Heart.

"Heart was the only planetoid, born into a loving and caring family. Her parents were extremely excited when she was finally formed because they had been trying to give birth to a planet for a long time. Her father boasted to all his friends about the Big Bang that made his young daughter possible, while his wife told her friends quietly, so as not to bruise his ego, that while it was indeed a bang, there was nothing big about it. In fact, she used to say it was more like a two-day effort that was hardly worth talking about.

Nonetheless, no matter what happened all those millions of years ago, they were extremely happy to have finally become parents, and loved their daughter very much.

"As the millenniums went by and Heart began to grow, they tried to instill in her proper manners, wholesome values, and respect for everything and everyone around her. Despite any shortcomings that their daughter might have had, causing her to not quite fulfill her parents term of endearment of 'our little angel', they were very proud of her, always boasting to their families, friends, and even the neighbors about what a wonderful girl she was turning out to be. She achieved well scholastically, bringing home excellent grades (at least most of the time), got along great with other kids at school, listened to everything her parents had to say without the customary rolling of the eyes, and performed all that was asked of her without delay or any obvious signs of disapproval. Heart was becoming a caring planet, and never displayed many characteristics of laziness or great mischief. Over all, no parents in the whole universe could have asked for a better child.

"However, not everything in Heart's life was as perfect as it might have appeared to a casual observer. Even though she usually had a smile on her face when her parents were around, deep down she was not extremely happy. While her feelings and state of mind were nowhere near what would be considered clinical depression, the young planet never had any real friends and therefore, felt sad and lonely. Despite her best efforts, she could not make any long-lasting friendships. Perhaps her social skills were poorly developed, or maybe the other planets did not like the atmosphere around her – it is not clear. There were a few planets that liked her enough to become her friends, but they always wound up moving away when their parents found more profitable universes, or just warmer suns to orbit around. Despite the fact that several of the other children did indeed talk to her at school, they all lived far away, and she usually wound up playing in the sandbox by herself, rode the bicycle alone, and had no best friend her age that she could talk to and share her deepest feelings with. The point here is this: that despite being a nice child, Heart had no close friends, and therefore, as billions of years went by, she was getting more and more lonely. If only she had a sibling. While her parents tried to fill that void, the fact remained that while she had several acquaintances, she had no real friends.

"Now Sonny, pay close attention because this is where the story gets really interesting. As any other living creature, for better or for worse, Heart grew into an adolescent, and then inevitably became a teenager. Quite often that phenomenon takes place to the detriment of at least one of the parental units (usually both). For a planet, that is quite a few billion years of age, not sure exactly, but to her parents, the eons just flew by.

"The young lady started high school and that is where my story really takes place. You see, for the first time in her life, Heart found some friends. In fact, she became part of a small clique of planets that hung around together almost all the time – or at least they did in the beginning. Let me briefly describe them for you.

"The first one, the one that she liked the most and got along with the best, was kind of similar to her. Although this planet's atmosphere was mostly made up of carbon dioxide and methane, the temperature on the surface closely resembled Heart's. It was a female planet, and when Heart introduced herself, the other one squeezed the funny looking cigarette even tighter with her lips and very slowly, with a deep crackly voice, said, 'Mmmmm.' Then she slowly reached up and removed the cigarette out of her mouth, looked Heart over from head to toe with her red puffy eyes, and with a barely perceptible wave of her hand said, 'I'm...' She took another long drag of the cigarette,

'I'm...mmmmmm...Ars.' For some unknown reason, Heart liked her right from the start. Her mannerism, self-confidence, and rebellious nature really appealed to her. They shook hands and eventually became the best of friends.

"Heart's new best friend then introduced her to Pluto, a midget planet that she was seeing from time to time on weekends. He was smoking the same type of a cigarette and turned out to be a very cold and somewhat angry individual. He preferred to mostly keep to himself and just always hung out on the periphery or the outskirts of the clique. Most said that he was just upset over the small size that he turned out to be, and the goofy name that he was given. Dark and icy, he proved to be very distant indeed, and the majority of the time he acted as if he was mad at the whole galaxy.

"Four of her other new friends were mostly gaseous and lacked any real substance. The one with the most gravitational pull was Jupiter, and he hoped to become a star someday.

"The second was Saturn, and she was really interested in mortuary sciences, always carried an empty urn with her, and was somewhat obsessed with death.

"The third was Neptune and he aspired to be a professional singer someday, and always carried a tuning fork in his pocket. No one had the spirit to tell him that he was tone deaf.

"The fourth gaseous planet was named Uranus and he was a strange one. He had psychiatric problems because, at the very least, he was bipolar. At times, he would stare off into the distance, and mumble something to himself that none of them could understand. They figured he had not taken any of his medications in quite a while.

"One of the other planets by the name of Mercury, liked to keep very warm. In fact, during the day, the temperatures on his surface became extremely hot, and approached approximately fifteen hundred degrees Fahrenheit. He always wore warm clothes, and added some mysterious spices to everything he ate. He said they were very hot and helped to warm him up from the inside. None of them were brave enough to try any of the spices.

"Finally, there was Venus. Venus was a very energetic planet and proved to be extremely talkative, although very little of what she said was pertinent. She loved to incorporate words such as 'like', 'totally', and 'whatever' in the middle of her sentences. She also liked to absorb a lot of the sun's radiation and her atmosphere was filled with greenhouse gases such as sulfur, carbon monoxide, and radical oxygen. She frequently asked a lot of unimportant questions that occasionally annoyed those around her, became involved in all kinds of rumors and various other exaggerations, repeatedly became moody and snappy, constantly changed her mind just about everything, was very hard to please, and sometimes liked to disagree just for the sake of argument, especially with the male planets. Quite often she also liked to nag, made mountains out of molehills, assumed facts that were not true, and regularly made situations and conversations more complicated than they actually had to be.

"Heart and the other eight planets became a tightly knit assembly of friends that did nearly everything as a group. They walked to school together in the mornings, talked to each other between classes, ate their lunches at the same table, and walked back home together in the afternoons. They often had 'group studies' (at least that's what Heart often told her parents when she went out to meet her friends), and frequently, aimlessly bummed around the galaxy in the evenings and on weekends. Heart was finally just as happy on the inside as she appeared to be on the outside. Perhaps that is why she was blind to the problems developing around her, or maybe she just didn't care. After all, peer pressure is often hard to notice and even harder to overcome, especially for a teenager.

"Heart began to smoke those funny cigarettes as well, and started to experiment with other mind-altering substances that Pluto supplied her and her best friend. Despite the fact that the other six planets stayed away from all that stuff, she saw no problem with it and, in no time at all, began to smoke anything that she could get her hands on – every day. She was no longer polite to her parents or anyone else around her. Skipping classes, or the whole day of school became regular practice, and needless to say, her grades suffered. Drinking became an everyday occurrence as well, with no regard to place or time, and I'm not referring to water, juice, or soda. Much like the other two that she spent increasingly more time with, Heart no longer cared about her personal hygiene, clean clothes, or school. She didn't even care when Mercury, Venus, Jupiter, Saturn, Uranus, and Neptune began to separate themselves from the three of them, and spent less and less time in their company. Their tastes in lifestyle, choices in personal behavior, and preferences for various activities began to differ more and more, and eventually their happy clique of nine was divided in two.

"Heart's parents tried to intervene by forcing her to stay away from her friends, study more, and be a better planet in general, but unfortunately she refused to listen. Like millions of other teenagers, she felt that she pretty much knew everything that there was to know, and that she knew it better than anyone else. When they did not allow her to leave the house, and even locked her in her room, she would sneak out at night, and if needed, she would climb out of her bedroom window to spend time with her two remaining friends. There was just no controlling the young and rebellious planet.

"Eventually, all three of them began to resort to crime in order to sustain the habits that they had developed, and Heart dropped out of school and ran away from home to live in the streets. She felt that she was mature and tough enough to make her own decisions; it was not a pretty picture for the three friends. However, none of them realized that they were spiraling out of control, traveling at a high rate of speed on a road that stops at a dead end. Although surprisingly none of them were arrested or died a premature death (at least not yet), the future did not look very bright for the three of them.

"Like all living creatures with a large number of hormones circulating through their bodies, Heart began to notice and take interest in the opposite sex. As time went on, she heard many girls talking incessantly about their varied experiences with male planets and passing comets. At times, they told very interesting, and often amusing, stories of their exploits, although Heart was pretty sure that a lot of those were greatly exaggerated. However, she was still fascinated by them and had a growing urge to try and make at least some of those stories a reality for herself. Even though she often blushed at such a topic, an ever-increasing mix of curiosity and desire spurred her on towards the opposite sex.

"Some girls wanted to fall into orbit with just one other planet and live out their lives submerged in deep love and multiple moments of pure joy and ecstasy. Others wanted to experiment with as many different planets, comets, and space debris, in as many galaxies as possible. Many just wanted to be somewhere in the middle of those two extremes.

"Her best friend constantly boasted how much fun she had when a passing comet touched her and how pleasurable the experience turned out to be. She even told her of the occasional rendezvous that she and Pluto had been having and how satisfying, at times, those activities turn out to be. Heart was amused remembering how the boys in her old clique liked to constantly tell stories of their obviously exaggerated exploits. She figured it might be fun to try some of the things that she had heard so much about, but was not sure what exactly she wanted in the long run, and to be honest, she did not really care. One thing that she was certain of, however, was that she definitely wanted to experiment.

"Back at school, and in many other parts of the universe, however, the many male planets that caught Heart's eye, to her chagrin, all stayed far away from her. Why, you ask? Well, at first it was simply because they were not mature enough for such activities. As the saying goes, they could talk the talk, but they were way too nervous to walk the walk.

"Then, as everyone became a little older and more mature, Heart's lifestyle changed, as did her outward appearance ... and it was not for the better. She constantly looked tired, frazzled, and depressed. Her eyes were red and puffy (on those occasions when she could fully open them), clothes dirty, hair disheveled, and well, she gave off a less than pleasing scent to stimulate those olfactory senses. To make matters worse, her speech was drawn out and her words were slurred. Much like her other two friends, she became quite unattractive, short-tempered, and somewhat dimwitted.

"After several centuries of rejections and disappointments at her attempts to get close and experiment with a member of the opposite sex, Heart began to get frustrated and upset. Once again, in spite of her friends, she felt alone and longed for a deeper, more meaningful relationship with a male companion. She felt a need in her that she wanted to fulfill more and more, and no longer cared about his personality or what he looked like.

She just wanted to try it out for herself and find out how much of those stories were true and would settle for any willing male subject.

"Then one day it finally happened. It was actually quite unexpected. Heart was just hanging around with her friends, smoking yet another one of those home-grown herbs, when a large, somewhat older comet happened to be passing by. He was no more than several million miles away and Heart moved towards him. As she approached, he noticed her and adjusted his trajectory. For the briefest of moments, they touched, fulfilling Heart's long held desire to experiment. He immediately continued on his way, never to be seen again. It was so brief, she never even learned his name, and was quite surprised by how short and not all that fulfilling or satisfying the experience turned out to be – hardly worth boasting about. However, life for Heart was never the same again.

"It took several million years for the signs and symptoms to be noticed, but once they flared out of control, there was no denying that she was, indeed, quite ill. At first, she tried to ignore it, convincing herself that after such a short contact, transmission of any disease was impossible. However, as time went on and the infection raged on, Heart became so sick that she had to confine herself to bed, drop all of her bad habits because they made her feel even worse, and obtain medical help since she was in so much discomfort. Heart had contracted a planetary transmitted disease, and this was quite a serious case.

"Not knowing what words of support she could say to make her feel better, Heart's best friend confessed to her that she had a similar infection after her second rendezvous with a passing comet as well. She admitted that she was frightened by it quite a bit, but was able to eventually fight off the infection and get healthy again. Heart was convinced that the same would happen to her since her signs and symptoms were very similar to those of her friend. The infection, after all, was localized to the bodies of water, and at first did not appear to be too dangerous. The doctor at the local clinic was convinced that the disease could be cured with proper treatments within a few centuries. However, for some inexplicable reason, the virus began to adapt to other environments, and to mutate into something strange and more exotic.

"To make the situation even worse, Heart found out that she was pregnant. Everything in her life was spinning out of control, and she turned to her parents for help. With open arms and undying love, they took her back, and did everything in their power to try to heal their daughter and ease the discomforts of pregnancy. She spent the next several million years in bed, with the best doctors in the galaxy looking out for her, doing their best to cure the infection, and assure the birth of a healthy planetoid. The problem, however, was that none of them had ever seen such a virus and were not sure how to treat it properly.

"Heart eventually gave birth to a very premature, extremely sick, baby girl rock. The doctors worked feverishly to save her life, and only through the miracles of modern medical sciences did the baby live long enough to become Heart's moon. However, shortly after falling into orbit around her mother, the baby died quietly while she slept one night. Heart cried for a very long time.

"In the meantime, her immune system finally organized itself into a cohesive defensive effort. Earthquakes, erupting volcanoes, tidal waves, hurricanes, mudslides, blizzards, avalanches, and unusually cold and icy conditions became less random, and more organized. Even the solar eclipse became a defensive tactic that the young planet tried to incorporate. The doctors were able to launch wave after wave of these attacks at the infection, and surprisingly enough, after about one hundred and twenty million years, the virus population began to decline and was nearly wiped out. Heart began to feel a little better.

"During a moment of clarity, she finally realized that her lifestyle and the choices she made were leading her into trouble and that she was living a life of dead ends. She decided that there would no longer be anymore drinking, smoking, or cigarettes of any kind in her life. She wanted to go back to school, take her studies much more seriously, and concentrate on obtaining good grades once again. Then, Heart wanted to go to college, and become a productive member of her galaxy, and a responsible adult. On occasion, she dreamed of marriage and, someday, perhaps motherhood once again. Even her best friend changed her ways, and developed very similar goals.

"However, as eons passed, she began to get sicker and sicker. The virus that lived upon her managed not only to survive, but to thrive. It was no longer weak or isolated. You see, it took about fifty to sixty million years for the virus to become an entity that no one had ever seen or heard of up to that point – becoming an ugly mutated creature that resembled a cancer in character and behavior. It began to multiply throughout most of her body and exhibited quite virulent properties, becoming extremely aggressive and multiplying at a very high rate of speed, until in a relatively short period of time, it spread over every part of Heart's surface – even underground.

"It had conquered or killed almost every other organism (and environment) that it encountered. Normal flora and their ecosystems in all parts of the planet began to be viciously and mercilessly destroyed. The virus conquered their environments and prospered in the valleys and mountains; at sea and deep underground; in the brutally cold conditions of the North and South poles, and the harsh environments of the overbearingly hot deserts near the equator.

"The virus proved to be a very resourceful infectious agent, able to overcome all of Heart's natural defenses. Every one of the doctors that her parents summoned were amazed at the rate with which the virus evolved and the speed with which the infection spread. None of them knew how to cure the dreaded disease, or even how to slow it down – everything they tried proved useless. It took them all by complete surprise when this radical virus quickly adapted to all of the antiviral agents that the physicians tried to introduce into their patient's system, and overcame the new challenges by developing more and more lethal defenses and counter attacks that made the planet only sicker. The physicians were left speechless when they observed the speed with which the pathogen was able to learn the unknowns, process the new information, and solve difficult problems.

"As the virus continued to evolve, it began to produce an exorbitant amount of regular and toxic wastes. Even though it proved to be very lethal to the virus itself, all throughout the entire planet deadly gases, radioactive byproducts, and other hazardous materials were being freely released, dumped, or buried. She became so polluted that it became dangerous even for the doctors themselves to be anywhere near their patient. With no regard for the consequences its actions might have on the planet or itself, the virus continued to produce a plethora of trash, and release it into the air, water, or deep (and sometimes shallow) ground. Even the blanket that Heart pulled over herself began to disintegrate, as huge holes began to appear in its layers.

"After thousands of years, the virus managed to build and organize itself into complex colonies and societies. The separations were mostly dictated by geographic areas, cultural traditions, certain similar practices, and the minute differences in the DNA and the resultant RNA complexes. At the heart of every one of these social orders, the components that all of them are based on and what makes them function in a relatively productive manner, are the core values often based on theological beliefs, much like a set of doctrines, and a kind of monetary system that has given rise to an unbalanced economy and unequal distribution of resources and power.

"Like I said Sonny, this is a highly evolved and mutated virus. Based on those two concepts, they killed each other almost from the moment they were able to organize themselves into groups. Perhaps, that pathogen is not that highly evolved after all. Anywhere from one individual virus in an isolated incident to thousands and millions of viruses in an all-out war, get killed every day. Pride, greed, jealousy, ethnocentrism, sense of justice, and several other attributes have contributed to this phenomenon. Sometimes it is accidental, but more often than not, they are purposeful acts of aggression. Overall, it amounts to greater viral population control than what doctors and Heart's immune system could provide in a combined effort. Who knows, perhaps if Heart hangs on long enough, the virus will exterminate itself out of existence and she will finally be able to make a complete recovery.

"Oh, I almost forgot to tell you about her friends. You were probably wondering what happened to the rest of them. Well, let me see now. Last I heard, Pluto became even angrier when Heart and her best friend quit smoking and both stopped being his friends. He decided that none of the fully developed planets were worth his time anyway, and befriended other dwarf planets. He, Ceres, Haumea, Makemake, and Eris formed their own clique and prefer to spend most of their time in darkness on the very edge of the galaxy – as far from the sun as possible. They still smoke all kinds of home-grown herbs, and don't even come close to understanding that their poor habits have most likely stunted their growth, made them social outcasts, and offered absolutely no opportunities for a better future. Of course, they lack the insight to see much further past today, and therefore, live only for the present.

"Jupiter has grown into an extremely large planet, and after settling down with a beautiful lady, fathered about forty moons. In fact, today all those planetoids can still be seen orbiting their father, and on occasion, driving him absolutely nuts.

"Saturn, who changed her mind about her mortuary science major half way through the program, managed to complete a degree in chemistry, and obtain a really good job. After that, she had more time for a social life, and managed to find the love of her life. I'm not sure who or what he is, but she proudly displays her engagement ring and is anxiously looking forward to her wedding.

"Mercury continues to enjoy his spices in even greater amounts today than he did as a teenager. They help him to have the biggest temperature swings in the galaxy, as his surface goes from extreme deep freeze at night to incredibly hot during the day. He finished college with a degree in physical education, but decided to open up his own shop where he sells a wide variety of culinary spices, seasonings and hot sauces, which he whips up in his own kitchen, to anyone brave enough to try them.

"Neptune finally figured out that he could not sing or carry a tune, even if his life depended on it. However, after refusing to give up on his dream of being in a band, he learned how to play the drums, and joined a band right after graduation from high school. They have actually had some moderate success, and have played at relatively popular concert venues. The large violent storms and ferocious winds on his surface closely resemble the mood and the tone of the music that they play.

"Uranus, despite being bipolar, managed to become a counselor for mentally disturbed individuals and moonlights with the suicide hot line. He is able to keep his cool under pressure by being consistently the coldest planet in the Solar System.

"Venus became a pretty popular planet. After spending several eons as a fashion designer, this young lady managed to become a trend setter for nearly all other women in the universe. Her fashions, character, mannerisms, and even personality were copied and popularized by most females in existence. Despite the fact that she still absorbs a lot of the sun's radiation, today, more than ever before, nearly all of them strive to be just like her. Heart's best friend eventually settled down, but not before she gave birth to two adorable and, luckily, healthy moons. Despite the fact that she might become infected with Heart's dreaded disease, they continue to be best friends, and she often comes to check up on her friend. She always tries to offer a comforting word, a shoulder to cry on, or just an ear to listen to the pain and suffering that Heart is going through.

"As for Heart, well Sonny, she is dying. Most of her days are spent in bed, agonizing in pain, coughing, sneezing, and experiencing shortness of breath because of the heavy pollution. She continues to run a high fever, and the temperature just keeps climbing. Her appearance is no longer vibrant or cheerful like it used to be all those years ago, and the virus doesn't show any major signs of slowing down. All of the doctors gave up on trying to cure the young planet a long time ago, and her immune system is slowly shutting down as well. There are still pretty strong earthquakes, blizzards, and hurricanes that develop over the oceans and come inland, but they provide extremely minimal protection and are not very effective at killing a large number of the virus since it has learned to adapt to them. All other natural disasters are not very common anymore, and do not amount to too much of a killing field for the infection. It is a very grim situation for Heart indeed.

"Sonny, you look a little confused. I guess that what I have been trying to say is that...well, let's not beat around the bush. Do not use drugs, stay in school, and wear protection when engaging in any kind of offspring producing rituals that involve sexual contact. You never know when a terminal microorganism may be transferred, and then deplete and poison your loins. And, of course, don't pollute. Plain and simple; straight to the point. You see, every person should always consider the costs of his or her actions and, unlike a small child, keep in mind that there will always be tomorrow and he or she will have to deal with the consequences of all the activities from today. Therefore, living only for the present is not a good way to function or exist. Oh yeah, and do not kill anybody either.

"Sonny, how is that for a pretty dark story? I just hope you enjoyed it. If you found it boring, look on the bright side: it was not that long. It is getting to be very late now and well past your bedtime (mine as well).

"Good night, sleep tight, and sweet dreams."

"**W**ell Sonny, sit back, relax, and listen to the story that I am going to tell you. It's about qualities that we all possess – appreciation, respect, and the ability to do good deeds for others. However, we all possess those qualities in varying quantities and express them in so many various ways that sometimes it may seem somewhat unorthodox, or simply may not be seen at all. Mostly though, this story is about being careful of our actions towards others, because they may be the most important individuals in our lives. In no time at all, this tale will clarify any confusion my previous words may have created.

"Although the majority of this tale takes place at a village in the middle of nowhere, located on the bottom of an ocean, I will begin this saga many miles from there, with a whale who was just a calf when these events began to unfold. His name was Eugene. He had big brown eyes, making him very endearing, and his extra-long eyelashes made him look even more adorable; in fact, he could melt the biggest iceberg heart with his cuteness, especially when raising his eyes to look up at something above.

"However, unfortunately, at the young age of just two-years-old, Eugene became on orphan. Both of his parents died in freak accidents, nearly leaving the poor baby whale to fend for himself. Eugene remembered almost nothing of them, and never knew that his father, Ronald, was an alcoholic who used to come home late at night and abuse his family. Ronald would blame his behavior on the stress of his job and the fact that he received no support – moral, physical, or spiritual – at home. He always emphasized the fact that his wife did not work, even though this was due to extremely limited opportunities in the job market for those without a college education, to earn enough to cover the exorbitant cost of infant childcare, let alone contribute to the household bills. Because of this, he began to believe that his wife and his only son, (who was too little to make a living), were nothing but a burden, and were only good for spending the hard-earned money that he brought home.

"Of course, Ronald was also involved in a few other unsavory activities, but that is another story for other time. One night, after yet another binge of loud music, hard liquor, and wild women, Ronald became disoriented, stumbled off his usual swimming route becoming hopelessly lost, caught in a strong current, and was, unfortunately, unceremoniously beached, where he died sometime later along with several other drunken whales. Hardly any tears were spilled at the news of his untimely demise. Thus, the world triumphed at getting rid of another unsavory character.

"Eugene's mother, Rose, died shortly thereafter in a more tragic way. She was caught in the nets of a fishing vessel while freeing her son of the same trap. You see, while playing around with a pod of whales from school, Eugene wandered off a bit too far from her while she was busy looking for the southern current, didn't see the nets and became entangled in them. He was badly frightened and screamed for his mother. Were it not for her, he surely would have perished. She immediately swam over, and in a panic, began to free her son. It took a considerable effort to finally accomplish that task, but in the process, her own tail and one of her flippers were ensnared by the heavy net. She struggled for hours, attempting to flip, dive, and roll and anything else that she could think of, but it was all to no avail. She was simply too exhausted from saving her son.

"The only one to witness this tragic, yet heroic event was a lone aging dolphin by the name of Matilda. Matilda tried to help in whatever way she could, but the whale was just too big, and the nets were too heavy. Shortly before Eugene's mother died, Matilda, with teary eyes and a quivering voice, promised Rose that she would look after Eugene, and raise him as her own son.

"You see Sonny, Matilda had never been able to have any children of her own, but nonetheless, her motherly instincts were very strong, and she took in poor Eugene, raising him as only a loving mother could.

"Thus, a bottlenose dolphin adopted a humpback baby whale, and Matilda was finally triumphant at becoming a mother. I would love to say that they lived happily ever after, but that is not the way it happened. Real life is never easy.

"Matilda raised Eugene the best way that she could, instilling in him positive values and proper morals. She taught him respect, courtesy, and good manners towards others, as well as himself. Most of all though, she stressed humility, and the difference between right and wrong. He quickly learned how to appreciate life and all that it has to offer. Eugene took everything in stride, carefully paying attention to everything she had to say, never questioning any aspects of his lessons, and always trying to be the son she could be proud of.

"Eugene was growing by leaps and bounds, and his ever-increasing size was matched only by his heart. He loved children, and would spend hours playing with them. He could usually be found building or digging in the sandbox with the toddlers, playing war, a game of tag, tug of war with the teenagers, or just giving rides on his back to kids of all ages. Sometimes he was "it" in the game of hide and seek all day long, and at other times he played board games with anyone that asked him to join in.

"As he approached his teen years, he hit a growth spurt and, at least physically, turned into an adult virtually overnight. His heart grew right along with him, and Eugene developed into a relatively straightforward, quite trusting, and very giving individual. He rarely questioned anything that he was told or asked to do, went about accomplishing his chores and tasks without complaint, and was always willing to lend a hand to anyone with anything; all they need do was ask.

"However, socially, things were slowly changing. Most of the kids did not like him anymore because he was becoming way too big and extremely clumsy – especially within the small confines of his neighborhood. He never realized that the reason nobody wanted to build sand castles or seaweed houses with him anymore was because one could always count on Eugene to accidently hit the structure in mid construction, and destroy everything that all the kids worked so hard to build. At times he was ridiculed and bullied by the older, more inconsiderate, and the less disciplined kids on the block, who mistook his large size for obesity. It never even occurred to him that he was much bigger and stronger than them and could have easily bullied them back. Feeling sad and left out, he always went home to the comforting words of his mother who knew all too well what the problem was, but was completely unable to do anything about his clumsiness or size. She comforted him the best that she knew how with encouraging words and a big warm hug, made him feel like he was somebody important once again and life moved slowly on.

"When Eugene started getting older, a bunch of stonefish and mosquitofish suddenly became his new friends, and he didn't grasp the concept that they were usually up to no good. Many of them were starting to take advantage of his size and good nature more and more in order to help them accomplish hooligan-type activities and then trick him into aiding them to escape from the local sheriff once mischievous conduct of some type, or a deviant act was committed. Matilda did not like any of his friends and worried about Eugene, knowing that her naïve son, probably had no idea of the undesirable nature of his actions or their consequences, and was, therefore, unknowingly heading for trouble.

"The last thing that anybody wanted, especially her or Eugene, was to commit any offenses against the laws of the ocean, set forth by his royal highness himself – The King of the Seas. He established laws and regulations for all sea creatures and ocean dwellers to live by, and breaking any of them was usually dealt with swiftly and, at times, quite harshly. It did not take long for Matilda to decide that in order to safeguard her son's future, and to perhaps improve their situation in general, they had to move. At this point, she felt that she needed a change of scenery almost as much as her son.

"You see Sonny, as any single parent might do, Matilda moved around from time to time, struggling to make ends meet. The financial burdens in her life seemed insurmountable at times, but as long as her son was there to brighten her day, she could survive any obstacle and tackle any pesky problem. Thus, when Eugene was thirteen years old, Matilda decided to move her family to the village in the middle of nowhere, on the bottom of an ocean, where there were promises of a job, better and safer housing, and a more stable financial future.

"The village was relatively small compared to all other communities of that time, but nevertheless, was considered quite modern. In it lived all sorts of fish: skates, cichlids, haddock, guppies, triggerfish, frogfish, salmon, perch, groupers, shrimp, tuna, octopi, certain species of squid, and a few others that I will get to shortly. On the village outskirts resided crabs, urchins, various slugs (one of them was The Spanish Dancer), and eels. There were even two families of manta rays residing among them. The villagers were a widely diversified group of individuals, all working together toward a common goal – survival. This involved improving their community, households, personal wealth, and well-being.

"After a long day of hard work, many of the inhabitants enjoyed an evening out. The Trumpetfish would put on a spectacular performance that constantly managed to delight the young and the old. When the circus came to town, which was quite often, the main attractions were always the lionfish and the tigerfish. Although, the little ones believed that the clownfish alone were worth the price of admission. Many of the villagers chose to unwind by taking long swims in the park and observing the sputtering sea moths, multicolored butterflyfish, and pretty flying fish. Some even tried to feed the ever-nutty squirrelfish. On some evenings, near the caves, the villagers could easily spot the batfish swimming by, minding their own business, but always startling one or two unsuspecting visitors.

"Some fish were nicknamed for their habits. The ones that always woke up before everybody else were named the sunfish. The cleanest ones in the village – probably due to compulsive obsessive disorder – were known as the soapfish. The ones that liked to cause trouble and exhibited poor abilities to conform to society standards – probably due to immaturity, secondary only to poor growth development – were called the devilfish.

"Just outside the village, there were farmers who raised porkfish, goatfish, cowfish, and relied heavily on seahorses during the harvest season. Others, mostly lobsters and swordfish, joined the military to protect the village from any threat that may exist in the wide-open spaces of the ocean.

"And now, these villagers also had a dolphin and a whale residing among them. Although there was no inside housing big enough for them to fit into, they were perfectly happy to live outdoors. They established their residence on the outskirts of the village, right next to one of the manta ray families on one side, and a large family of sardines living in a one-bedroom apartment on the other. Eugene made new friends, ones that were not going to get him into trouble, and Matilda was able to obtain the new job that she had hoped for. Thus, for the only two mammals of the village things were moving along quite nicely. They were both content with their new lives, and enjoyed the relative peace and quiet that this village had to offer.

"Eugene completed his education with acceptable grades, always making his mom proud with his academic and sports achievements, handmade gifts for birthdays and other holidays, and most of all, with his attention and caring towards his aging mother. He continued to grow some more, becoming, upon his graduation from high school, an absolutely huge whale. Seemingly within a blink of an eye, the years went by unnoticed.

"By the time Eugene became a fully-grown and developmentally matured adult, he was a pretty large creature even by whale standards. Unfortunately, not many residents of the village were familiar with whales, and believed him to be simply, grotesquely overweight, much like the kids that he had to deal with in his youth. That made his life quite difficult in the public eye. As cruel as kids can be, adults can often be even more childish, and at times, worse than a rotten, spoiled adolescent. And as I said before, Eugene was very trusting of all who were around him and had a very big heart. He learned not to pay attention to the unpleasant statements that were directed in his general direction, and believed that the individuals who felt that way were in the minority. Instead, he preferred to concentrate on the huge soft spot that he had for children.

"After securing a minimum wage paying job, and discovering that he had little use for the small amounts of money that he was making, the big-hearted mammal decided to donate most of his earnings to various children's charities. He regularly stopped by to spread cheer at the local orphanage as well. The very young ones loved his simplicity and were easily amused by his clumsiness. However, due to his trusting nature, he was never able to figure out, and therefore, never knew, that all of his neighbors really disliked having him around. They thought he was nothing but a clumsy oaf and detested his size, personality, and mannerisms. Since the village wasn't very big, that sentiment spread throughout the entire town, and was eventually shared by almost all that lived there. However, they all tolerated him out of respect for his aging mother.

"One day, as life was perking along, tragedy struck once again in the relatively quiet life that Eugene led. He awoke one morning to find his mother would not wake up. Matilda had died in her sleep at the ripe old age of forty-eight. Eugene was absolutely devastated and his heart ached mercilessly. He held one of her fins with both of his flippers, pressing it tight to his cheek, and wept like he had never done before. His big brown eyes were filled with tears for a long time, and he believed that going on without his mother would be impossible. He was sure that with her death, his life had ended as well, and it proved to be quite difficult to eat, sleep, or function in any productive manner for days. He felt lost, and numb all over. It was a truly sad time for the oversized whale.

"Despite his seemingly never-ending grief, Eugene remembered three important lessons that his mother had taught him: time does not stand still, all things must someday come to an end, and that, no matter what, life does go on. Six days later, as the sun began to rise, in a quiet ceremony that was not attended by anyone else, Eugene buried his mother at a local cemetery. Standing over her grave, he bowed down his head and said a little prayer. He asked her spirit to help him in his missions and to watch over him in times of danger. Mostly though, he asked for her continued guidance in being a generous, and good individual overall. Every week, on the same day, he brought fresh flowers to her gravesite, and said the same little prayer.

"Eugene did not want to live in the same place where he had resided with his mother because it just seemed too empty without her, and the memories depressed him greatly. He decided to move to the center of the village, creating a whole new controversy and causing an outrage from all the citizens that lived there.

"You see Sonny, it was already a pretty heavily populated part of town, and there was absolutely no room for a creature the size of a whale. While Eugene saw no problem with such a move, the townspeople were quite displeased with his decision and vehemently protested his choice of a new residence. But, after considerable yelling and debate, much to their great discontent, the huge whale settled down – so to speak – and made his home just above the center of the village.

"However, instead of things settling down, anger and resentments subsiding, relationships improving, and life getting back to normal, the opposite took place. All of the citizens of the tiny village, and especially those that lived under the large orphan, became more and more frustrated, their tempers flared way out of control, and the dislike for their neighbor escalated nightly. You see, over the years, as Eugene lived and worked above the village – and it was a pretty large area that he occupied – accidents continued to happen, and this time they were a little more serious than knocking down a seaweed house.

"To begin with, he was the only citizen of the village who did not fully sleep at night. Nobody realized that Eugene was a mammal, and mammals that live in the water never fully fall asleep. On many occasions, as the fine residents of the tiny village were snuggled cozily in their beds, a scuffling noise just outside their windows made by the oversized whale would invariably awaken even the deepest of sleepers. Needless to say, many of the villagers were quite upset about that, especially if they had to work in the morning.

"Quite often, many of the pets that lived in that village – catfish and parrotfish were the most popular – would become hysterically frightened at the sight of Eugene's enormous body, especially after bedtime. There was even one old herring that claimed her 'precious had a coronary, and died on the spot' after witnessing Eugene swim by their living room windows at night.

"And, then, there was a bigger, more serious problem to deal with. As you can very well imagine, Sonny, Eugene had a very large tail, and every now and then, like a very excited puppy, he would wag it. When the currents in the sea flowed just right, and Eugene flapped his tail at just the right speed and angle, he managed to create a powerful and somewhat destructive turbulence. It was widely believed that he had even been solely responsible for a tidal wave or two. Although under the sea the rushing water was not strong enough to destroy any of the houses, it always shook many of them so violently, that everyone and everything inside was twirled and swirled and twisted into a whirlpool like a human trailer home during a tornado. With increasing frequency, much to the escalating dismay and furious frustration of the residents, Eugene did his tail wagging mostly at night.

"One fine day, after yet several more fish neighbors lost quite a few hours of sleep and a pet bit its owner, the inhabitants of the little village in the middle of nowhere on the bottom of the ocean decided that they had enough. Something needed to be done and fast! The whale was, literally and metaphorically, a huge problem that needed to be rectified immediately if they ever hoped for their lives to get back to normal. They all felt that Eugene's menacing presence had to be dealt with, and a plan of action needed to be designed and implemented as soon as possible, in order to keep the village from becoming a wasteland.

"One night, a secret meeting of the villagers, the sheriff, and the mayor was held at the City Hall. Everybody had something to say. They conferred for hours, discussing options, analyzing various ideas, and trying to formulate a solution. Some wanted to trick the whale into swimming right next to a whaling ship where death would be swift and certain. However, that idea was quickly vetoed because they believed themselves to be civilized and could not bestow such a fate even onto Eugene. Besides, there was a distinct possibility that Eugene would be bigger than the ship, and might accidently sink it in the process. Others wanted to attack him with their existing army, which would not necessarily kill him, but definitely get the point across. That plan was vetoed even quicker than the first since suicide missions were a thing of the past, and matching brawn with such a creature was just that, even when incorporating the element of surprise. One individual, a flying fish, brought up an idea to simply pack up the whole village and move it to a different location when Eugene was not looking. That idea received no consideration at all because it was absolutely absurd.

"A long time went by before everybody settled on a simple, yet effective, idea. In fact, it was so simple and straightforward that some were not sure that it would work. One citizen argued against it, saying something to the effect that only the world's biggest simpleton would fall for something so direct. However, upon everyone giving him the 'who is it that you think we are dealing with here?' look, he changed his mind, and endorsed the deceitful idea with all the enthusiasm that he could muster. A draft of the plan was quickly typed up, officially approved by the sheriff, and a seal of approval affixed by the mayor. Everybody was excited at the prospect of peace and quiet once again, and the very next morning the plan was thrust into action. Everyone held their breath to see what the big whale would do next.

"Eugene was busy being 'it', once again, in a game of tag with a bunch of kids at the orphanage, when an urgent telegram arrived. Surprised to receive any kind of mail for the first time in his life, he quickly opened it and carefully read the content. It was from some lawyer that specialized in wills and estate management. The message stated that a sister-in-law to his long dead mother Matilda – that he had never heard of before – had recently passed away. Having no other surviving family members, she left Eugene, her only existing relative, a very large sum of money. It further went on to say that to claim the fortune, he must come to the town of Tsol where his distant relative had lived for many years, and give her a proper burial. It was very shocking to Eugene, and exhilarating at the same time. He felt saddened by the loss of yet another family member but happy to have finally found the money that the orphanage needed to build a new playground. You see, after trying to save up his own money for that purpose for quite a while and only scratching the surface of what was actually needed to accomplish such a big task, he was about to be triumphant in that long-anticipated endeavor. Two days later he set forth on a search for a town by the name of Tsol. For the citizens of that village it was a triumph the likes of which they had never experienced before.

"A parade was quickly organized upon Eugene's departure, resulting in a celebration so big, that the village in the middle of nowhere, at the bottom of an ocean, could easily claim as the grandest that it had ever seen. The mayor declared it a holiday and everyone took the day off from work. Huge banners proclaimed the return of peace and quiet. Everyone was feeling happy and smiling as they ate heartily from the feast-laden tables and drank their finest ales. The monster was finally gone, and there was joy in the air.

"This joy lasted exactly three days before disaster struck. No, Eugene did not come back. It was a lot worse than that.

"In the middle of the night, everybody was awakened by the ear-piercing siren of impending doom. However, even with the early detection systems that they possessed, and the well-equipped troops that they were able to mobilize, very little could have been done to prevent the deadly assault. The tiny village was brutally attacked by a gam of sharks. No one really knows how many there actually were. Some said ten totally ruthless great whites, while others claimed to have seen dozens of tiger sharks and a few hammer heads, but that mattered very little. What did matter was that all night long, wave after wave, they assaulted the defenses that the army scrambled to put up, inflicting heavy losses, and destroying a great deal of property. They were determined and relentless in their attacks, sending most of the citizens scrambling for cover in sheer terror. Many of them suffered great personal losses, and many more did not survive. The sharks outflanked, outmaneuvered, and quickly overwhelmed their much slower defenses until there was almost nothing left of them, and the tiny village lay in ruins. The sharks were decidedly triumphant that night.

"The deadly assault continued for the next thirteen nights. When the sharks finally ceased their attacks for a couple of days, the weary survivors gathered at City Hall to discuss their critical status and very limited options. Everybody had something to say. Some thought that they should stay, fortify whatever was left of their defenses, and fight to the last fish and at least die honorably. Others believed they should regroup their remaining military and counter-attack, since that would surprise the sharks and catch them off guard. Quite a few argued that everyone should sprint out of the village at the same time, and head out in various directions as quickly as possible, giving at least a few citizens a decent chance at survival should the sharks choose to pursue them. The flying fish opened his mouth again, bringing up an idea that they should all just play dead when the sharks come back, but that only earned him a few dirty looks and he was politely asked not to speak at any public forums ever again. The debates continued late into the night, and shortly before the crack of dawn, they agreed to a plan of action that was suitable for all. The time to act was now, and they wasted no time in doing it.

"Quickly packing what they could recover from their destroyed homes and carry on their backs, everybody gathered on the edge of the village. In fact, it was right where Eugene used to live when he and his mother first moved there. When everyone that survived was accounted for, the mayor waved his shaky arm, and very quietly led his citizens away from the village and unto the long journey towards the castle walls. They all decided to go see the King of the Seas, hoping that perhaps he could offer some help, and explain the shark's brutality towards their tiny village in the middle of nowhere. They sincerely hoped that he could shine a light on the darkness that settled over them, and help put back the pieces of their tragically shattered lives. Going to see the king was the only true option that they still had.

"Five days and five nights they walked, or rather swam, towards the castle, in a single file, with their heads bowed down low, and their spirits dragging on the ground. Very little was said as they made their way, mulling over the events of the previous two weeks. Some thought of the terrible luck that forced its way into their lives and invaded their village. Others thanked the forces that watched over them, and could not believe how lucky they were to still be alive. Mostly though, the one thought that bothered them the most, was the simple fact that in a very short time every one of them had lost at least one family member or friend in the unexpected attacks. Although it is hard to tell in the water, it was pretty obvious that many of the villagers cried as they swam on. Every now and then some of them glanced back to see if they could spot the sharks, but saw nothing. They finally reached the castle's main gate late at night, without further incidents.

"Feeling safe for the first time in a long time, and being physically, mentally, and emotionally exhausted beyond anything they had ever experienced before, they decided to rest first, and then appear before the king. Most fell into a sound sleep almost immediately; however, there were still some that could do nothing but nervously swim back and forth, pondering their uncertain future.

"At sunrise, the gate was swung open, and everybody was let inside a very large room to wait. It was a long-standing tradition that the king saw his subjects every morning to hear their problems, concerns, and suggestions, and to see if at least some of them could be resolved. He was widely regarded as a fair and just king. On that particular morning, they did not have to wait long since no one else arrived to voice their grudges, and they were escorted into the King's Throne Chamber.

"'Speak your minds my fair travelers,' the king said in a deep, booming voice. 'Tell me what it is that troubles you on such a fine day!' Very patiently he listened to each and every member of the surviving party tell his or her version of the horrors that bestowed the tiny village, the hardships they had endured, and the injustices of the shark's behavior. The king did not say a word until the last one finished, displaying only concern and surprise on his face. Only then, once everyone was done, did he take a few moments to think things over. Furrowing his eyebrows in deep concentration, he took a deep breath and said the following:

"'My dear friends, what can I say? My sympathies and condolences, and those of my kingdom, are extended to you. All of you have been through a lot, and suffered more than any sea creatures should ever have to. Unfortunately, the sharks in our waters have a mind of their own. They do not listen to a word I say. They do as they please, and the things they do are usually not good. To make things even worse, at this time I simply do not have the means with which to police, or even control their actions. However, one day, when the economy rebounds and things become better financially, I will increase the number of sheriffs to patrol those waters, restore order, and bring them to justice. That I promise you.

"'There is still one thing that puzzles me. Whatever happened to that oversized whale living with you? What's his name again? Eugene, that's right! Whatever happened to Eugene? I do not see him here among you, and none of you mentioned his name. Did he stop defending your village against those sharks? Why did he suddenly stop? Is he ill, or perhaps injured?' The King took a closer look at the faces of his subjects.

"'All of you look so surprised, and confused. Didn't you know that he has been fighting those sharks nearly every night for the past fifteen years? About two years after he and his mother moved to your village, the sharks stumbled onto it, and Eugene has been defending it, single-handedly, ever since. And you must admit, those sharks are very persistent. They never quit after losing every battle to him all this time. That's why I never worried about your village. Why, you had the best protection money could buy living right there with you, and he did it without asking for anything in return. He always did have a big heart! None of you knew this? So, whatever did happen to Eugene? Where has he been during all of this?'

"The news of Eugene's nightly shark battles sent shock waves through the ranks of the villagers, causing many to nearly faint, and giving many others headaches the likes of which would make the worst of migraines pale in comparison. All who came from the tiny village in the middle of nowhere on the bottom of the ocean stood with their eyes wide open and their jaws on the ground. No one had anything to say, as karma proved to be triumphant on that day.

"I guess that what I have been trying to say is that no matter how big or clumsy the whale in your life gets, even if you hardly know him (or her), do not cast him away. Someday, he may help you out, maybe even save your life. I'm sure you're well familiar with the saying, 'you don't know what you have until it's gone.' It is one of the truest sayings around. And unfortunately, by the time we find out, it is often too late. That's why sometimes, despite any unwavering confidence and irrefutable knowledge, you really do need to be careful of what you wish for. While negative events or experiences could be a blessing in disguise, triumphs could, just as easily, be mistakes in disguise as well. So be careful. And also remember that doing something good for others without any gratitude in return, especially if it is because they know nothing of it, is the highest form of altruism and honor. Even though very few individuals are capable of it, they do exist.

"Well Sonny, that's all I have for you for tonight. Your face tells me that you have some questions, but we'll get to those tomorrow – I promise. It is awfully late already and you need your sleep – it will keep you looking younger you know.

"Good night, sleep tight, and sweet dreams."

SLEEP TIGHT

LOVE STORIES

*T*ony lay in bed and continued to stare at the ceiling, as sleep proved to be quite elusive on that night. He also continued to contemplate the uncertain future and the myriad of possibilities that it had to offer. Some of those variants were rather happy and uplifting, while others threatened to be gloomy and sad. He sincerely hoped for the former. After inhaling deeply for what seemed like the millionth time that night, he rubbed his tired eyes once again and looked at the clock on his bedside table. It was 5:47 in the morning. The question that kept him awake and incessantly plagued his mind for the last fifteen hours was whether the project that he started in the basement of his house over forty years ago could somehow affect one of those uncertain outcomes and make the coming years bright and warm, because dark times were threatening the not too distant future. The love of his life, lying next to him, was in peril from within.

He turned his head and looked at his wife who was still sleeping deeply after staying up for most of the night herself. Her name was Julianna, although Tony always called her Jules, and he was absolutely, head over heels, in love with her. She was beautiful, smart, adventurous, caring, possessed a sharp wit, and had an excellent sense of humor. Jules was the woman of his dreams, and he knew that from the moment he met her.

Tony looked back up at the ceiling and thought about that blessed day. By the time Jules entered his life, he was already in his early sixties, having given up on finding the "right one" to grow old with about a decade earlier. He strongly believed that, for him, there were no more eligible women left in the world – at least he had never met one that he liked enough to marry – and was absolutely convinced that his life path would no longer cross with a lady that could melt his heart. By the age of fifty-five he simply stopped looking and came to terms with the fact that he was going to grow old alone. With no expectations for any further romance, Tony was swept off his feet when, out of nowhere, Jules waltzed into his life, and right into his heart. He never even realized how miserable he was for all of those decades until she made him – and he was totally convinced of the fact – the happiest man in the world. Quite often, he thought of her as his little angel.

It all began nearly five years ago when he begrudgingly went to a New Year's Eve party at a friend's house. Enjoying early retirement for the past six months after having a very lucrative career as a mechanical engineer at a private company for nearly thirty-five years; Tony didn't do much socializing, and favored the life of a recluse rather than a social butterfly. He preferred the world to see him as an enigmatic person. He tried to keep a healthy diet as much as possible without going too much out of his way, stayed active with various exercises that happened to be the flavor of the month, and occasionally dabbled in a hobby or two until losing interest a few weeks or months later. Most of the time Tony chose to spend it in the basement, working on this crazy project that he started in his early twenties. At times, he thought of it as his early onset midlife crisis venture.

While at that party, he found himself sipping a glass of wine in a corner of a room, immersed in the best conversation that he had ever had with a lady who took his breath away from the moment he laid his eyes on her. There was undeniable chemistry between them and Tony couldn't get enough of her. They talked for hours, interrupting their conversation only once to awkwardly kiss under the mistletoe at midnight. Ever since that night, whenever Tony talked to Jules, stood next to her, or just simply thought of her, he felt re-energized and vibrant. He noticed himself experiencing a reawakening for romance as his soul re-emerged from hibernation. Even his heart sped up at the smell of her perfume, and there was no sign of that effect fading away any time soon.

Julianna was enamored with Tony as well. He made her laugh over and over, something that she had not done in decades. She also found him to be a chivalrous gentleman and a genuinely caring person. Unlike many of the men she had met in the past, Tony was not self-centered, and proved to be quite a good listener. They dated for exactly a year before he proposed. The very next December thirty-first, he asked for her hand in marriage while down on one knee at a bench in a park about five minutes after they dismounted a horse drawn sled. They exchanged their vows and became officially married, and had the reception, at a ballroom in a local banquet facility in front of fourteen of his family and friends and fifty-four of hers.

Tony took another deep breath, and slowly swung his legs down, sitting up as quietly as he could, so as not to disturb Jules. After putting on his robe and slipping his feet into his favorite slippers, he made his way down to the kitchen and set the coffee maker to brew up some much-needed beverage. He was pretty hungry as well by that point, since his appetite disappeared the previous afternoon, and he had not eaten anything since lunch the day before. He wanted a small snack or something to munch on while sipping his coffee, but nothing grabbed his fancy on that particular morning.

He rummaged through a few pretty depleted cupboards and the nearly empty fridge, finding only a few leftovers from a party they hosted three days ago, however nothing called out to him. Finally, he opened up the freezer and immediately settled on the several miniature éclairs that were still there. As Tony began to close the door, he noticed the nearly empty container of vanilla ice cream. He stared at it for a moment as it brought a happy memory to the forefront of his mind. Vanilla ice cream was Jules's Kryptonite. She absolutely loved it. He reflected back to the first date that they went on after the New Year's Eve party. At some point during that night, she let it be known that vanilla ice cream is her absolute favorite food in the world. So, when Tony showed up at her door for their first official date a couple of days later, he was holding a pint of vanilla ice cream and a package of waffle cones. She was highly amazed that he paid attention to such a small detail, and laughed heartily at his attempt to impress her. In fact, she found that gesture to be adorable and somewhat endearing. They both laughed about it, and had a serving of the ice cream before going out to dinner. Ever since then, whenever he committed any mistakes, in addition to an over the top bouquet of flowers, Tony did his apologizing with ice cream in his hands. And whenever he needed her to agree to something that she did not readily accept, along with kisses and an extra dose of terms of endearments that he had for her, ice cream would invariably be presented in order to persuade her to accept whatever seemingly controversial idea or proposal that popped into his head.

When the coffeemaker finished its job, Tony poured himself a cup and sat down at the kitchen table. Unsuccessfully he rubbed the back of his neck to try and work the knots out and then massaged his temples. He shook his head. It was hard to fathom that Jules was about to embark on a fight for her life. After waiting for nearly two long weeks, they finally saw the doctor. Yesterday's appointment proved to be both shocking and quite upsetting. Jules began to suffer from a cough, occasional mild shortness of breath, decreased appetite, and slightly increased fatigue about a month before. Their worst fears were realized when the doctor informed them that they found multiple spots in the lungs and that Jules had small cell carcinoma. They immediately scheduled radiation and chemotherapy, but the doctor gave her a fifty-fifty chance at best.

Tony experienced outrage and ire towards the diagnoses. He felt helpless and extremely frustrated, which made him even more indignant. He wanted to blame the environment, the government, her work conditions, the chemical processing plant that was about one hundred and sixty miles away, and even his next-door neighbor, but he knew all too well the real reason why Jules most likely developed the heinous disease. There was no one to blame but herself. However, deep down in his gut, Tony was blaming one individual for it and his name was Gregory. Although Jules didn't like talking about that aspect of her life, he did learn from her about the ugly detour that her life took many years ago.

When she was only twenty-years-old, Jules met Greg and he became her first love. She fell hard for him and thought that she had actually found her life partner. She spent all her free time with him and eventually moved into his one-bedroom apartment. There is a belief that when we first date someone, we meet their representative, and not the actual person. Greg was the epitome of that concept. As far as Tony was concerned, based on what Jules had told him, Greg metamorphosed into a monster.

Jules felt that she had moved in with a totally different person than the one she had dated previous to that. Greg became very possessive of her, extremely controlling, and soon began to be verbally abusive. He manipulated her into breaking up with all her friends, made sure he was aware of her whereabouts at all times, and made all of the decisions in her life. She was not allowed to even keep in touch with her family as often as she would have liked. With increasing frequency, he would come home drunk late at night and keep her up until morning with temper tantrums and violent outburst towards their dishes and furniture. On quite a few occasions the neighbors called for the police to settle him down, even taking him away in handcuffs a few times. Jules hoped that it was just a phase and felt sure that things would soon change for the better. However, things continued to get worse.

Jules found herself in unfamiliar territory and was not sure how to deal with her situation. She felt extremely stressed out, and became a nervous wreck. Her appetite virtually disappeared and she began to slowly lose weight. She found herself getting progressively weaker physically, emotionally, and psychologically, and began spending the majority of her days in a stupor, either wandering around the apartment aimlessly for hours at a time, or lying around in bed or on the couch watching the television all day long and often late into the night. To make things even worse, a little less than a year later, at the age of twenty-one, Jules became pregnant.

At first it was a blessing, and she was very excited at the prospect of becoming a mother. She looked forward to the birth of their, as the doctor pointed out during a sonogram, baby daughter. A list of names was picked out within a week and narrowed down to two by the time her next sonogram came around. Greg, on the other hand, was quite a bit less enthusiastic about that development, claiming that he was not ready to be a father. Tony could not remember all of the excuses that her boyfriend came up with, however, after a few months, he begrudgingly accepted the inevitable eventually of parenthood.

Tony took a big gulp of his coffee and took another bite of an éclair. He pursed his lips and stared at the black liquid in front of him. He couldn't help but wonder what would have become of Jules had she managed to carry that child to full term. She took her vitamins, really concentrated on eating right, went for her monthly OB checkups, and even walked out of the apartment whenever Greg smoked there.

But sometime during the late second trimester she woke up one morning and could not feel the baby move. Jules assumed that her daughter was still sleeping, even though prior to that the baby always said "good morning" to Jules by kicking her in the stomach. By that afternoon, she became quite concerned and went to see the doctor. There, it was confirmed that the fetus was no longer alive and a date to remove it was set. Jules was devastated by the loss of her baby, and had often said that was the lowest point in her life.

She had reached a whole new level of depression, and lacking any constructive coping mechanisms at that age, and finding no support from Greg or anyone else, she began to smoke, developing a pack and a half a day habit in under a month. She also began to drink quite a bit, but hated the way it made her feel. That habit did not last too long. However, smoking was not as easy to give up. Even though, a year later, she finally broke up with Greg and moved back home, she continued to smoke for the next forty years – at times up to two packs a day. Therefore, while it was very upsetting and quite frustrating to learn of her diagnosis the day before, it was not awfully surprising. She finally managed to kick that habit only three years before meeting Tony. On quite a few occasions she confided in him that she wanted to try and have kids again later on in life, and even considered adoption, but the right circumstances never presented themselves.

Tony finished off the cup of coffee and rubbed his eyes. The next few months, and even years, were going to be trying, but he and Jules had already decided to just take it one day at a time. They were going to face this new challenge together, side by side, and emerge through all of the upcoming trials and tribulations with their hands held up high in victory. On the drive home from the doctor's office, he promised her that during her moments of weakness, or any other times for that matter, he will always be her pillar of strength, a beam of support, and a ray of sunshine. He reassured her once again that no matter what the future held in store for them, she will always be able to count on him to be there, even if it's just to hold her hand, and if needed, to hold her hair if the chemotherapy wreaked havoc on her stomach. She simply smiled back and quietly wrapped her arms around him, holding on tight, not letting go until they were parked in their driveway.

Tony looked at the clock on the oven. It was almost seven in the morning, and he decided that he might as well get things started. He put the mug in the sink and walked back upstairs as quietly as he could. Jules was still sound asleep, although it was obvious that she had tossed and turned at least a couple of times. He dressed himself in the oldest clothes that he possessed. Despite being very timeworn and totally out of fashion, they were still in great shape, and that was exactly the point that Tony was aiming for. It was time to go grocery shopping. He wanted to fill up the refrigerator and the cupboards with food and other sundry items. There were also other household items that he wanted to buy as well.

Once he was dressed, Tony went to his office and pulled out the second drawer on the right side of his desk. After removing a few folders, lose papers, various notes, rubber bands, and pens, he lifted up the false bottom to reveal a secret compartment. Out of it, he produced quite a bit of cash. Just like his clothes, the money was very old but in relatively good condition. Tony counted how much he had, replaced about half of it, and put the other half into his wallet that he kept in the back pocket of his pants. He then placed everything back into the drawer and closed it.

Unlike most other people that proceed to their cars, other forms of public transportation, or who walk in order to get to a store, Tony proceeded to a small room in his basement. He always kept it securely locked and the only key in existence that could unlock it was always in his pocket. Access to the door was hidden behind revolving rows of shelves that appeared to be a permanent fixture firmly attached to the wall. Tony constructed it himself once all of his schemes, stipulations, and theoretical concepts became a working reality, and the dangerous consequences that could be unleashed if discovered by anyone else became a possibility. Tony never told any of his friends or family, and even Jules did not know about the secret room or what was inside of it. It was the only secret that he kept from her.

Tony entered the room, flipped on the lights, and looked over the project that had consumed several decades of his life.

After graduating MIT with a master's degree in mechanical engineering and securing a well-paying job, Tony began dedicating a significant amount of time to his hobbies and secondary interests. He started to read up and study the fields of theoretical engineering, quantum physics, quantum mathematics, and Einstein's theories of relativity. He studied each of those quite intensively and even succeeded in contacting several leading scholars in those fields to pick their brains and to clarify some of the concepts. He began to form his own ideas on the topics, construct and execute a myriad of unconventional experiments, and even invented a specialized computer processor and something that he called the biphasic modulator. He proved to be a very persistent and diligent individual, because after many years of failed attempts and near disastrous results, he eventually succeeded in building something right out of the world of science-fiction.

Tony managed to build a time machine.

Some days he found it difficult to believe himself that he accomplished such a feat, but he was getting used to the idea by the time he met Jules. He knew well that with this machine he was in control of great power, but he also realized that his invention possessed the possibility for a disaster and perhaps even presented a danger to his character, personality, physical wellbeing, and the world in general, if one was to incorporate even a little bit of imagination with such a thing. He certainly could have used it to make millions of dollars, become an eccentric and influential individual, and perhaps even shape the history of the world. However, Tony had no desire for any of those things. He considered himself a simple man and strived to be modest and inconspicuous. He preferred a quiet existence, living a comfortable and a very happy life. As far as he was concerned, Jules completed him and no further actions, objects, or status in the world would make him any happier. Plus, he was afraid that accumulating great wealth would eventually change him into a person that he did not want to be. Greed, distrust of the few friends that he had and people in general, and feelings of ethnocentricity were at the top of the list of traits that he wanted to avoid. One thing that indubitably was etched in his brain after studying medieval European history back in High School was that wealth and power (especially absolute power) invariably corrupts, and Tony wanted no part of it. He also did not want to catch the eye of the government due to any wealth, or anybody else's for that matter. He was afraid that if the word of the machine leaked out to the public, then sooner or later, unsavory characters would come looking for it. Therefore, he never had the urge to bet on any sporting events, invest in stocks, buy rookie sports cards of future super stars, acquire any valuable antiques, or capitalize on any other idea or concept that would turn out to be quite profitable in the future. Besides, in the beginning, he just wanted to see if he could actually make his crazy ideas into reality and built one, not to accumulate fame and fortunes. He often philosophized that the past should be learned from, not taken advantage of.

There was only one thing that he used the machine for. It was kind of silly, but it was the secret to his early retirement. Tony returned back in time exactly forty-five years in order to do all kinds of shopping. Everything from various cooking supplies, snacks, fruits and vegetables, meats, and desserts, to cleaning supplies, laundry detergents, some personal hygiene products, socks, hats, and gloves were procured whenever the need would arise. To keep Julianna from questioning the outdated packaging or expiration dates from a long time ago, most of the foods were quickly distributed among glass jars, plasticware, and other containers. It actually did help to keep their food fresher and for longer. And besides, Tony did the majority of cooking anyway. From the past, he also purchased and brought back to the future the wood to rebuild his back yard deck, several pieces of artwork that hanged on his walls, a lot of the furniture throughout the house (some of which were considered to be valued antiques), and the carpeting that lined the floor of the living room and the guest room. The roses, lilacs, bleeding hearts, lavenders, tulips, geraniums, and plumeria growing in the front lawn were all acquired a long time ago, but planted and tended by Tony much more recently. He even managed to buy a muscle car in the past, store it in a safe place, and pick it up in the present in nearly perfect condition. The reason he kept going back for just about everything was rather simple – the price. All stores and markets sold their wares at a much lower price many years ago as compared to the present. The inflation had increased the cost for all items more than ten-fold in the last forty years, so Tony decided to save a hefty amount of money by shopping in the past. His dollar went a lot further forty-five years ago. He even enjoyed the less polluted air.

Tony managed to calculate the date in the past when the house would be empty. He knew that the construction was completed two years prior to his family buying it, and that they moved into it shortly thereafter. He clearly remembered all of them going away for three weeks on a vacation to Europe, while he was away at college taking summer classes. Tony's arrival date in the past was always somewhere in that three-week period. That way he was afforded the opportunity to just appear in an empty house and move around freely, without the possibility of getting caught and questioned. It all worked out quite well since the machine was capable of traveling through time, but not space. Getting back to the future at nearly the same time as he left proved to be a much easier calculation as compared to the complicated linear calculus problems he had to solve in order to arrive at an approximate date in the past. He always managed to return to the present within five to ten seconds of his departure time, and since he always did it while Jules was either out of the house or asleep, she had never noticed his absences.

Standing in the basement, looking at his machine, Tony considered getting another cup of coffee before returning to the past, but decided not to waste any more time in the present, especially since he wasn't sure how much longer Jules would stay asleep. Besides, he figured that he'll just buy a cup in the past if he really needed it.

Like a pilot performing his pre-flight check before taking off, Tony meticulously looked over the main cooling shafts and the hoses of the machine, double checked some connections, wiped off the dust on some other parts, and finally flipped several switches. The soft hum of the engine indicated that the propulsion mechanisms of the engine were on and warming up. Tony turned a few knobs and inspected the outside of his apparatus for any obvious cracks and leaks. Everything appeared to be in order, and he stepped into the capsule, closing the door behind him. After looking over the control panel and adjusting a few more dials, he was satisfied with what he saw - all of the gages showed that the electronic and mechanical systems powering the machine were within normal ranges and operating properly. It took another twenty-seven seconds for a small green light in the bottom left corner of the control board to turn on, signifying that the machine was ready for time travel. Tony took a deep breath and pulled down a large lever in the middle of the board.

Everything outside the capsule began to get blurry and shift as if he was slowly spinning. It took another minute before the outside became so out of focus that Tony couldn't even tell anymore what he was looking at. He also realized that he was feeling very strange. There was a sensation throughout his whole body that he had never experienced before. At first, he tried to ignore it, but the feeling was intensifying by the second. He did not have any pain, nausea, or dizziness, but rather he felt flushed, followed by a surge of energy. Then he felt tightness, first in his chest, and then in a wave like fashion, spread out throughout his whole body. His toes tingled as a sense of weightlessness surrounded him and he began to feel almost euphoric. Tony had no clue what was causing him to feel like that. All of his previous trips into the past were quite benign and uneventful. He considered pushing the lever in the middle of the control board back up and aborting the trip but, instead, decided to see what would happen next.

Suddenly he heard a loud whine in the engine which was followed by an even louder snap. An ear-piercing grinding noise came after that, and Tony noticed some smoke inside the capsule. He spun around and, with horror on his face, realized that the entrance into the capsule was not completely sealed. He immediately understood that in his distracted and very tired state of mind he did not close it properly before engaging the mechanisms. He wasn't sure what the ramifications of that were going to be, but he was positive that whatever was happening to the machine and himself was because of the small crack that was clearly visible between the door and the capsule wall. Then he heard an even louder pop and a plethora of multicolored sparks emanated from the electrical system of the apparatus, as if a miniature lightning storm was taking place within the engine and thick smoke began to emanate from a panel outside the machine. All of the lights on the control board were flashing rapidly as Tony reached out his hand to pull the lever in the middle of it back up. However, the whole capsule suddenly started to shake violently, and Tony fell to the floor. He attempted to get back up but inhaled some smoke, began to cough, and lost his footing, falling back down once again.

Before he could make another attempt to get back on his feet, the shaking stopped, and he could clearly hear the engine wind down and turn itself off. Except for slight ringing in his ears and some crackling, everything was quiet. The smoke was quickly dissipating thanks to the still functioning ventilation system and he was able to take a few breaths without any further problems. Tony stood up in time to see a few more sparks and arching electricity as they faded and disappeared completely. He noticed that there was still some black smoke rising up from some of the wires, so he grabbed a small fire extinguisher from the wall, and made sure that ended promptly.

Then he examined the control board. Many of the lights were burned out and some of the switches and dials did not respond when Tony tried to activate them. Despite a few remaining functioning parts, the machine was essentially dead. However, the display console did have enough power in it to confirm that Tony managed to arrive at his target date. He quickly turned everything off to make sure that there was no more sparking or arcing that could produce additional smoke or cause a fire.

Despite the rough ride back into the past, Tony felt great – energized and vibrant. It was as if he had drunk a cup of really strong coffee with two shots of espresso. Even his right hand which developed early onset arthritis where he had broken it in his early thirties during a skiing accident, was not hurting. However, he hardly noticed any of that.

The time machine was in rough shape, to say the least, and Tony was much more concerned with how he was going to get back to the future. If he became stuck in the past, Jules would be facing her dreaded disease for weeks, months, and even years alone. She would think that he had abandoned her in her time of need, and none of that was acceptable. He wanted to be by her side, knowing that he needed her as much as she needed him. The machine must be repaired so that he could get back to the love of his life at any cost. He couldn't even fathom being away from her for an extended period of time.

He quickly exited the capsule and began to inspect the machine. All but three of the fuses had burned out, the triangulating stabilizer looked to be obliterated, and the influx generator was cracked right down the middle. There was oil splashed all over the wires that connected the main modulator to the distributor caps, which was quite disastrous in itself, and he couldn't even find the time delineator that should have been right in between the capsule and the exhaust pods. Things were not looking good. The computer board was not functioning either, and that had Tony the most concerned. Still, he was confident that even though it would take a long time, he could either fix or replace the majority of the damaged parts. Although he knew that many of the things he needed were not invented yet, he was confident in his engineering abilities, ingenuity, and creativity to do just that. He would simply have to adapt and overcome; there were no other options.

However, in this era, computers were just beginning to be introduced and were nowhere near powerful enough to run the machine; the majority of them were bigger than the time machine itself, and were used mostly by government agencies and several major corporations. Tony decided that for the first time in a very long time, he was going to have to figure out several complex algorithms using an adding machine, a slide ruler, lots of paper and ink, and rely on just a bit of luck.

After taking another deep breath, he looked over all of the damage again and made a mental note of the preliminary things that he would need to start the repairs. Later on, he would have to make a list of all of the other materials and parts that would have to be obtained, and try to figure out the best places to appropriate all those things. He knew for a fact that several of the parts he needed were in existence but not as readily available in that time period. The next few days were promising to be interesting and very challenging indeed.

He began to walk towards the front door, passing relatively close to a mirror that was hanging on a wall. Out of the corner of his eye he saw his reflection and, almost as an afterthought, his brain registered that something was wrong. It took him another second to react to it, and jump back in front of the mirror. A wave of shock ran down from his head to his toes, as Tony stared at what initially appeared to be a stranger. For what seemed like hours, with nearly bulging eyes and his mouth twisted into a silent scream, Tony could not move as he stared at a face that he had not seen in over forty years. It was a young man's face staring back at him, the face that Tony had when he was still in college. Finally, he blinked several times and slowly raised his hands to his face. It all felt very surreal, yet it was all very real. He could hardly believe that it was him in the reflection, and after several more minutes sank down to the floor, still in awe, but already starting to figure out what must have happened.

Since the door to the capsule was not closed all the way when the time machine mechanisms engaged, the time continuum must have been stretched well beyond what the machine could handle, putting significantly excess stress on the stabilizer rods, which must have caused the time shift paradox not just outside the capsule, as it was supposed to happen, but inside as well. As the machine traveled back in time, for some reason that he could not explain yet, the duplicating particles of the paradox within the capsule became charged (probably positively, Tony surmised) and apparently reversed the aging process of the biological entity caught within, making him young once again. When the rods finally snapped, it set off a chain reaction that destroyed the rest of the engine, and caused him to reverse age by the same amount of years as that which he set the machine to go back in time for. That meant that he was forty-five years younger now.

Tony was twenty-one once again.

He slowly stood back up and looked at himself again. He could hardly believe it. However, now he understood why he felt so much more energetic and why he no longer felt the arthritis in his hand. Even the surgical scar on it was no longer there. After blinking a few more times, he finally smiled and breathed a sigh of relief at the fact that he did not set the machine to go back in time any further than what he had. It was also easy for him to deduce that the machine would have probably exploded if it had continued its journey any longer.

Of course, this presented a whole new set of problems. Once the machine was fixed, then he would have to figure out how to age himself again. He was pretty sure that Jules would not be very accepting of a twenty-one-year-old kid attempting to convince her that he is indeed her husband. He also began to theorize that the capsule door would have to be left ajar once again when he goes back. The number of rods would have to be doubled and they would have to be extra reinforced. He just wasn't sure yet how he was going to accomplish all that.

Tony exited the house and, in deep thought, proceeded to walk down the street. A lot was weighing on his mind. He was trying to deduce which parts were going to be the easier ones to obtain, how to maximize their mechanical value, which stores would have them, and the locations of these stores. He could not decide whether the duplicating particles of the paradox would have to be positively or negatively charged for his trip back to the future, what the proper distance between the door and the capsule should be, and if he should try to repair or completely replace the transmonometer within the guidance system.

Since he never bothered to shop at any specialty stores as a teenager, he could not remember where half of them were. So, after deciding that he needed a set of tools in the first place to even start the repairs, and feeling that the local hardware store was as good a place to start as any, he stopped and asked for directions at a local gas station. As it turned out, the closest hardware store was only eight short blocks away. He proceeded there at a relatively fast pace.

Tony was nearly running by the time he reached the store, and sweat began to form on his forehead. It was a hot and humid day, and he was very anxious to get started. He entered the store and proceeded to walk up and down the aisles grabbing whatever he felt was necessary to accomplish his goals. Over by one of the walls he saw a bunch of fuses hanging on a hook, and stopped to examine them a little closer. They were not exactly the kind he was hoping for, but he removed them from the hook, examining them closely in his hands, and wondered if he could modify the spark enhancer module so that it would not destroy these fuses during the warming up of the engine phase.

"Can I help you find anything?" was suddenly spoken in a soft and pleasant voice next to Tony. Surprised that he didn't see or hear anyone approach him, Tony looked up to find a very pretty sales associate standing next to him. She was smiling pleasantly and repeated her question again after Tony seemed to hesitate with his response. There was something about this girl that seemed strangely familiar, but Tony could not figure out why. He desperately searched his memory for who she could be, but could not remember meeting anyone like her in his early twenties. He found her to be quite attractive and felt very drawn to her. Beyond any shadow of a doubt, he was convinced that if he had met her before, he would have remembered her. Her green eyes were mesmerizing and would have been impossible to forget. It took another two seconds for Tony to stop staring.

"Sorry, it's been a long day," he finally answered with a smile of his own. "I think I'm all set for now though. But thank you very ..." Tony stopped in mid–sentence and for the second time on that day a wave of shock ran down his body. Once again, he was frozen stiff and could not believe his eyes. He could not inhale for what seemed like hours, felt the blood drain from his face, and his heart seemed to forget to beat for an even longer period of time. He was tongue tied and could not even move his lips to form any sounds.

The sales girl standing in front of Tony was Julianna. At that moment, he vaguely recalled that she had once mentioned working at a hardware store that was no longer there for a short time after her freshmen year of college. An insatiable desire began to burn in his chest for his love more than ever before, and he ached for her touch like he had never done before. It took Tony all of his willpower to restrain and control his impulse to step over to Jules, and to hug and kiss her. After that he desired nothing else but to hold her in his arms and to never let go.

Suddenly, as if hit by lightning, Tony realized that there is no need for him to go back to the future; that this is where he belonged. The love of his life was standing right in front of him. There was no need for him to wait until his early sixties to be truly happy. He could achieve that happiness right here in his twenties. It also dawned on him that this might save Jules as well. If he was twenty-one, that meant that Jules was nineteen. She had not met Greg yet, and if she never does, she will most likely never start smoking, and therefore, most likely will not develop cancer. Plus, he knew, beyond any shadow of a doubt, that he could make her happy for the rest of her life. That if he could just convince her to go out with him on one date, she would see all the things in him that she so adores in the future. They could build their lives together right from the start, experience the joy and love that they bring into each other's hearts now, without having to wait another forty-five years, and be truly happy from a younger age. Perhaps they could even have children together at some point.

But this was not the New Year's Eve party, and there was no mistletoe to stand under at midnight.

"Are you okay?" she asked, her smile replaced with a look of concern. It took Tony another split second to regain his composure.

"I ... I ... Yeah, I'm ok," he stammered and tried to smile again. Jules looked relieved.

"You looked like you saw a ghost. For a second there, I thought you were going to pass out." She added with a smirk on her face.

"I thought I would as well." Tony said, making eye contact with her and concentrating on a smirk of his own.

"Well," she responded with a straight face, "don't do that. Passing out in the store during business hours is not allowed." And in a nonchalant sort of way, as if it was the last thing on her mind, added, "Management's rules, not mine." Then she immediately smiled and looked at Tony closer to see how he would react to the joke. He smiled back with a wide grin. That dry sense of humor was just one of the many things that he loved about her. One of the reasons they were so successful together in the future was because their sense of humor was very similar and they often enjoyed long exchanges of dry wit amongst themselves.

Tony did not hesitate this time. He stopped smiling and with a straight face of his own said, "I guess I'm going to have to come back after hours to do that then." At that point neither one of them could keep a straight face and they both smiled.

"I'll make sure to leave the back door unlocked for you when we close," she said. Tony took a small bow.

"That is most accommodating of you. Thank you very much." Jules did a slight bow of her own. Unfortunately, before Tony could say anything else, another customer asked her for some help and Jules excused herself to go help the would-be consumer. Tony waited for her to come back and aimlessly walked up and down the aisles for what seemed like hours, but did not see her again.

There were many other staff members that were willing to help him, but none of them were the one that he was hoping to run into. Eventually he left the store in deep thought once again. This time however, his mind was not on the time machine and how to fix it. He had no intentions of ever going back to the future again. All he could think about now was Jules and how to get her to go out with him.

Tony walked to nowhere in particular, contemplating the dilemma ahead of him. He wanted to just ask her out, but did not want to come across as some creep. Just about anything that he would say to her referring to a date at this juncture would be seen with a negative connotation, and would surely put him in poor standing with Jules. He was sure that if such a thing were to happen, he would not have a second chance, so therefore, he could not afford to scare her off in the first place. After all, as far as she was concerned, he was still a stranger to her, and just accepting a date with somebody that she doesn't really know was definitely not her style.

He must have walked for miles, but no easy solution came to mind, except to go back to the hardware store the following day and start a conversation with her again. Perhaps it wouldn't be as busy and he would be able to talk with her for a while longer.

After spending a restless night back at the house, Tony was up relatively early and felt quite anxious to get to his destination, and hopefully, his destiny. He knew that the store wouldn't open for another two and a half hours, and being way too nervous to eat breakfast, he paced back and forth at a slow stride, and contemplated how he would approach the love of his life and what he would say to her once they came face to face again. At least a dozen times he liked various lines that he came up with, and then felt that most of them were awful a few minutes later. Like a professional actor warming up for a role, he practiced his intonation and pronunciation of those lines while they were still in his good graces. From time to time, he checked himself in the mirror to make sure he still looked his best, and kept trying out different smiles in an attempt to figure out which one Jules would like the best. He was also uncertain if his eyebrows should be raised just a little when he smiled at her, or raised as high up as he could get them, or not raised at all. Sometimes he fixed his hair when it was not really needed, or brushed his teeth yet again, or sprayed a little more cologne on his neck and wrists.

Not having settled on any particular look or line, Tony finally left the house and walked towards the store. About halfway there he stopped at a flower shop and purchased a single plumeria to possibly give to Jules. He knew that they were her favorite flowers and decided to take a calculated risk. He was well aware of the fact that giving flowers at such an early stage of their relationship, which didn't even exist yet, might scare her off, but if the talk with her went well today and the vibe was right, he might give it to her later on.

Tony walked into the store with his heart beating about a thousand times a minute. He could hardly breath and kept wiping his sweaty palms on his pants. After looking around for a while, Jules was nowhere to be found. Tony continued to walk up and down the isles for hours in hopes of spotting her, but she never appeared. He considered asking another employee to see if she was there, perhaps working in the back somewhere, but thought it might scare her off having some, for all intents and purposes, stranger ask for her by name. He stayed there for as long as he could, desperately searching, hoping to see that beautiful face, but he never did spot Jules.

He finally had to leave when the store was closing down for the night. Depressed, tired, and hungry, Tony dragged himself to a local diner across the street that he used to go to on rare occasions after class with some of his schoolmates when he was still in High School. He ordered dinner that he barely ate and pondered the situation. Eventually he concluded that he had no choice but to keep going back to the store. He sincerely hoped that Jules just had a day off and would be back to work the following day.

To his great disappointment, the next day was exactly like the previous one. Tony even bought another flower to make sure it was as fresh as possible. However, once again, he did not see the woman that he was so in love with. By late afternoon he knew that she wouldn't be there but, not knowing what else to do, continued his vigilance in desperate hope of spotting her. His luck turned for the worse, however, when he started getting weird looks from the other staff members who noticed him aimlessly wandering through the aisles for hours, without buying anything. One of the store managers eventually asked Tony to leave and not to come back, having wrongly assumed that he was there either to case the store or attempt to shoplift.

Depression and despair threatened to consume the young lover. Tony felt frustrated and helpless in his quest, but refused to give up that easily. He went back to the diner, grabbed a seat by the window after ordering a cup of coffee, and watched the store for any signs of Jules. He refused to crumble up and wither away due to some bumps in the road that fate threw in his way. Instead, he decided that the diner was his next best option, and became determined to sit at that window for as long as it took to spot her. He even came up with a whole new set of pickup lines that he would rely on, and just as before, in his head, kept debating their usefulness and effectiveness. But to Tony's great disappointment, that day ended just as the previous one had.

Jules was nowhere to be seen.

The following morning Tony bought a fresh flower once more and proceeded straight to the diner. He ordered a poppy seed roulette, a cup of coffee, and watched the front door of the store like a hawk. Even his bathroom breaks were taken in as short a time as possible. He hardly blinked as he nursed his food for the next several hours. The store opened, several staff arrived, but Jules was not among them.

Lunch had come and gone, and Tony nursed a sandwich for another several hours. By the time dinner time arrived and the store was beginning to close, Tony's upbeat spirit and determination were being put to the test. He began to doubt that he would ever see her again. A nagging thought kept chipping away at his resolve when he remembered her telling him that she had worked at that store for only a short period of time, and Tony sincerely hoped that when he saw her two days ago, it was not her last day of employment. Worry began to overtake his normally calm mind and passive demeanor, and eventually, Tony went back home feeling more depressed than he had ever felt in his life. He knew that it was still too early to panic, but every hour in that diner seemed like an eternity. That night he hardly slept, tossing and turning, wondering if he would ever experience another day of happiness.

When the morning came, Tony felt tired and beaten. He slowly dragged himself out of bed, and methodically went through his morning routine. After dressing himself, he brushed his hair in the mirror without really seeing himself or thinking about what he was doing. His mind was elsewhere, constantly thinking about that beautiful face that he saw so briefly at the store. His spirit was deflated and subdued by the ache in his heart, and despite what his mind was telling him, Tony could do nothing to elevate his mood or to lessen the ache in his heart. Methodically he reviewed a few of the old lines, but had no energy left to debate their efficacy. After leaving the house, he stared at the ground as he dragged his feet back to the diner. He bought another flower, now out of habit, and in a robot-like state proceeded to his destination. He sat in the familiar seat once again and sipped his cup of coffee.

He watched the door just as vigilantly as the day before, and contemplated his options. He could certainly find out where she lived from a phone book, but then what? Showing up at her front door out of the blue would not endear him to her in the least. If anything, it would only make him look like a stalker, and that was way worse than anything he would try at the store. Serenading a girl only worked in movies, television shows, novels, and perhaps in some short stories. This was real life, and going to her house was just not a very good option. Besides, he definitely knew that he did not have a good voice for singing. No other prudent options were popping into his head.

Tony sat there all day with no success. Once again, he saw the familiar routine of the main lights being turned off inside the store and eventually one of the managers locking the front door. Jules was nowhere to be seen once again. Tony closed his eyes and exhaled. He felt no desire to breath the air back into his lungs, as the happiness that he now pursued so desperately seemed to be slipping away. He felt like he was trying to hold a handful of sand that kept trickling through his fingers.

The natural instinct to survive and live forced him to take another breath. Tony opened his eyes and stared at the flower that was laying on the table in front of him. He hardly blinked and pondered his no longer certain future. At one time, it appeared that he had figured out and knew the direction that his life was heading, but now, it no longer looked certain or bright. Jules was the elixir of life for him, a lifeline for his spirit and soul, the cure for all the ailments in the world, his angel, and his light on the path of life, especially at times of darkness. And now, the times were becoming darker by the minute; but his light had disappeared. Tony pondered if he was destined to be unhappy before his sixties.

Suddenly a familiar voice snapped him out of his nearly hypnotic state, and as another shock wave ran down his body, without even realizing it, he jumped to his feet and smiled like he had never smiled before.

"A penny for your thoughts?" Jules said. "Perhaps two? You were really lost in thought there. When was the last time you blinked?" She smirked. "Can't find a good place to pass out or what?"

It took Tony a couple of seconds to get his breathing back under control and to restart his brain. He could not remember any of the lines he came up with and practiced so diligently the previous couple of days. In a split second he decided that they were all bad anyways, and spontaneous improvisation was the best way to proceed. However, he had to clear his throat because the first attempt at speaking was rather unsuccessful. Finally, as the shock of seeing Jules standing in front of him began to wear off, just enough to allow him to start regaining control of his body, he was able to manipulate his mouth and vocal cords enough to make normal sounds once again and form comprehensible speech.

"Hi," Tony finally uttered, "Yes, I was feeling a little depressed. I went to several places around here, but it looks like it's illegal to pass out anywhere in this town. Apparently, there is legislation prohibiting that from happening anywhere within the city limits. So unfair. I was hoping to break that law in here, but they won't let me do it either. What's a guy to do?" Tony pursed his lips. "So, I was just sitting here contemplating my dilemma. Figured I might as well get some food while I'm at it." Jules smiled wider, but then became serious.

"That is an unfortunate dilemma. I agree with you, it's just not fair. Well, when I become the mayor, I'll be sure to designate at least several spots for people to pass out at. Do you think you could hold on for a few more years?"

"A few years?" Tony answered and pretended to think really hard, "I guess I could do that, but if you could do it sooner, I'd really appreciate it." Tony's face was absolutely beaming by this time, and he felt more excited and energized than he thought was humanly possible. He wanted nothing more than to sweep Jules into his arms, spin her around, and then kiss her. He wanted to kiss her like he had never done before; just one kiss that would never end.

"Well, I'll see what I can do," she said. "I guess I have your vote then, no need to campaign in your neck of the woods."

"Oh yes," Tony answered, "you have my vote. I'll even make a monetary contribution to your campaign."

"Well, thank you." Jules bowed slightly and looked at the table that Tony was sitting at. "What's with the flower? I don't think I've ever seen anyone in here before with a single flower."

"Oh, that ..." Tony hesitated for just a second, having forgotten that it was laying there on the table. "I figured that would enhance the ambiance of my dining experience. What do you think, did I buy the right flower for such a purpose?" Jules took a closer look at the botanical decoration.

"I think you made the right decision. Plumerias are my favorite. Don't see guys buying those too often these days." Tony tried to appear surprised without overacting. Jules had just presented him with an opening.

"Well," he said, "in that case I would like to make my first contribution to your campaign right now." He picked up the flower and, with a slight head bow of his own, extended it to her. A slight blush colored her cheeks, as Jules took it and gently smelled the petals.

"Thank you," she said. "It's beautiful. Are you sure you want me to have it?"

"Oh yes," Tony quickly responded. "This particular plumeria is a good luck charm. It will help you win your run for mayor, and improve the ambiance of your future dining experiences – both equally important contributions." Jules smiled at that.

"Sounds like this flower will save me many long hours of shaking hands and kissing babies." After a short pause, she added, "but in the meantime, speaking of dining, I came in here to get dinner. After working all day, I'm famished." Now Tony looked surprised without any acting.

"You worked today? You must be exhausted." He looked somewhat perplexed. "And this is where you came to eat dinner?" Tony immediately realized that the last comment he made was pretty self-explanatory and probably not very helpful in achieving his goal, but Jules either chose to ignore it or didn't notice.

"Yeah," she answered, "I worked in the back for the last two days, unloading the supply truck. It arrived three days ago, but I was off then. Nobody ever likes to unload it because a lot of the boxes are heavy and have to be unloaded by hand. I don't mind doing it though. Went in through the back door this morning before the store even opened and spent all day there. Left through the back as well because I didn't finish till after the front door was all locked up. On days like this, I'm just too tired to cook, so I stop in here to eat before going home." Tony nodded in understanding. It all made sense now. He decided that the time had come to finally get to the point. Jules had not walked away yet, so perhaps she was attracted to him at this juncture as well. There was no reason to continue pussyfooting around the subject. He took a deep breath as his hands became clammy one more time.

"That is an excellent reason to stop in here," he said, "I was about to order as well. Would you care to join me? My treat, of course."

"That's very sweet of you." she answered as an uncomfortable smile formed on her face. "Thank you," she began to stammer as if the words were hard to come by, "but I can't. I was actually getting my dinner to go. Have to get to bed early because tomorrow another truck is arriving." Tony felt as if his heart was being ripped out of his chest. His shoulders visibly sank and he felt as if tears might form at any second. He was staring at the counter behind Jules, unsuccessfully attempting to formulate a sentence that would allow him to ask her for a date on another night, without sounding too desperate. It took another second for his eyes to refocus on the counter and the sign that sat on it to realize that it was a display case for various desserts. Suddenly he had another ace up his sleeve. This was going to be his last-ditch effort, but he felt surprisingly confident. Like a puppy, Tony tilted his head a little to the side, and added,

"That dinner offer includes vanilla ice cream for dessert ... or ... or chocolate, or strawberry – whichever one you prefer, of course." The sign on the counter that Tony never noticed until that moment read "Homemade Ice Cream: Vanilla, Chocolate, Strawberry." Even though he played that ace with confidence and displayed that on his face, inside he began to feel terrified and felt weak in the knees. For what seemed like a very long time, Jules just stood there frozen, her face displaying no emotion of any kind. Her eyes did not reveal her feelings either. But then she smiled and extended her hand.

"By the way, my name is Julianna," she said. "Make it vanilla and you got yourself a deal." Tony smiled back. The world had just fell off his shoulders, the spirit that he had been dragging on the ground for the last two days was back in his chest, and he felt as if he could fly. He took her hand in his and exhaled a sigh of relief. Her touch felt like a warm cup of hot chocolate on a cold snowy day.

"Tony" he answered, "nice to meet you Jules...Julianna. Mind if I call you Jules?"

"Not at all," she said, "that would be nice." They both sat down at the booth that Tony had pretty much made his own over the previous two and a half days, and continued a conversation full of dry humor jokes, compliments, and small talk that most first dates are full of.

Tony could not stop looking or smiling at Jules. Very few people get a second chance at life, and he knew that this one was quite unique. The future for the two of them was uncertain once again, but one thing that Tony was convinced of was that he would spend very little time in the basement this time. Now the main projects of his life would be centered around Jules and the life that they would build together; perhaps they would even start a family. He wanted to grow old with her – surrounded by an awesome family and good friends. Most importantly though, there would be plenty of love and true happiness for many years to come.

And then Tony had an epiphany ... It occurred to him that, either forwards or backwards, love really does transcend time.

I was sitting quietly, deep in thought. My eyes were lowered to the ground, staring at the swaying grass in front of me. I experienced the saddest, most uncomfortable feelings I had ever felt. A dull, almost ruthless pain tormented my heart – as if a part of me was torn away and lost forever. A look of deep sorrow covered my face, and a knot sat defiantly in my throat. However, for some inexplicable reason, I could not cry. It was a warm sunny day, and the breeze, disrespectful of the melancholy mood that enveloped the knoll, played gently with our hair. There were only three of us.

I slowly raised my eyes and looked at a fallen tree that I could clearly see in the not too great distance, and then at the open casket and the body inside.

Henry Klein died peacefully three days ago in his house at the age of ninety-seven. He was the quietest, most secluded person this town had ever known. Having outlived all his family and never making any real friends, he mostly kept to himself – never asking for anything, never getting in anybody's way, and always avoiding the town's multiple gossip mills that the market and church gatherings were notorious for. He had been that way for as long as anybody could remember. He had never even attended the corn festival in the fall nor the squash festival in the spring – both quite large celebrations that the town was extremely proud of; notwithstanding an extreme circumstance, just about every person here attended those two events.

Every morning people would see Henry walking to the market for groceries, quickly vacating the premises after the purchases, and in the afternoons working on his garden – tending to a beautiful rose bush, or relaxing on his porch. Residing in a single-family house across the street from me, on the edge of town, outside of a cursory "hello" and a nod of his head with a friendly smile on his face, I had never seen Henry speak to anyone any more than he absolutely had to. He always gave the shortest answer possible if anyone asked him anything, and then quickly retreated back to the serenity of his rose bush or the sanctity of his home. It was just widely assumed that Henry either suffered from agoraphobia or was a social recluse, and was happy in his semi-seclusion.

There are about two thousand people residing here, and in a small farm town like ours, secrets are seldom kept; however, Henry was an exception. It was not an easy phenomenon to notice, or perhaps no one cared, or they were too busy to realize, that Henry mysteriously disappeared every year, on the same day, for the whole day. Nobody saw him walking to the market, or anywhere else for that matter. Nobody saw him working in the yard, or sitting on the porch. In fact, on June 27th of every year nobody saw him anywhere - except me. I discovered his secret out of curiosity, but decided that it could never be revealed, that even Henry could not know that another person is aware of his secret. Privacy is a treasured and scarce commodity in our small town, and that day belonged to Henry Klein, and him alone. Perhaps that is why I felt so close to him.

Although June 27th is just another day for most people, for me it is special because that is the day that I was born. That is how I noticed Henry's disappearances. He was just about the only person in my neighborhood not to wish me a happy birthday. Quite a few years went by before I realized that he was the only person on my block that I did not run into first thing in the morning, on that day. Eventually I discovered that nobody saw Henry – not just in the morning, but all day long.

I knew that it was none of my business, that I should not be so vain and inquisitive, but sometimes curiosity knows no bounds, and in the end, proved to be too strong. Therefore, I decided to find out what happened to Henry on June 27th of every year.

I wanted to know his secret.

I could easily see Henry's house from my living room window. On the eve of his disappearance, I was wide awake staring at his home when I saw him turn off the lights and retire for the night. After sleeping most of the afternoon, it was not difficult for me to stay alert, and wait for my neighbor to awaken. Always being a patient individual, I calmly spent the long hours at my window, waiting for a man I hardly knew to begin his disappearing act. Keeping busy with card tricks, and a few other mundane activities, to help pass the time, I often pondered the possibility of abandoning my pursuit of the unknown, but I guess it is in my nature to solve all mysteries that I come across. So once again, curiosity overwhelmed my sense of dignity and respect, and I resolved to discover Henry's secret once and for all.

As the first rays of daylight appeared, Henry's kitchen light was turned on, and I could see him eating breakfast. As quickly and quietly as possible, I snuck out of my house, and hid behind the bushes in my front yard. I felt like a kid playing hide and seek, and it was really hard to contain the excitement that engulfed me. I was ten-years-old all over again.

After what seemed like an eternity, Henry's front door swung open and he stepped onto the porch wearing a large blue backpack.

I crouched closer to the ground. My heart was beating so fast it felt as if my chest would burst. My neighbor calmly locked the door, and upon reaching the sidewalk, carefully looked around, making sure nobody saw him. Except for the two of us, the whole town was still asleep. In the cool misty air, he took a deep breath, looked up at the crimson sky, closed his eyes for a moment, and began walking east. I cautiously followed, making sure to stay off the sidewalks, and to stay hidden as much as possible. It did not seem to matter, because Henry never turned around.

Twenty minutes later he was still walking calmly down the road, leaving the town far behind. A forest stretched out on the left side of the road, and a lake on the right. My imagination ran wild as I pondered what Henry's destination was. Would he wind up meeting with extra-terrestrials? Was he conducting some secret government work? Was he part of some weird experiment? Or was he stalking someone like I was stalking him? There seemed to be no limit to what my imagination envisioned. I guess, I just failed to see the simplicity of it all, and looked instead for something complicated and bizarre. Perhaps I was simply too young and foolish – too inexperienced with the cruelties of life.

Suddenly, Henry turned into the forest and was out of my view. Without hesitation, I came out onto the road and ran to the spot where my neighbor made his unexpected move. Although it was hard to notice at first, a small trail weaved its way among the trees, disappearing somewhere into the forest. Wasting no time, I quickly moved along the grass-covered ground, following the barely perceptible path. Suddenly I realized that despite the fact that I lived in this town all my life, I had never set foot this deep into the forest. And for that matter, I could probably say the same for most of the townspeople. While some liked to occasionally fish in the lake, going deep into the forest had never become a popular activity.

As I continued to walk, Henry was nowhere to be seen. I began to worry that I had lost him and would have to abandon my quest when the loud crack of a branch caused me to spin around and crouch down. Not more than fifty yards ahead of me, completely unaware that somebody had followed him, was Henry, looking down at the ground in front of him, walking calmly at his own pace, lost deep in thought. My heart skipped a beat and sweat formed on my forehead. I could not believe that he did not see me. Perhaps Lady Luck was stalking me.

The day was becoming hot, when Henry reached his destination. At the bottom of a small hill a huge, uprooted tree was lying in the middle of a small clearing. Slowly, Henry sank down onto the grass, dropped his backpack, leaned against the trunk, and rested. At the top of the hill, I crawled to a spot from which I could easily observe, yet not be seen. With great anticipation I watched the events unfold in front of me. This was not what I expected.

Henry was breathing heavily from the long walk, and I could see that he was sweating profusely. Eventually he opened his backpack, and pulled out a large multicolored blanket. Spreading it out neatly on the grass next to the tree, Henry appeared to be lost in thought, like he was trying to recall something from the past. Next, he removed two sandwiches, a bottle of what appeared to be whiskey, and a tumbler. Then, from a different pocket, he pulled out a portable cassette player and a cassette case. He placed everything on the blanket very carefully, and took a few moments to double check his work. Satisfied, he stood up, walked over to a different part of the tree trunk and put his hands on it.

Amazed, I saw Henry open a secret compartment on the side of the trunk and from it he removed a few objects wrapped in plastic. With trembling hands, he carefully removed the plastic wrapping, and I could clearly see that he now was holding some kind of a picture and a sheaf of papers. He put them all down on the blanket, sat down next to them, leaned against the trunk once again, and filled the tumbler halfway with whiskey.

Then Henry just sat there for quite a while, reading the papers, interspersed with staring sadly at the picture, while holding the glass on his lap. I felt badly for him at that moment because he looked like he was in great emotional distress and wanted nothing more than to cry. Taking a deep breath, he downed the whiskey, took the cassette from its case and inserted it into the player. After fumbling with the buttons for a bit, he sat the player back down and closed his eyes. Although the sound quality was somewhat distorted, suddenly the beautiful music of Glenn Miller's Moonlight Serenade filled the air. I did not know what all of that meant, but I knew that it had to be a magical moment for Henry. Keeping his eyes closed ever so slightly, he swayed back and forth, and for some reason, the emotions that I saw displayed on his face and in his body language touched my heart. I wanted to go to him, offer a shoulder to lean on, a soothing word, or lend my ear to listen to what troubled him.

He stared at the picture once again and then, with a shaking hand, brought it up to his lips and kissed it. Suddenly, like a match caught on fire, a new, more intense pain surfaced on his face, and ever so slowly, he raised his knees to his chest, lowered his head, set the picture down, and pressed his hands tightly against his face.

A long time passed. Getting my own thoughts and emotions under control, I tried to reevaluate the events that I had witnessed, but was unable to draw any conclusions. Eventually, Henry lowered his hands, and I saw that his eyes were red and puffy – full of pain and suffering, the likes of which I had never seen before. The torment that he clearly displayed on his face melted my heart and my own eyes filled with tears. He looked like the world had just crashed in on him, like there was nothing left worthwhile in the world, like there would be no tomorrow. Soon, tears began to roll down his cheeks and he began to openly cry. A different side of Henry was displayed before my eyes, one that I believe no one alive today had ever seen. He was no longer a stoic, almost robot-like individual, but one with overwhelming emotions – full of pain and frustration. In a mesmerized state, I observed it all, taking in every single detail as if they were the most important events of my own life. Perhaps, they were.

After rewinding the cassette and playing the song for a second time, Henry filled the tumbler again, arranged the papers in a neat pile, and picked up the picture. Quickly he swallowed the whiskey in one gulp, rewound the cassette once more, and played the song from the beginning for the third time. When it finished, he was still staring at the picture. Without shifting his eyes, he turned off the player, and ever so slowly, with a barely audible, quivering voice, recited the following:

As the sun begins to rise, and disperse the night,

In a dream a vision is born and takes off on a flight.

A vision of such charm and beauty as to be paralleled by none,

A vision so precious, I dare not blink for it may be gone.

I see you walking on petals so graceful and free,

So soothing and sweet your vision appears to me.

Your face, so refreshing and gentle, like the morning dew,

To lay your head down, a bed of roses I have planted for you.

Each day and each night my heart beats in pain,

I live in torment, looking for peace is in vain.

Like a child born without bonding, devoid of caring and love,

My soul withers away; you are everything that I am, my white dove.

Sweet tastes and smells have had no meaning for me for a long time,

Misery and loneliness have me surrounded, like a box holding a mime.

Filling a river of pain, I shed a tear each morning that you are not here,

Perhaps soon we will be together, that is the thought that quiets my fear.

I stumble through darkness as my life moves on,

The gentle hands that held the light are forever gone.

The days we spent together, ever so happy, were few,

Garbled as they may be, hear these words – I love you!

He then played the song again, poured another shot of whiskey, and quickly emptied the tumbler. Leaning back against the dead tree, he closed his eyes once again, and just sat there, as if meditating on something vitally important. After staying like that for a while, he slowly opened his eyes and stared off into the distance. He hardly blinked as he ate one of the sandwiches, finished the last of the whiskey, and set to play the song for the last time on that day. When it finished, he turned off the player, laid down on the blanket, and before long, I could hear the soft sounds of his gentle snoring.

Since I forgot my watch at home, it was hard to tell how many hours went by before Henry fell asleep. He reminded me of a child who was playing all day, became very tired, and now was sleeping to get his energies back for another day full of exhausting activities. I did not even realize that my own eyes were slowly closing. The ground beneath me was rather soft, and the heat wore me out, leaving my own reserves at nearly nothing.

The sun was well on its way to the west when Henry awoke. A loud cough aroused me out of my own slumber, and I opened my eyes to find him neatly wrapping the picture and the papers back with plastic and carefully putting them back into the secret compartment in the side of the uprooted tree. I slowly rolled over onto my side, realizing that everything in my body was stiff and hurting from lying in the same position for so long.

Henry repacked his backpack and put it on his back. Lowering his head as if in prayer, he stood there for a moment, and then began to walk back the way we had come. Looking back at the tree trunk, I noticed that Henry had left a rose and the other sandwich on top of it. Fighting back the stiffness that overtook my body, I followed him even more carefully, making sure he would not see me in case he decided to turn around on the return trip, but just as before, he never did.

It was already dark by the time we reached the village. Henry walked at his own pace – never stopping or slowing down. He headed straight home and went right to bed. I felt extreme hunger, thirst, and exhaustion. Many questions and concerns about my neighbor buzzed around my head, but it all had to wait until morning. As the tension of the day began to wind down, I could feel all the major muscles in my body screaming in pain, and a headache pounding mercilessly at my temples. After grabbing a quick snack, I spent the next nine hours in bed recuperating.

The sun was already high in the sky by the time I opened my eyes. I slept well that night – there were no dreams, no nightmares, not a single noise to disturb my rest. I woke up refreshed, with a clear idea of what I had to do to get to the bottom of this mystery. A long hot shower relieved a lot of the stiffness and aches that I still felt, and a big breakfast made me feel better still.

First thing I wanted to check out was the place in the forest where Henry and I had spent the previous day. A theory of what I saw, and the reasons for it, formed in my head, but I had to find and confirm a few facts to verify it. Grabbing a bottle of water, I headed out for my destination.

When I stepped onto the porch, I saw my neighbor across the street working diligently in his garden. He paused just long enough to nod a courteous hello, and went on about his business. Everything was back to normal, and yesterday seemed like a long time ago – quickly turning into a surreal memory. I returned the greeting and stared at Henry for a few long moments while he intently removed the dried-up twigs from a rose bush. Less than twenty-four hours earlier he was a totally different man – a man full of frustration, desperation, and most of all pain. And now, his face would not betray a single emotion.

The walk back into the forest was pretty uneventful, and I reached the top of the hill rather quickly. The scene was just the way we had left it the day before. I descended to the bottom of the hill and slowly walked up to the trunk, hearing an echo of my heartbeat in my ears. With a few feet to go, I noticed that there was something carved into the side of it. I kneeled down to take a closer look, and cranked my head to the right since it became immediately apparent that the carving was made when the tree still stood upright.

The edges of the carving were no longer well delineated, but there was no denying the fact that it was a heart with two sets of initials in the middle, connected with a plus sign. After several seconds of staring at them, I saw that it read HK + EM. Not sure what to make of it at that time, I decided to proceed with my investigation, stood back up, and carefully laid my hands on the spot where the trap door was supposed to be. It gave way with a considerable amount of pressure when I pushed it open. Inside was a larger compartment, and in the middle of that, wrapped in multiple layers of plastic, was a cloth bag containing the picture and stack of papers.

The anticipation and excitement were nerve wrecking and I fought to keep my hands from trembling as I took them out of the trunk. The old plastic wrapping had a few small tears in it, performing its duty to perfection well beyond its life expectancy. Forcing myself to relax, I took a deep breath and unwrapped the items of interest. Both were quite old and I handled them as carefully as possible, especially since it was obvious that time had not been kind to quite a few of the items and their integrity was becoming fragile.

The bunch of papers turned out to be old letters, all addressed to Henry. The careful cursive penmanship talked a bit about the hardships that even a civilian life can bring into a home during a war. Mostly though, the letters abundantly stressed the author's undying love for Henry, the nearly insurmountable amount of stress that his absence was putting on everyone back home, the fact that he was being missed very much, and the excitement over his inevitable return. I carefully set those down, and looked at the picture. It was an old, yellowish photograph on a thick, cardboard-like paper. Although it was somewhat blurry, I could clearly see a couple on it, a bride and a groom, wearing a conservative wedding dress and a three-piece tuxedo, holding hands, joyfully, posing and smiling for the camera. It was actually a very nice picture of them. Both looked full of life, excitement, and perhaps even mischief. I wondered who these people were.

Suddenly it hit me.

I held my breath as I brought the picture closer to examine it better. Time had taken its toll, and the lack of color made it even harder, but there was no doubt about it. The groom in that picture was Henry – young and vibrant, with his whole life still ahead of him. Young Henry.

Then I noticed something else. Pinned to her wedding dress was a beautiful rose – just like the ones Henry was growing in his front yard. Intensely I examined the picture, trying to put the pieces together.

After several long minutes, I rewrapped everything, put it away just as it was found, and headed home. Sipping the water, I pondered the significance of what I had discovered – some of it pretty simple to figure out and self-explanatory; while certain other areas still remained a mystery, requiring further investigation. The next few days proved to be quite interesting, especially since the events I was investigating took place prior to the invention of the internet.

Over the next three weeks I spent long hours on my computer, at City Hall, the town library, and the local clinic doing research of old records – putting together pieces of a puzzle that sprung its roots long before I was even born. Once I obtained everything that those resources had to offer, I spent several evenings talking to some of the oldest residents of our town, and in a nonchalant way inquired about Henry's youth - always finding myself very intrigued by what I heard. Most people turned out to be very helpful and were eager to tell me many bits of history from their youth and what life in this town used to be like.

Often sitting on the porch and enjoying the sunsets, we talked over tea, lemonade, or cake, while they eagerly remembered many useful details, some facts and some rumors, but all painting a grim picture. Eventually I connected the clues and unraveled the mystery of Henry Klein. My heart and never-ending sorrow went out to him, but there was nothing I could do. No word of comfort could I give him, or even reveal that I know his tragedy. Now I understood why that day belonged to him, and him alone.

It happened decades ago. On June 27, 1945, Henry M. Klein married a young lady by the name of Elizabeth K. McDougal. They met at one of the town festivals in the spring of 1941 and began dating shortly thereafter, often spending time in a forest – on day-long picnics, away from everybody else - always treasuring the few moments of privacy that were so seldom found. They were a vibrant couple looking forward to a long and happy life together.

However, their romance was suddenly interrupted when on December seventh Pearl Harbor was bombed and the United States entered World War II. Two months later Henry was drafted to fight on the European front. The day before he left, he proposed to Elizabeth somewhere in the forest – no one knew exactly where they went – they just knew that the young couple liked to spend time alone somewhere in the forest.

Later, after he was deployed, she told others how Henry went down on one knee and asked for her hand in marriage. He told her how she made his heart sing, how her smile made the gloomiest of days bright once again, and how much joy her mere presence brought into his life. He promised to always take care of her, but mostly, he stressed his unwavering love for her and that he would love her unconditionally forever and ever. She always had a smile on her face whenever she recounted that moment for anyone. He also promised her to come back just as soon as he could. She wrote letters to him nearly every week while he was gone.

In the early days of May, 1945 Henry upheld his promise and returned home. They immediately set a date for their marriage, and a couple of months later, exchanged their vows in a quiet ceremony at the local church.

At the wedding reception, everybody was enjoying themselves – dancing to the sounds of the big bands. The first dance, however, belonged to the young couple. With just the two of them on the floor, holding each other tightly, they glided effortlessly to their wedding song, the enchanting sound of Glenn Miller's Moonlight Serenade. It was a truly magical moment. But then the unexpected happened.

As the evening was winding down, the beautiful bride walked from person to person thanking them and saying goodbye, when suddenly she collapsed, never to regain consciousness again. She was rushed to the local clinic, and then transferred to the closest hospital, which, at that time, was about fifty miles away. However, it was all to no avail, and she died a short time later. The doctors at either facility could do nothing for her. They attributed her death to a ruptured cerebral aneurism. I was unable to ascertain any more details, but it was not difficult to infer the rest. Henry must have been devastated. An old nurse, long retired from her profession, told me that he was at her bedside the entire time, lovingly whispering into her ear, tightly grasping her hand, holding onto hope with her every breath. As per his wishes, she was buried in an unmarked grave in the forest next to a recently uprooted tree.

After that, Henry moved into the house where he had planned to live happily ever after. I imagine that he began disappearing the following year, spending some time alone at their picnic sight, listening to their wedding song and talking to her spirit, remembering in private – reliving the happiest and saddest day of his life. He recited a new poem every year – each one more beautiful than before.

They say that a young spirit never rests. Perhaps she talked back to him.

I never figured out when he managed to make the secret compartment in the tree, or why he decided to keep that picture and the letters there. I imagine it was just too painful for him to keep them in the house, and seeing them once a year probably made that day more special for him. I do know for sure though that Henry was never seen with another woman again. Even after all this time, he remained faithful to his one true love.

I admired his commitment and idolized his resolve. As much as I wanted to help him, the best thing to do was to keep my mouth shut, and allow Henry the privacy he so desperately wanted and needed. But I refused to just idly sit back and forget all that I discovered. That was just simply impossible. So, I began to do the only thing that I could think of.

Every year, on June 27th, I followed Henry into the forest, to keep an eye on him. To make sure that nothing bad happened to him while he cried, talked, prayed, and slept. To make sure that he reached his destination and came back safely. To make sure his secret remained just that – a private affair. Every now and then, I went to the forest to check that everything was still there, safe from man, animal, and the elements. Several times I had to replace the old plastic wrappings with slightly less old plastic wrapping, clean, perform minor repairs, and weather-proof the hidden compartment in the tree, but thankfully Henry never noticed.

Despite his age, Henry's death three days ago was unexpected. Without giving it a second thought, I took it upon myself to organize his funeral and burial site. I felt that no one else would be able to provide him with the proper final goodbye. After quite a bit of effort, I was finally able to make the desired arrangements that he so rightly deserved. Since all of it was a bit unusual and the rules and regulations have become more strict since the 1940's, and with no immediate family present to support my decisions, I wound up doing a lot of running around, paid extra money for some services, and even asked for several favors. Eventually though, I managed to arrange the funeral in the middle of a forest, at the top of a small hill, and Henry was going to be buried in the only place he saw himself: in an unmarked grave next to an old uprooted tree, right in front of the long-ago heart carved on the side of it.

I took my eyes off the casket and looked at the other two people, both sitting by themselves. One of them, staring at the ground in front of his feet, was the mayor of our town. The other one, looking straight ahead and not blinking, was the lawyer that helped me make that funeral possible. It occurred to me that neither one of them knew his secret, and at that moment I vowed that nobody ever would.

I looked towards the clear blue sky. They are finally together again.

I slowly rose to my feet and looked at Henry's body for the last time. There was no great mystery to solve, no perilous danger, no exciting adventures. Just a man who profoundly loved his wife. I walked over to the casket, and pulled out of my pocket an old, yellowing photograph and papers. I realized that physically this was the closest I had ever been to him. Maybe it was my grief, or the wetness building up in my eyes, or just my imagination, but I could swear the rose in that picture looked more vibrant – almost bigger than I remembered it to be and far less faded as compared to the rest of the picture. It almost looked red on that black and white print. Quietly, I slid the picture and the letters inside the left breast pocket of his three-piece tuxedo, and laid a single, long stemmed rose just above his crossed hands. I closed my eyes as a tear rolled down my cheek.

Perhaps someday when I find true love, I will take her to a small clearing somewhere in the forest, at the base of a small hill by a fallen tree. And I will pin a rose to her dress, and we will laugh and play together, and eat a couple of sandwiches. And perhaps someday, I will propose to her out there, while listening to the soft sound of Moonlight Serenade on a compact disc player or some other electronic device. And after we marry, we'll move into our own home with a garden, and live full and loving lives. Someday, perhaps. If I am lucky.

Fleeting Moments

Stifling a yawn, I rubbed my eyes and took a deep breath, as the antique clock in the gallery's marbled vestibule chimed right on time - one melodious tone, followed by seven more. My shift was over, but the day was just beginning. The tiny radio sitting on the desk quietly emitted the meteorologist's forecast for the day. He called for sunny skies and a temperature in the low eighties. Ralph, the day watchman, took another sip of his coffee, polished his badge, and then squared his hat. He always had a grin on his face that, for no particular reason, tended to annoy me from time to time, and this morning was one of those times.

"Everything go alright on the night shift?" he asked, knowing what the answer was going to be. I nodded. Everything always goes alright on my shifts. I had read my book for a bit and solved another puzzle. Mostly though, it was another night full of daydreams and a lot of art admiration. The night shifts allowed me to be the number one fan of the masterpieces on display at the museum, and to admire them in complete peace and quiet. In a trance-like state, I often took advantage of that opportunity and truly appreciated the various strokes of the brushes on canvases, adored the details of the landscapes and the various characters depicted there, and became one with the myriad of talent hanging on those walls. As Ralph began his rounds, I shot him a begrudging look.

Before leaving, I looked around with awe and saluted the Masters. Why couldn't this perfection exist beyond these hallowed halls?

The employee lot was nearly empty at this early hour (as it should be). It would be another forty-five minutes before the rest of the staff would start arriving. I started my 1967

Chevy Nova, put the top down with some effort, and headed home to my comfortable bed.

Not far from the art museum, I encountered a traffic light that was changing from green to yellow. I thought of speeding up to make it, but begrudgingly decided to err on the side of caution. So, I stopped at the crosswalk and waited. I was glad I did because after checking the rearview mirror, I saw a police car slightly behind me in the next lane.

I looked around at the neighborhood bathed in the early morning sunshine. Before me, in panorama, was Monet's Impression, Sunrise. Never before had I felt such peace as I did at that moment, caring nothing for the world around me. It was magnificent! But I was able to enjoy it for only a fleeting moment. A tractor-trailer traveling on the cross road pulled into the intersection blocking my glorious view. I inhaled deeply and pursed my lips. Monet once commented, "Landscape is nothing but an impression, and an instantaneous one." Claude, you are so right – a master of arts and smart philosopher to boot.

Something – or someone – on the sidewalk caught my attention. For a fleeting moment I saw her – Degas's The Star. She was slender, smiling, and sensational! Wearing a fitted flowery blouse which showed modest cleavage, she was hurriedly dodging in and out of the throng of pedestrians on the street. As she ran gracefully among the people, her long shapely legs were accentuated as her skirt swept up and floated down. Her personage radiated sexuality just as the sun radiates heat. Time stood still as I stared at this marvelous sight and I dared not blink. My heart melted a thousand times over and I could not speak though I desperately wanted to call out to her. Then, she was gone, swallowed by the crowd.

I blinked several times and looked back at the traffic light.

Still red.

To my left I heard the voice of an angel speaking into her cell phone. Like a smoothly conducted Romantic Period symphonic orchestra – piano, violin, saxophone, harp – every nerve in my body and every ounce of my being were played to the sweet tune of soul-satisfying fulfillment. For a fleeting moment, I watched as her lips moved in unison, with her angelic voice. Her tongue darting in and out of her mouth, licking those succulent bright pink lips. A hint of a smile materialized on my face as I willed us to be the ardent lovers in Hayez's The Kiss. Cradling her beautiful oval face in my arms, I would cover her lips, cheeks, and neck with passionate never-ending kisses. I would hold her and never let go. Then, she hailed a taxi cab, jumped in, and was gone.

Just like that.

Slowly exhaling, I looked back at the traffic light.

Still red.

The sudden pounding of a jack hammer and the yelling of definitive commands caused me to look down the street. For a fleeting moment, there was Rockwell's Rosie the Riveter. I watched as a woman dressed in blue overalls, a hard hat, a reflective vest, and heavy work boots hollered commands over the noise. Although I could not hear the exact words that she was shouting, her intonation was confident and competent. There was a seriousness about her that could not be denied nor should it be. I was captivated by her. For a fleeting moment, time slowed down to eternity and everything around me stood still. Then she moved on to the next work crew and was gone.

A polite toot sounded from the car behind me. I looked up at the traffic light. It was green, but for how long? The police car had already driven past.

I glanced in my rear-view mirror. A spark flashed somewhere deep inside me setting my soul on fire, engulfing my whole being in a blazing white inferno that burned brighter than the sun above. For a fleeting moment, I saw her. A woman so exquisite that she stole my breath away and caused my heart to skip a beat. She was Botticelli's Venus from The Birth of Venus, a goddess the likes of whom I had never seen before. She was a natural beauty – alabaster skin, long flowing strawberry-blond hair, luscious ruby lips. Her ample bosom was accentuated by her tight sweater that I could see above the dashboard. Simply gorgeous! She gave me a friendly wave and I moved my car forward. Then she turned at the intersection and was gone.

After that, driving home everything seemed different – a little less sad, a lot less empty, and a whole lot more exciting. I realized that for a few fleeting moments, true beauty existed and love filled my heart. Life really is an imitation of art – even if it is for only a few fleeting moments at a time.

Thank you.

"*R*hapsody in Blue" was quietly playing on the radio as I stared out the front windshield of my car - hardly blinking, aimlessly driving, my mind traveling back to what now seemed like a different life in the not too distant past. I was a long way from anywhere and my funds were dwindling quickly. The last of my life savings was being held hostage in my back pocket. However, I did not care anymore as long as the wide-open space of the deserted road was in front of me. For hours, I saw no cars on that two-lane highway. The half empty bottle of whiskey on the passenger seat began to call out to me. My faithful companion and one true friend.

I pulled over to the side of the road, opened the sun roof, and took several big gulps. The warm liquid felt good going down my throat as it softened the aches of my heart and quieted that macabre scream which kept haunting me day after day and night after night. Ever since my wife died, liquor helped soothe everything in my life. But tears welled up once again as the memories of that dreadful night swept across my conscious stirring up emotions that I have tried so hard to suppress. The living nightmare was temporarily tamed, but redemption was nowhere to be found. Numbness settled over me as the last drops of the bittersweet poison rolled down my tongue.

The blowing wind carried the sound of a howling wolf. I lifted my heavy eyelids to look at the world around me. Dark threatening storm clouds played bumper cars across the sky. They looked angry. "I know how you feel!" I yelled at them.

As my bloodshot eyes refocused on the earth, suddenly I saw her. Standing by the side of the road, dressed all in white, was a beautiful vision. What was such a lovely creature doing on this God forsaken road in the middle of nowhere? I clumsily opened the door and stepped onto the dusty road.

She stood motionless, as if waiting for me to sweep her off her feet. Trying to clear my head, I stumbled toward her. Drawing nearer, I was mystified by what I saw. She was the most incredible woman I had ever laid my eyes upon, glowing under the starlit sky and enchanting moonlight. Where did the clouds go? Her long auburn hair gently swayed in the breeze, while her soft curls fell and framed her smiling face. I was in awe. Her presence brought back memories of those long-gone days when Celeste and I would lie on the beach, and I would run my fingers through her long brown hair.

Coming back to the present, I became mesmerized by the sparkling pool of sapphire eyes that were before me now. They were surrounded by long dark lashes and arched eyebrows. Her oval face and high cheekbones complemented the small nose on her delicate visage. She had full, luscious, ruby-red lips that left me breathless. Her soft and gentle Mona Lisa smile was mysterious, yet inviting. The long, flowing, silken dress accentuated the contour of her womanly curves. Feelings long forgotten were aroused and I felt my head spinning as time stood still.

"Hello," she said in a melodious voice that sounded more like heavenly harps than a sound made by a mere mortal. "You must be lost because hardly anybody travels down this road." My mind was stuttering and I could not think of anything intelligent to say. I barely responded with a nod of my head.

In a voice not quite my own, I finally muttered, "Who are you? What's your name? Are you lost too?" She smiled shyly at me and came a little closer.

"My name is Angela." She answered in that musical voice and extended her hand. I took it and held it in mine for what seemed to be a very long time. It felt warm to the touch, and I did not want to let go. "I enjoy being out here in the open, bathed by the moonlight, with only the starry sky above me. This wilderness is absolutely beautiful at night." Calmness settled over me as she spoke, dissolving my apprehension. For some inexplicable reason, it no longer felt odd to be talking to this goddess. After a momentary pause, she said, "What's your name and what brings you all the way out here?" All of my pain and guilt swept over me again like a tidal wave. It made me wish I had another bottle of whiskey in the car.

"I'm Sam." I answered fighting the knot in my throat and barely holding back the tears. "I guess I'm out here to ... escape reality. This may sound like the ravings of a lunatic, but demons haunt me every time I close my eyes. And so, I try desperately to get away. So far, not so good." I trailed off on the last several words and stopped, unable to explain it any further.

"You look so unhappy. Misery is evident all over your face." Pulling away her hand, she stepped a bit closer. Her sweet fragrance sent a shiver down my spine and made my body tingle. "Take a walk with me. Let's share the beauty of this night together. The fresh air always helps me clear my mind, maybe it will do the same for you." I was surprised by her invitation. There was no good reason to refuse so I nodded and followed her lead.

Slowly we walked along the side of the road. Angela looked straight ahead, while I stared at my feet pondering my sorry existence. We did not talk for a while, but strangely, I found some comfort in the silence. Angela appeared very relaxed in that calm setting and her mere presence radiated tranquility and peace. She was truly enjoying her surroundings and I envied her free spirit. My nerves began to unwind, and I lifted my head. She was right. The scenery was indeed breathtaking. The forest stretched out on both sides of the road as far as the eye could see. From somewhere in the distance, among the trees, a cricket's soft stridulating reached my ears, and I saw the shimmering moon's reflection in a small shallow pond ahead of us. I felt like a stranger, an intruder, among the delicate balance of nature and beauty.

"It's so delightful out here, isn't it?" she said.

"It is," I answered, but words did not come easily.

"Where are you heading?" Her voice floated to my ears, sounding soft and compassionate. Once again, I was not sure what to say.

"Well, wherever the day takes me, I guess," I eventually mumbled and sighed. She seemed to understand.

"How long have you been on the road?" I smirked at her question and was momentarily lost in visions of the past.

"I have been running for one year, eleven months, and seventeen days." She looked at me with a frown on her face. I realized that I had already said too much, but looking back into her eyes made me feel as if she already knew my whole story.

"Who or what are you running from? What's making you so miserable? Pain and suffering emanate from you like heat from a fire. I have never seen so much sadness on one person's face. Would you like to share your story with me?" She gave me an encouraging look.

"It would be too painful to relive that night. I'm sorry." I answered in anguish. Grief began to slowly creep to the surface and I longed once again for my wife's soft caring touch.

"It's okay," Angela responded. "It is I who should apologize. I didn't mean to upset you." I nodded my head and just kept walking. Angela remained quiet.

A fox ran across the road and disappeared into the darkness. My chaotic thoughts were in a tug of war. Although I did not want to share my experiences with anybody, I felt a strong attraction to this unexpected companion and a desire to release my tortured soul.

My love for Celeste only deepened my distressed state, but Angela seemed to want to alleviate my pain.

"Look at the deer over there by the pond," she redirected my attention. "Don't they appear to be peaceful?" I followed her gaze and saw two deer illuminated by the tranquil moon. They slowly approached the water and cautiously began to drink. We watched in admiration the innocence of those shy creatures. I admired the scene with fondness and envy, while Angela enjoyed the pure simplicity of it.

"They look magnificent," I said. "It all reminds me of a time long ago, when things were quite different, and, for me, life was full of meaning." She looked right into my eyes for several long seconds, appeared to be considering something, then took my hand and gently tugged on it.

"Let's sit on that grassy patch," she suggested and pointed to a small knoll. "I need a rest and we can get a better view from there." It was an unexpected invitation, but I followed her without hesitation. Quietly, so as not to disturb the deer, we made our way to the mound and sat down on the soft grass.

At that moment, watching the deer, I felt more at peace than I had in the last year. Keeping an eye on them, I rested on my elbows and took a deep breath. My mind began to wander as I tried to relax the stiff muscles and joints of my drained body. However, tension did not withdraw its crippling hand that easily, and I felt very tired, wishing tomorrow would never come.

The two animals finished drinking and after a moment's hesitation ran off into the forest. I looked at the infinite sky filled with billions of diamonds. The whole universe was in front of me, and at that moment I felt very small and insignificant in its seemingly boundless infinity. Angela looked at me and smiled.

"I'm glad to see that you like the serenity of this night. I like coming here to unwind and relieve my mind of unwanted stress. Perhaps, even set my spirit free."

"This whole scene is truly captivating, and it feels like there is a pleasing aura around this place, almost surreal." Angela smiled even wider at my response, and settled down next to me.

"What do you see when you look up at the sky?" she asked in a quiet tone.

"I see a ghost," I said even quieter. "A ghost of my one true love – Celeste. Unfortunately, she is gone forever." Angela took my hand and squeezed it tightly.

"I am very sorry," she said gently. "I can see that you are a good and caring man and I know your love for her will never die. She must have been a very special person."

"Yes, she was," I answered, remembering her relaxed demeanor, delightful sense of humor, and keen intellect. "She was always cheerful, caring, compassionate, and loving. She would have made a great mother."

Angela fell silent for a while. She appeared lost in thought, and I wondered what kind of images her mind formed from my descriptions. She looked at me thoughtfully. It felt odd to have a stranger show interest in my misfortunes and care about my feelings. That reminded me of Celeste. Once again, I saw my beloved's face in front of me.

"How long were you together?" Angela asked and sat up without taking her eyes from mine. I sensed the beginning of a special, yet unexplainable, bond between us.

"Seven gloriously magical years," I answered. "They were the best years of my life." The memories of those days filled my mind and tugged at my heart. "Now it all seems so distant and remote, like it was all part of a wonderful dream that literally overnight became a hideous nightmare."

"It must have been horrible." Angela said in a very soft tone, pulling me away from the frightful image.

"It still is," I murmured. "Every day I feel like I'm falling deeper into this darkened abyss. Most of the time, I don't want to share this burden with anyone and I feel like the weight of the world is on my shoulders." Angela pulled me up next to her and put her arm around me.

"Perhaps tomorrow it will be better." She said it with such conviction that I really wanted to believe her. My lips attempted a smile.

"I want to believe that with all my heart," my reply finally came, "but she was my guiding light, my bright tomorrow, and my future beyond that. Now that she's gone, I have no hope left." I dropped my eyes to the ground and tried to imagine what it would be like if Celeste were still here. The children we would have had and the memories we would have shared. I could only dream. Angela was quiet again, and with a sigh, looked at the ground as well.

I rewound my mind's memories – romantic walks in the moonlight, tranquil country getaways, quiet evenings in front of the fireplace, candlelight dinners after a hard day at work, intimate moments. I closed my eyes and saw Celeste, ever so close, reaching for me, searching into my soul with that familiar smile that took my worries away. I could smell the scent of her perfume once again and it sent a tingle down my body. I took a deep breath and tried to hold on to the moment as long as I could.

"We met in college," I slowly whispered. Angela leaned her head over and gave me an encouraging nod, as if to say, "Go on, I'm listening. I'm here for you."

"One day," I began, "my classes ended early, and on the way to my car I saw her from a distance and immediately knew that she was something special. Her car, with the hood popped open, was parked next to mine, and she was leaning up against it with her arms folded across her chest, cheeks puffed out – like crying was the next inevitable step. I fell in love with her at the very moment I looked into her deep blue eyes.

"I offered her my assistance and she seemed grateful for it. She had left her headlights on and now the car would not start. After grabbing the jumper cables out of my trunk, I connected the batteries, and her car sprang back to life. She was very appreciative and offered to buy me a cup of coffee. It was the best mocha I had ever had. We talked for hours, finally agreeing to see each other again. I felt like a little boy in a candy store. Sleeping, concentrating, and, at times, even eating became more and more difficult. All I could think about was Celeste, and my whole world began to revolve around her. We saw each other every day. We would take long walks in the park at sunset, have picnics on the weekends, and talk for hours. We were meant to be together.

"Although her grades suffered slightly, Celeste graduated that May with honors. Within two months she found a job, while I stayed in school for another year finishing my dissertation. She was very helpful and supportive when I needed it. I finished my studies successfully and was offered a position in a genetic engineering laboratory. Everything was going great and our love grew stronger every day. I was so thankful that destiny had brought us together." I briefly paused and reflected on the fact that I was sharing my deepest feelings with a complete stranger, but it felt surprisingly liberating, and Angela appeared sincerely interested.

"In the winter that followed," I continued, "we moved into a beautiful flat overlooking the bay. We were both making good money, and at times, felt as if the world was at our feet. However, when Celeste left to visit her parents, I realized that everything we had meant nothing without her. I needed her at my side almost as much as I needed air. Two days after she came back, I proposed to her. She immediately accepted and a date was set for that summer.

"It was a clear sunny day late in June, the happiest of my life. A tent was set up inside the botanical gardens where the ceremony and reception took place. Twelve round tables were arranged around a dance floor, and the wedding party sat at a long table on the west side of the tent. About one hundred and fifteen guests attended, and as funny as it may sound, I knew only about a quarter of them. They all seemed to enjoy themselves – dancing and singing. There was a five-piece band that played a variety of music and the party went on late into the night. We even hired a magician to entertain the guests with close up magic during the cocktail hour.

"But the most spectacular sight at the wedding was Celeste. She took everybody's breath away when she walked down the aisle. A tiara crowned her queen for the day, and the sweetheart-neckline gown flowed down to the floor, spreading into a full skirt. The six-foot long train was carried by her two nieces. My bride was a picture of perfection in her wedding dress – a vision of loveliness in satin and lace. My knees turned to jelly when I saw her. She floated towards me like an angel sent from above to brighten my life. Even the roses in the garden seemed pale compared to Celeste's beauty.

"Two years after becoming husband and wife, I was nervously pacing our living room, while Celeste sat on the sofa tapping her foot – anxiously awaiting THE phone call. An eternity seemed to pass before the phone rang and when it finally did, we both jumped in anticipation. Exchanging a hopeful look, she picked up the receiver and closed her eyes. After a few intense moments, a triumphant smile stretched across her face while tears ran down her cheeks. She threw the phone down and we passionately embraced. After trying for a little over a year, we were finally going to have a baby." I stopped and lowered my head. The temporary feeling of contentment began to dissipate and the pain of loss was slowly overtaking me.

"She died soon thereafter," I whispered. Taking a deep breath, I looked at Angela who seemed fascinated by my story.

"Please," she said in a voice barely audible, touching my arm. "Please go on." Her expression confirmed the feeling of sincerity and compassion that I felt from her since the beginning. Inhaling deeply, I nodded and attempted to smile, but just as before it did not work.

"It happened on a Friday night, about two months later." I slowly began and clenched my hands. "It was pretty late, and we were driving home from a dinner at her parents' house. Both of us were tired and looked forward to getting some rest. The streets we drove on were mostly deserted and we quickly covered the seven miles to our house – except for the last two blocks." Frustration began to edge its way into my emotions and my hands curled into tight fists.

The desire to cry out and run as fast and as long as I could welled up inside me. Angela did not say anything, just continued looking at me sympathetically. She then took my hand and gently squeezed it. I tried to relax and be strong, but controlling my emotions without a drink was becoming tougher by the minute. With considerable effort, I continued.

"There was a traffic light two blocks from where we lived." I stared at the ground, seeing the events unfold in front of me as if they were just now happening. "We drove through there many times; never imagining something like that could happen so close to our home. The light was green, so I gently pushed the accelerator. We were driving no more than two or three miles over the speed limit when our car entered the intersection." I squeezed my hands into even tighter fists as it became increasingly harder to get the words out. "I looked into my side mirror and saw an empty street. Suddenly, a scream from Celeste pierced the air. I quickly spun my head, but there was nothing I could do. A pair of headlights shone brightly on us for what seemed like a lifetime. I will never forget that moment."

Pain began to materialize inside my heart.

"The speeding pick-up truck hit us on the passenger side. I don't remember much of the collision itself or the moments that followed."

A tear ran down my cheek and my voice began to quiver. Sadness, rooted deep inside, began to seep to the surface and melancholy, like I never experienced before, settled over me. I no longer wished for a bottle, I wished for a gun.

Angela put her arm around my shoulders once again, and gave me a gentle hug. "I'm sorry," she whispered. There was no need for more. We sat there for a few quiet moments.

The sky seemed closer and the stars twinkled and winked at us as if they were keeping a secret. Lowering my head, I closed my eyes, and attempted to compose myself. For the first time in my life, I wanted to finish telling the story of my love for Celeste and the tragedy that separated us.

"The driver of that truck had been drinking. His blood alcohol level was more than twice the legal limit and he was convicted of vehicular manslaughter. However, I found no comfort in that." My breaths were getting deep and rapid. "I woke up four days later in a surgical ICU. Besides a severe concussion, I had four broken ribs which perforated and collapsed the right lung, a fractured pelvis, and both of my lower legs were crushed. It took five surgeries to put me back together and months of rehabilitation.

"Celeste was not as fortunate. From what I understand, the trauma team worked on her for nearly an hour in the Emergency Room, before she was rushed to the operating room where they spent another three hours trying to save her life. She had severe head injuries, among many others, and two days later, at four in the morning, she went into cardiac arrest for the third time. They could not bring her back." I held my breath for as long as I could, forcing back the tears that wanted to come out in a flood of emotion, pain and suffering.

"Six months later I was discharged from the hospital," the words were getting garbled, "but I was a broken man and nothing has been the same. Everywhere I turned, everything I did, reminded me of her. I found only more despair and agony in all of our friends and even in our families. I didn't know where to turn or who to go to. Many times, I've considered just ending it all, but have never been able to go through with it." I thought I could go no further with my story, but the words just poured out on their own.

"I have not spoken to my family or friends since being discharged from the hospital, and shortly thereafter, I lost my job and my apartment. I drive my car now wherever the roads take me, finding comfort in the bottle. Life can be funny. The very thing that took her life is keeping me from going insane and helps me to numb the memory of that night – at least for a little while. Even today, it seems that I can still reach out and touch her, waiting for me to hug and kiss her, as if nothing has changed."

I lifted my head and stared into Angela's eyes. She seemed to understand exactly how I felt, as if the story that I had just finished had happened to her. "Even now as I look into your eyes, I can see Celeste's face in front of me – full of love and understanding."

A tidal wave of sorrow surfaced from the sea of whiskey in which I tried to drown it. Anguish and desolation welled up within, extinguishing all other emotions, and dissipated completely the few minutes of relative peace that I experienced not so long ago. I desperately wished for Celeste to be here so we could hold each other and share life's happiness and sorrow. I needed her to put meaning back into my life.

Squeezing Angela's hand, an aura of sympathy and compassion enveloped me and I felt my defenses weakening. I felt like Angela perceived my thoughts and experienced my emotions. In a final attempt to control them, I lifted my head to the sky sparkling with diamonds, and through clenched teeth I cried, "Why did it have to be her?"

My raw emotions and insurmountable pain erupted like a volcano that has been dormant much too long. I could not help myself as tears rolled freely down my cheeks, and I cried as never before. Angela consoled me, and I clung to her like a child. All the bottled up anger, frustration, guilt, sadness, and helplessness that I kept prisoner inside of me for almost two years finally surfaced and began to escape in a wave of emotion which made my soul give in to the fact that we have been separated, but my life must go on.

As I cried, a blanket of peace and contentment began to wrap itself around me. Angela gently pushed me back onto the grass, and I continued to sob into her shoulder, clinging to her as if I stood on the precipice of a cliff and she was a solid rock. I was no longer able to open my red puffy eyes, as the gentle hands of deep slumber caressed my consciousness, eventually winning out over any resistance I might have tried to put up.

When I opened my eyes, the sun was shining directly over me. The clouds were gone and the sky was a perfect sapphire blue. A steady headache pounded at my temples and I massaged them briefly in hopes of alleviating the discomfort. Squinting my eyes, I clumsily looked around and tried to gather my thoughts. Like the pieces of a puzzle, the events of the previous night began to come together. I felt drained and weak, physically and emotionally exhausted as if I had been engaged in a fierce battle. Strangely though, the desire for more liquor was not there. I called out, "Angela!"

There was no answer.

Lying next to me was the empty bottle of whiskey. Slowly picking it up and rising to my feet, I realized that I was on the grassy knoll which Angela had led me to last night. I looked around one more time, but saw nothing except the pond, the forest, and my car parked right where I left it. Where was Angela?

Many nights I have stayed awake staring at that mysterious moon and trying to figure out exactly what took place on the side of that road. Yet, even now, after all these years, I still do not know. Did it really happen? Was Angela a figment of my imagination brought on by demon alcohol and a sleep deprived mind? Was she sent from the heavens to save me? Was she Celeste?

My life is different now. I am slowly putting it back together – one small piece at a time. My urges for alcohol and the desire to stay away from people are gone. Once again, I managed to find a rewarding job and an apartment. I even made new friends and reconnected with some of my old ones. I still have a long way to go, but I am slowly moving on. On occasion, I even notice that I have a smile on my face for no particular reason.

Every now and then, with "Rhapsody in Blue" quietly playing on the radio, I drive out to where I saw Angela, hoping to see that beauty walking by the side of the road dressed all in white. Maybe she was an angel sent to rescue lost souls and shine a light on the darkness that surrounded them, or a ghost forever searching out those in need of guidance and helping them to overcome those misfortunes of life. Perhaps, Angela was a real caring person out for a walk whose path just happened to cross mine. Whoever or whatever she was, I will never forget her and for that night, I thank her.

THE YOUNG POET

"Alright men, fall in and listen up!" the captain shouted with an authoritative voice over the buzz produced by the mass of the gathered soldiers, startling every one of them. The captain was already a mature white blood cell having graduated basic training himself three days ago. He managed to quickly rise up through the ranks, and has been dealing with the newly graduated stem cells from basic training ever since. For him, retirement was in the not too distant future. After all of the soldiers quickly fell into formation, he briefly looked over the young men and being apparently satisfied with what he saw, he continued. "The moment that we all have been training and bred for is finally upon us. That's right, we are going into battle! According to the latest data from Intelligence, the enemy has managed to invade our lands by incorporating the Trojan horse method. They hid in a slightly undercooked piece of hamburger, using it as a vector to get past our initial security measures, and they are now laying siege in the South." The captain stretched out a part of his cytoplasm to point in the southerly direction. "The word has come down from High Command to attack this enemy as soon as possible because they are depleting us of water at an alarmingly high rate. The temperature is on the rise throughout our homeland, so the time to act is now. Gentlemen, they came here to start a war, but we will bring the battle to them. Now, I know the smell is not very pleasant down there, but we all have a duty to act, and I'm sure all of you will prove worthy of the challenge. You will be dealing with the dreaded Coli population that must be eradicated immediately. They are not the ones that we have a signed Peace Treaty with. These are their nasty cousins. They are rounded Prokaryotes that are mean, unforgiving, and can replicate to boost their numbers with extreme speed and efficiency. In fact, be warned, they have found a large nutrient source and, therefore, managed to amass a large army. This campaign will not be easy!

"All of you have been well trained and conditioned for an occasion such as this. I know that you men will prove to be lethal and precise killing machines and we will be victorious on this day. We will launch our first strike in exactly one hour which should give all of you plenty of time to divide into more stem cells, and consequently, mature into combat worthy leukocytes. Remember, strength and success lie in our numbers. All of you know what you have to do. That is all gentlemen. Good day and good luck!" He then turned around and slowly slithered away.

Everyone was dismissed. They were all in a state of shock and disbelief. While knowing that this day would come sooner or later, it was nonetheless, very stressful to go into your first battle. The rumor mill had it that rookies were always the first to die, and for all these soldiers, basic training finished only an hour and a half ago. Many of them formed close friendships, developing bonds that would last their lifetime and many subsequent generations to come. The added pressure that they all felt since joining the military two days ago made almost all of them buddies.

"I don't know about this, Andy," one of them was saying, "going into battle, at such an early age. War is such a big commitment, and I just don't feel ready for it yet. Fighting is messy and strenuous. I could get dirty, break a nail, or my hair could get disheveled. Not that I have either one of those, but it's just the idea of it that scares me so much. So many bad things could happen. I mean, what if I get killed? That just doesn't fit nicely into my long-term future plans. Not to mention, that it would totally ruin my social life. Not that I have one of those at this time either, but there is that one osteoblast that I was checking out the other day, and I think she winked at me. Who knows, she's sitting there all alone in that lacunae and would probably love to have some company. She might find me attractive and then some chemistry might start brewing between us."

Andy raised his eyebrows and pursed his lips, but his friend just continued to ramble on. "I just don't feel like I'm cut out for this kind of stuff. Killing pathogens and other foreign things, that's ... that is a big responsibility at this point in my life. Maybe we could just give them a stern talking to and a warning? Or we could calmly explain to them that at this time their presence here is simply not welcome. These particular strains are reasonable and understandable pathogens, aren't they? Perhaps some of us could make fists and wave them aggressively in their general direction to get the point across? What if we just swat or punch a few of them. Perhaps a gentle, but yet firm, slap across the face will do the trick? Or...or finger pointing! That has always worked on me. But killing? I just don't know if I can do that. And this 'divide and mature into a leukocyte' business, what is that all about? I've never been able to do that in my life. And now they expect me to do it under these circumstances?!?! Within an hour?!?! I am definitely not capable of handling all this."

"Oh Sparky," Andy answered as convincingly as he could. After all, it is hard to sound sincere when one does not believe in the words that are coming out of one's mouth. "I know it's hard, but you are a soldier now. Be strong. It is your duty to fight and kill." He found the idea of Sparky being a killer almost as amusing as any other semi entertaining oxymoron that life has to offer. "After all," Andy tried to point to something positive, "it's not like we are the lowly Paramecia being outmatched by the Didinia. We have excellent odds of winning this one. Maybe you will find your calling once the fighting starts. Who knows, maybe your fighter spirit and instincts are just hidden deep ... way deep, inside." They both almost broke out laughing at the last comment.

"No," Sparky said in a melancholic manner after a brief moment of silence. "I strongly doubt that. I mean look at me. It doesn't take a genius to see that I'm a pretty pathetic soldier. I was born and trained to be a ruthless killer, but I cannot do even the most basic, and the most important, task that is required of every soldier. I have not been able to divide even once, let alone mature into a leukocyte fighter. I have contributed absolutely nothing to this platoon as far as increasing its numbers, or, for that matter, in any other way either. Look at you though. You and every other individual here have divided at least five times already, and I'm still the same old Sparky."

Andy wished that there was something more that he could do to help his friend find the fighting spirit he knew was hidden somewhere deep inside. "Why is that Sparky?" Andy asked. "I have been meaning to ask you about that for a long time. What is preventing you from dividing? Like you said, everyone else in the whole army has done it multiple times. There is plenty of food, the temperature is perfect (even if it is rising), the bone is healthy, and we're surrounded by all the materials a budding soldier could ever want."

Sparky inhaled deeply and pondered on that mystery for the millionth time that day. They both knew that it was their duty to do so, and they both knew that if Sparky cannot multiply by the time the attack on the invaders commences, the captain would come down hard on him, and neither one wanted to contemplate the consequences of that action.

"I guess that I just don't have it in me, Andy." Sparky thought about it some more. "You know, I wish I was trained to be a red cell, not white. They lead such a peaceful lifestyle and no one demands anything great from them. They just lay back and relax in the lazy rivers, or splash around in the rapids of the slightly more turbulent flow. Always playing around with gases, and meeting so many beautiful ladies. Andy, all I want to do is sit back, relax, and write some beautiful poetry, one for every beautiful lady in the world. I guess, I'm a lover, not a fighter."

Andy smiled. "In case you have not noticed, Casanova, there are not a whole lot of ladies trying to break down your door. In fact, there has never been one."

"I know, I know." Sparky quickly responded with a hint of excitement in his voice. "There is this poem that I have been working on though, and it is sure to melt the heart of any lady that hears it. They will turn to potty in my pseudopods if I will read it to them in person. It will be an absolutely awesome piece of poetry. And this will be the first of many more to come. Well, to be perfectly honest with you, I just started working on it. There are only two stanzas, but it is already really good. Want to hear it? It's called The One." Andy knew that his friend's excitement went up another notch when he agreed to listen to the first two stanzas, which some day would undoubtedly become a part of a masterpiece.

After clearing his throat, with as much enthusiasm and emotions as Sparky could muster, he began to recite:

"Lonely and sad was my heart.

I couldn't find love from the start.

Then grace and beauty I finally saw.

Her melodious voice held me in awe.

My heart does not have boundaries when it comes to love,

It aches for her gentle hand to caress it, and bring it to life.

Her eyes are mesmerizing; those eyebrows are like a dove,

But she loves another, a wound in my chest with a knife."

Suddenly they heard a voice behind them.

"Well what do you expect? He's a man, where's you ... you're still just a boy." Quickly spinning around, they saw another soldier standing a pseudopod's length away, on the brink of bursting into wild laughter. They realized that he probably overheard the entire conversation. "You know Spanky, that almost made me cry." With that he began to laugh hysterically and slowly crawled away.

Feeling quite a bit embarrassed, they exchanged a quick look and then stared at the ground. Andy tried to tell his friend that the poem sounded really good, and that he should not pay attention to all the jerks in the platoon. He tried to tell him that at least they were going to leave the cramped marrow tube that they currently lived in and will finally get to travel and explore the wide-open spaces of the motherland, meet new cells, and create new bonds and friendships that will last for hours. He even pointed out that some of those will be ladies, but it was all to no avail.

Time was working against Sparky and they both could feel the incredible pressure of the imminent march to war. Sparky could feel a sinking sensation manifest itself deep in his gut, one that he experienced several times before but never this severe, a feeling so strong this time around that it could begin a growth process, which if not controlled, can easily terminate in a state of panic. For a split second, Andy felt like he was already involved in a losing battle trying to get his friend to cheer up and to accomplish his military duties. Sparky, for the briefest of moments, felt utterly alone. Then they both raised their eyes, knowing that the captain would show up any minute. That sinking feeling was starting to really turn Sparky's stomach.

Suddenly Sparky saw her, slowly crawling up to him. He had no idea what she was, but as far as he was concerned, she was absolutely beautiful. The military beret on her head made her face look even more stunning, the military uniform she wore accentuated the roundness of her amoeba-like body beautifully, and her bigger than life aura was simply breathtaking. Her smoothly flowing cytoplasm, the long flagellum that she moved in such a sexy way, the cute little dimple of a newly forming vacuole, and the gentle curves of her cilia, made his heart skip a beat. Sparky could not blink or take his eyes off of her, and as he let out a low moaning groan, he knew that he was in love. Stopping no more than ten nanometers away from him, she dropped a large hanky to the ground, and in a cooing voice, which sounded more like music to Sparky's ears, uttered, "Oops!"

Sparky was paralyzed and no longer aware of the world around him. He wasn't sure if she was real or just a figment of his imagination, but at that moment he didn't really care. Since he resembled a statue more than a living organism, she bent down to pick up the square of cloth that she had dropped. Unconsciously Sparky began to experience a myriad of new sensations building up inside of him – sensations he never experienced before. A combination of excitement and happiness enveloped his body, and for the first time in his short life he felt completely free as adrenaline circulated throughout his whole cytoplasm. Stripped of societal chains of burden, Sparky felt his soul fill with joy and begin to soar ever higher. He was not even aware that he slowly floated towards her. The vision of his dreams was now standing just a short micron away. He could hardly contain himself. All of the mitochondrion that he possessed were working at full capacity, and every RNA strand within his body was utilized at a feverish pitch.

She slowly stood back up after retrieving her handkerchief, and came even closer to Sparky, her cilia gently touching his cell membrane, which sent a shock wave throughout his entire cytoplasm.

"That was a beautiful beginning to your poem," she said in a mesmerizing voice. Sparky could not breathe now either. "It stole my breath away, tugged at the strings of my heart, and I can't wait to hear more. By the way, my name is Sherry." Sparky felt like he was going to explode. His macronucleus was beating so hard by this time, he thought it would break right out of his ectoplasm.

"Hi," he was finally able to barely mumble after a long moment of silence had passed. "I'm Sparky. Thank you. I...I..." Sparky found himself tongue tied, unable to finish the sentence.

"Tell me something, Sparky," she whispered seductively in his ear, "I prefer gentlemen whose intellectual capacity is equal to mine. Do you know what McLeanser means?"

Sparky was not sure what to say. His mind raced to find that word in his limited vocabulary, but utterly failed. He tried to mumble something under his breath, but words were getting caught in his throat. It was becoming increasingly hard to swallow around the lump that formed there. With his heart ripped to shreds and his spirits at an all-time low, he slowly shook his head, barely suppressing the tears. However, much to his surprise, a big smile stretched across Sherry's face.

"Perfect," she said. "I have no idea what that means either because it's not a real word. I just made it up. And thanks for being honest about that and not trying to make up some silly definition or a ridiculous excuse." And then, in an even more seductive sort of way, she added, "Perhaps we can write the rest of that poem together. I want it to have a happy ending." Sparky gave her a barely perceptible nod.

"I'll see you when you get back." She said and slowly leaned forward. Their cell membranes touched for what seemed like a blissful eternity, hers feeling so silky smooth against his, that Sparky was in ecstasy.

Euphoria settled over the young poet and he was finally at peace with the world. As he separated from Sherry, everything seemed somehow different. He was floating through the clouds, looking at the world in a different light, from a slightly different angle. He never even noticed that his nucleic acid began to replicate, and his cytoplasm began to pinch in on opposite ends of his body. Mitosis was well on its way and change into a powerful leukocyte was just around the corner. Nothing was ever the same again for Sparky.

SWEET DREAMS

MOSTLY RHYMING STORIES

A DROP

A powerful mixture of salt and water,
A single drop capable of many things.

Denoting wide spectrum of extreme emotions,
Relaying feelings to another human being.

Oozing when depression and despair consume the soul,
Gushing when happiness and hope embraces the spirit.

Obstructs the vision when crying calls upon a drop,
Dangles on an eye lash at the never-ending smile.

A single drop can melt a heart, diffuse rage and anger,
A single drop can make one feel, and make one's love stronger.

The wind and sun can coax it out of hiding,
Hysterical laughter can make it suddenly appear.

Rolling down the cheek, leaving a wet streak,
There is nothing more powerful than a solitary tear.

BEAUTIFUL FOOD

*I*n the middle of a hot and steamy day,

I live to aimlessly fly and soar away,

In search of bright colors, beauty and dismay,

It's summer, and I feel so wonderful today.

It is flowers and grass I search for each time,

But benches and humans' heads suit me just fine,

I am attracted to perfection worthy of mine,

I know when I die, they will build me a shrine.

No longer am I sluggish, slimy and green,

Now I am a thing of beauty, color and zing,

Soaring through the air I belong among kings,

It's a sight to cherish when I spread my wings.

There is a man running at me with a net,

He wants me as his award-winning pet,

Flying whenever and wherever I choose,

Is my right to freedom I will never loose.

Good Night, Sleep Tight, Sweet Dreams

So off I soar towards the big blue sky,

It is simply wonderful to be able to fly,

I could rest in a tall tree over there,

Free of worries, concerns, and care.

It's truly exciting being magnificent me,

I can sense jealousy coming from a flea,

You probably think that I'm full of conceit,

But without me the beauty would not be complete.

There is a rainbow of color I add to this world,

My wings are rare and should be seen unfurled.

Life without me would be so misunderstood,

Like the fossilized remains of petrified wood.

All other insects adore me in flight,

Sadly, their wings are lesser in might,

They do not compare to the beauty I weave,

Nothing can contribute to all I conceive.

Michael Kugel

The flowers below me sway in the breeze,

They are colorful too, but that is only a tease,

When captured by humans and put in a vase,

I'll still be gliding, so full of my grace.

There is an ugly bird flying this way,

Its eyes are looking at me in dismay,

Its mouth is starting to open in awe,

And I can clearly see it extending a claw.

This bird is getting too close for my taste,

It's flying right at me in a very quick haste,

Please Help! Somebody! It wants something to munch,

It's time to soar, for beauty is a lousy lunch.

FAIRY TALE OF AN OLD CHAIR

An old forgotten chair, standing under a window in the corner of a room,

In the light of a starry night, illuminated brightly by the rays of a dim moon.

The color has faded, the varnish is dull, and the fabric has long been torn,

The old chair stands vigilant, quietly witnessing each day as it is born.

The family of the house is no longer aware that the chair still exists,

Unable to realize that the quality, durability, and reliance still persists.

They have no idea that the springs are not stretched or worn out,

No clue that the curvy legs are strong and can perform without a pout.

Its pulse is strong and steady, there's plenty of life force within its heart,

The brain, sharp as ever, furnishes the personality, a pretty important part.

Michael Kugel

Although the soul is still young and vibrant, it no longer smiles at the room,

Despair and depression have engulfed it; the corner has become its doom.

The last time someone set in the chair, the world was at war,

The owner was called to fight, and the chair saw him no more.

Many handled the old chair since then, moving it here and there,

Never sitting in it, just using it once to help a girl get on a mare.

No one seems to appreciate the strength and comfort that the chair brings,

No one seems to realize there's a beauty, among other plainer things.

As if invisible, all people ignore the chair and just walk on by,

Many times, promises of a better new home were nothing but a lie.

And so melancholy surrounds the quiet, but still proud chair,

Life has not always been so kind, and often not very fair.

Relegated to the obscure, it no longer serves a purpose of any kind,

Collecting dust, and wondering if its best days are far behind.

As time passes by, decades disappear and become relegated to the past,

Seems like only yesterday it was made and sold, years sure do go by fast.

But something good and unexpected can happen to anyone, at any time,

Something that picks us up, rebuilds the core, and wipes the dust and grime.

So, it was with this chair, sitting there for sale as a man came walking by,

He was out for a walk, when he spotted it out of the corner of his eye.

It looked rather haggard, having suffered from neglect and some harm,

But there was undeniable elegance, and quite a good amount of charm.

Despite the chair's undesirable appearance, there was no doubt in his mind,

There was an indescribable connection, perhaps an inexpressible bind.

He purchased the chair and speedily took it back to his shop,

There was lots of work to be done, and he started right at the top.

He worked on the fabric for hours, and he refurbished the wood,

Replenished the stuffing, and began to elevate the chair's mood.

He washed and scrubbed the grime out of the creases and folds,

Slowly revealing the beautiful soul that the old chair still holds.

The varnish is no longer dull, and the colors are bright once more,

The fabric has no holes in it, and the chair is sturdy at the core.

It is comfortable as ever, and the owner sits in it as much as he can,

Even the visitors and guests adore it, all thanks to the handy man.

No more standing in the musky corners, watching the time slowly pass by,

Not relegated to the wings of a stage to collect the dust, waiting for it to die.

The chair now occupies the center of the stage, as it stands proud and tall,

Alive and vibrant, ready to answer at a moment's notice, a tired man's call.

It's a strange phenomenon that some dwell on, and assume that old equates to bad,

The process of thinking that older means not valuable, is undeniably rather sad.

Some of the younger ones today tend to forget that age is just a state of mind,

That there is experience, wisdom, and even mischief; it can indeed be quite a find.

FIRST DATE

As she stepped through the door and I saw her, there was a spark in my eye,

Suddenly, I began to hope that she wouldn't look at me as just another guy.

It was a blind date that had brought us together on that warm summer night,

I was slowly becoming nervous, wanting her to like me with all my might.

We shook hands, and I opened the car door for her with a smile on my face,

She liked the gesture and proceeded to get inside with elegance and grace.

Walking to the other side of the car, I had to concentrate on my feet,

Did not want to trip over them and wind up face down in the street.

She looked very nice and I told her so, hoping she felt the same about me,

I wanted to unlock her heart, and wondered what would be the right key.

Which words of wisdom would make me sound witty to her ears,

Which jokes would make her laugh and subdue my fears.

We pulled up to a restaurant and went inside to feast,

The food was good and the conversation great to say the least.

I enjoyed her sense of humor, sarcasm, and a very sharp wit,

Tried hard to keep up, but kept wondering if I sounded like a twit.

After the dinner we decided to get some drinks at a bar,

There was music playing in there, we heard it from afar.

Dance lessons were given to anyone willing to learn,

Then the floor was open to anyone willing to take a turn.

Latin dancing was the theme of the night, good news indeed,

I can dance those, so I asked her to join me and took the lead.

Bachata, Salsa, and of course Merengue, we danced them all,

A festive aura surrounded us, as if we were dancing at a ball.

Drinks, dancing, and laughter, we were having lots of fun,

Seemingly in a blink of an eye the night passed and was gone.

Michael Kugel

We had to vacate the floor as it was getting rather late,

Time to return to reality, it was time to end our first date.

Did she enjoy the evening? Was her time with me full of fun?

Would she see me again? Accept my future calls or would she run?

As I drove her back, I wondered if I hit the mark or did I miss?

My questions were answered, when the night was sealed with a kiss.

IN THE FOREBODING QUIET DARKNESS OF A LONELY NIGHT

In the foreboding quiet darkness of a lonely night,

In the deepest crevice of a slowly beating heart,

A bleeding stone lies dying, hidden from the light,

A life once so sweet has suddenly become so tart.

Disillusioned and trapped in a torpid state of mind,

Tormented in anguish, for pain is life's small fee,

The stone, once again realizes that life is not so kind,

That need for privacy is a cruel deception of fate to be.

In a pool of steadily increasing misery and sorrow,

Brightly illuminated by the shine of the black light,

Lies happiness in desperate need of "life to borrow",

No longer capable of rising up and putting up a fight.

In a cascading wave of sadness, unable to stop the fall,

The stone floats up in misguided hope of anticipation,

But only to find the damn loneliness still proud and tall,

On the floor, happiness lays lifeless, in total devastation.

Michael Kugel

Blanketed by the deafening quiet within four empty walls,

Too weak to yell out loud, to cry for help, or even moan,

Falling deeper into a dream, unaware of the slowing pulse,

In the black night, death finally finds the peaceful stone.

THE ANGRY SKY

The all-seeing sky frowned and shuddered as the angry clouds slowly rolled in,

It opened up and bled with tears of acid, crying, the heart aching for its kin.

The globe below was slowly withering and dying, while accosted by the rain,

Stoically awaiting the final days in the vacuum of space, and suffering in pain.

The abused sacred soil holds the secrets of wrong desires over the years,

The air, once thought to be so precious, now denotes all kinds of fears.

There is a myriad of undesirables in the multitudes of great watery depth,

The ever-present sky screaming at the guilty, as it reveals a ferocious wrath.

Oh the guilty go unpunished; the crimson sky knows this all too well,

Watching the crimes committed, echoing the anger as it continues to swell.

They are busy rearranging and destroying, often killing anything they touch,

Below, the system is disrupted often, causing the innocents to suffer much.

Through millions of eons, the sky was happy as it observed from afar,

Until one day it appeared, bleeding as it became bigger, an ugly scar.

Then there was another lashing, and many more appeared quite fast,

Decidedly an unpleasant feeling not knowing how long it will all last.

Individuals deposit the offensive substance where their sanctum no longer exists,

And the multitudes still spread the seeds of sorrow to where beauty still persists.

The morose sky again cannot help but wonder why the hypocrisy is so great,

It's obvious that ignorance, greed, and laziness prevail, soon to seal their fate.

The fruit is no longer ripe, but rotten, the taste entrenching on every bud,

The foul stench, the dirty water, cannot displace it, all tastes like moldy mud.

The consequences are aplenty, the choking throats of innocent's attest to that,

The lost have become the guilty, now standing at disaster's door welcome mat.

"The future is for the children", or so the guilty seem to always claim,

But the will is getting smaller by the pound, as desolation regains fame.

So, the angry sky quietly yells and bares its teeth, snarling at the events down below,

For it has a young child to gaze upon, as it wakes up each morning, and says "hello."

THE DARKNESS

This poem was inspired by Robin Williams, whose untimely death shook the world and his fans. I am a fan. While he was not able to overcome the darkness, there are many others who have or are currently struggling. This poem is for them.

For years, the black night surrounded all that could be,

And the light was engulfed by the darkness around me.

No advice or words of wisdom would brighten the day,

Not even birdsong or the soothing waters of the bay.

No one sees the misery and sorrow in my heart,

No one seems to care that my heart is not that hard.

I am alone at all hours of the day and night,

To this indifference there is no relief, no end in sight.

The candle of life burns in the vacuum of all that exists,

The wick is getting shorter, but the flame still persists.

Perhaps, if the wind extinguishes this particular light,

Someone else will continue the race and excel in the fight.

The tiredness overwhelms the senses, and the desire to live,

The world surrounds me, but there's nothing more that I could give.

No more interests, no wants, or needs, no more fun,

My soul is becoming a supernova, much like an exploding sun.

I stagger through darkness, and suddenly my foot touches the edge,

I stand on the precipice of a cliff, ready to jump from its ledge.

The choice is mine; it can all be resolved in a blink of an eye,

My last chance to endure the struggle and stop living a lie...

In my eyes, the solution is close, obvious, and easy.

The smile on my face makes others happy, but I feel dizzy.

The end to my hell is just under my feet, that much is clear,

Such a simple gesture, but there is a spark of doubt and fear.

My head is spinning and my sweaty hands shake at my side,

A battle rages inside me, but no winner emerges in this fight.

Indecision makes everything worse, as tears roll down the cheeks,

My life flashes through my mind – the low points and the peaks.

A gust of wind knocks me off balance, and I stumble taking a step back,

It allows me to look at the world from a new angle and grasp what I lack.

From this point there is plenty of light that I can see,

The darkness fades to grayness, and this life is not taxing my soul a fee.

Another step back and the devotion of my friends becomes clear,

Losing the family that I love materializes into my greatest fear.

There is much to explore and live for, I finally realize,

Many beautiful things to accomplish and finalize.

It was not easy to change the perspective and re-examine my life,

Hard to come back from the edge, and not plunge into that dive.

No matter how lonely I felt, someone will miss me if I fall,

So, take a step back, inhale deep, and choose to rise up above all.

THE FOG

Stumbling through a forest, attempting to make way through thick fog,

Blinded by useless ambitions, tripping over unseen roots of a dead log.

Unable to see the enlightened direction so obvious to most,

Hopelessly lost on the trail that proves to be a rather poor host.

For years I have wandered among the trees, not finding the responses I seek,

The forest does not whisper the answers, the fog does not offer a peek.

Extending arms forward, picking a direction, slowly moving on,

Wondering if depression is close behind or perhaps forever gone.

Suddenly out of the fog, a beautiful hand is extended to me,

Offering love and guidance, promises of bliss and lifelong glee.

Gently I take the hand into mine, mesmerized by her beauty and wit,

My heart is on fire and it is hard to believe, but my soul is brightly lit.

The fog in the forest dissipates and the path becomes clear,

Walking by her side, there is no apprehension, no more fear.

Happiness engulfs my being and a smile materializes on my face,

Love is a strange and unfamiliar feeling, but I like its hands of lace.

Time stands still as we talk at the playground in the park,

And hold each other close, as we whisper nothings in the dark.

Holding my breath in trepidation, ever so softly I kiss her strawberry lips,

Our hearts begin to beat in unison, dancing all night in twirls and dips.

For the first time in my life three little words burst forth from my chest,

"I love you" I whisper, happy to have found the one in a world so vast.

Excitement, desire, admiration fill my mind and flow through my blood,

And all the missing pieces of my life float away, swept by a great flood.

Walking on air sometimes I forget to exhale and in a blink of an eye,

Before either one of us has time to notice, nine fantastic months go by.

But suddenly something unexpected happens and shocks me to my core,

She releases my hand, pulls herself away, and says that she wants no more.

Her sultry voice as melodious as ever and so sweet to my ears,

Is surprisingly full of despise, as my eyes nearly fill with tears.

"It's one of your friends that you keep, plus I feel that you lie,

You don't do enough little things; this is our final good-bye."

She quickly explains her fears and doubts, and one thing becomes clear,

Nothing I do is good enough for her; there is no way to keep her near.

Despite my best efforts to convince her and to prove my love,

The hand stays withdrawn and she vanishes into the clouds far above.

To this day I wonder if there was more that I should have said or done,

What gestures would have made her happy and her eyes see me as the one?

Should I have committed no mistakes? Seems quite impossible to me.

She was not materialistic, but her love was anything but free.

And so once again I find myself back in the forest surrounded by the fog,

Stumbling blindly on the same unfriendly trail, tripping over the same log.

Is it truly better to have loved and lost, than to have never loved at all?

I hope to have the answer someday when I hit bottom and stop the fall.

THE INTERMISSION

This world is full of many different people, all of them are actors on some stage,

Complex interactions, roles, and lines, like reading a novel and turning a page.

Some play major roles, some minor, and a few do nothing but fill in the gaps,

The crowd always appreciating a good performance with many thunderous claps.

And so, I find myself on stage, falling in love with a beautiful girl I know,

Hardly able to speak whenever I see her, words get stuck somewhere low.

My heart beats fast, the hands begin to sweat, and my mouth becomes dry,

I find myself floating high among the clouds, seems like I can actually fly.

I want to hold her gently in my arms and land feathery kisses unto her crimson lips,

I want to stare into her eyes, and hope that I can handle my own heart doing the flips.

Just to see that sweet smile on her face, the one that makes my spirit soar and purr,

Every day, I would want to buy all the flowers in the world and present them to her.

I want to hold her hand in mine and walk on the beach as the sun touches the waves,

Perhaps whisk her away to some paradise, and tie a bow around all that she craves.

I would write her poetry, love songs, and tell her jokes to brighten a gloomy day,

Carry her over any puddles that life may present, limit the dark times and the gray.

However, the world in her eyes is vastly different; she's interested in other things,

All the main characters in her play are at center stage, as I watch from the wings.

Although she knows of my existence, for her my role is that of a fill-in at best,

Relegated to the background full of extras, observing from there her life's quest.

The man she adores has a pierced tongue, and several earrings in his ears and lip,

He has a colorful Mohawk haircut, many tattoos, and wears a chain on his hip.

His boots are stained, and his old leather jacket is faded and torn in several spots,

His language skills are abhorring, and his treatment of her leaves me in knots.

She's attracted to the "bad boy" image that he exudes, the whole cast can easily tell,

I'm happy for her, but on the inside, it tears me to pieces, and in pain I quietly yell.

It's only a matter of time before he gets her in trouble and causes her needless pain,

Putting himself first does not allow him to see that, his blood too full of vain.

I'm sure that it is only a silly phase in her life, one I hope will not last long.

Perhaps then I'll be able to release the words in my heart, and she will hear my song.

I will tell her how I feel and tremble on the inside, for that will be my greatest audition,

Till then, I will stand in the wings and in her play, be happy to fill in the intermission.

THE LIGHT OF HOPE

*I*t's midnight.

The night is cool and,

a lonely stranger comes forth into the light.

What is this strange phenomenon?

What is the source of such a thing?

Oh! I think he knows the answer!

It's the light of happiness and wonder.

It's the light of utopia for human kind.

But the human ugliness prevails.

It brings their race far below.

They think they might be getting stronger.

But all they do is weaken themselves.

The light seems farther now.

And soon it is no longer seen.

It's leaking through fingers like water,

It's falling to the ground like sand.

Oh! How difficult it all seems!

Is there no hope for betterment?

Won't the light ever comeback?

A lonely stranger wanders off into the darkness

and the warm day appears.

It's noon.

THE STORM

Outside, the irate wind was hollowing, talking within the cracks of an old wall,

The water smashing at the bricks, chipping at the mortar, screaming for it to fall.

Straining harder than it ever had before, the storm resurged its efforts at the core,

Vehemently it attacked the structure, knowing it could not stand for much more.

But the wall stood there defiant, quietly staring down the fury of the storm,

It was old and stubborn, unyielding in substance, durability, or form.

It stood there unflinching as the wind whipped around and screamed,

Inside, the open eyes were glazed over, the mind lost as it dreamed.

And so, the storm eased back its fury, the wind began to resemble a breeze,

But it was determined, the eye staring at the wall in an unwavering freeze.

It regrouped and concentrated, gathering its strength in a rather large pool,

And then again it unleashed its fury, charging at the wall like an angry bull.

The battle went on for hours, the storm could not get the upper hand,

There were large waves of sand and water, and winds that shook the land.

Suddenly there was a small chip in the mortar, and an idea crawled through,

It was closely followed by another, but more was needed to get a clue.

A hurricane had formed outside, and the old wall began to shake,

It had been there a long time, like a sunken ship on the bottom of a lake.

Another chip soon occurred, bigger this time, followed by many more,

Piece by little piece the wall began to crumble, parts falling on the floor.

More and more ideas came, until they turned into a flood,

Eventually whole concepts formed, as the wall lay destroyed in mud.

The brain was wide awake now, and the eyes were free of glaze,

The writer was free to create, his mind and imagination no longer a haze.

The storm was triumphant in the end, defeating the dreaded writer's block,

No need to dream the day away, watching the seconds tick on the face of a clock.

A masterpiece will surely be found in the prose that the writer can now invent,

And the reader can enjoy these fruits of labor, then comment, criticize it, or just vent.

THANK YOU

First and foremost, I would like to thank you, the reader, for purchasing my book. It was a lot of fun to write, and I sincerely hope that you will enjoy everything that I have included in here. There have been many people whose lives had crossed my path. I'm sure beyond any shadow of a doubt that every single one of them influenced me and shaped me into the person that I am today. Being that person has allowed me to explore my creative side, first on paper, and then in front of my computer, and eventually write the passages contained within this book. I could probably thank hundreds, and even thousands of them, but in the interest of saving a tree or two, I'll limit myself to just eight.

First, I would like to thank my senior year High School English teacher Chuck LaChiusa, who afforded me the opportunity to discover and ignite the spark for creative writing that was hidden deep within me. Prior to that, I never imagined that I might have any inkling of a talent for this kind of work. Thank you, Mr. LaChiusa, for giving me the opportunity to rub the two, proverbial, sticks together.

Madelyn Levy was kind enough to fan that spark, and provide plenty of oxygen to it. Thank you for helping me to keep the spark alive.

A good friend of mine at that time, Ken Gibson, poured gasoline on it (as well as many other accelerants), and helped me ignite that spark into a hot burning flame. Thank you Ken (and all of the unpublished writers of the science-fiction writing group) for teaching me about short stories, creative writing, plot development, and helping me drive my imagination in various directions that it had never even dreamed of going, and the myriad of explorations that I would have never made on my own.

I would also like to thank Yadira Garcia for her contributions to the short story *Thank You*. Without her, it would have never been written. Thank you for that and your grammatical guidance with many of the other ones.

As the flames were burning out of control, one of my friends bravely stepped up to the challenge and helped me rein in the fire, and make it a controlled burn. Thank you, Jeannette Estronza, for being my first editor. Without your help many readers would probably have suffered, at the very least, first degree burns from reading my "stuff".

None of this would have been possible without the tremendous effort of Rosemary Maloney-Hoffman. She put in countless hours readjusting the flame, surrounding it with just the right amount of oxygen and air, forming and guiding it towards a comforting and beautiful glow that all can cozy up to, and warm up with. Additionally, she also had invaluable input on the story *Fleeting Moments*. Thanks to her, the flame became a gentle spark that is quite beautiful and mesmerizing (at least it is in my opinion). As a writer, I should possess the knowledge, vocabulary, and skills to express just about anything with words. However, words are simply not enough to express all of my gratitude for all the hard work that she put forth into my stories. Thank you, Rosemary. All of your efforts have been greatly appreciated.

Next, I would like to thank Jeff Perdziak for his wonderful illustrations. They have added an amazing feel to the flame, adding a dimension to this book that has enhanced the ambiance by making it pleasing to the eye. Jeff, you are truly talented.

Finally, a big thank you goes out to my wife Elena, who continuously encourages me to be better, even when I tell her that I already did my best. Thanks to her, I've discovered that there is no ceiling to the quality of writing that I am capable of when she does the proof reading. She was an inspiration for several aspects of this book and thanks to her, that flame will burn for a long time into the future – I began to work on other literary projects. You are the best and I love you.

If I missed anyone, I sincerely apologize. Stop by with a bottle of wine and some finger foods, and we can discuss how to fit your name into the second edition.

CPSIA information can be obtained
at www.ICGtesting.com
Printed in the USA
LVHW030036211220
674728LV00001B/114